Haley laughed at her newborn baby. "Are you giving your mom 'tude already?"

"I wonder where he'd get that from?" Mateo said. He'd spoken softly, but the baby gave a startle reflex, his tiny hands splaying out. Mateo held his finger toward the infant and the boy grabbed on. A feeling of power and peace and absolute terror spread through Mateo.

If he was experiencing this, he could only imagine what Haley was experiencing. Her eyes were on him, and she smiled quietly. "Pretty cool, eh?"

He cleared his throat. "Yeah."

He wiggled his finger as if in a handshake. "Hello there. My name is Mateo. What's yours?"

There was a slight hesitation from Haley and then she said, "Mateo, I'd like you to meet Jonah."

"But that's—"

"—your middle name. I know. I've always liked that name. I'm not naming him after you."

He thumbed baby Jonah's soft hand.

They hadn't seen each other in twelve years, so he believed her. Still. Still...

Dear Reader,

It's a brand-new series! *A Ranch to Call Home* expands from my previous two series set in the small fictional town of Spirit Lake into the surrounding countryside. Then in the third book, the series heads south into the deep ranching country of the Alberta foothills.

This first story belongs to a lonely cowboy and the best friend he left behind. Also, there's a baby. I had so much fun bringing them to life, visiting with people from my other series and introducing ones set to enter the story arena in the next two books.

I am grateful to Lukacs Performance Horses for letting me observe a training session led by Keith Stewart and sponsored by the Central Alberta Cutting Horse Club. The language of the cutting horse world fell straight from Keith's lips, and the suggestion for a typical but recoverable injury came from horseman John Lukacs. His daughter and a cutting horse owner beside me on the bleachers also provided a wealth of information, but I failed to scribble down their names. I'm so sorry! This is why I'm a novelist and not a journalist.

Come visit me on Facebook or at my website! I also gobble up any feedback. Consider leaving a review on Amazon, Goodreads or both.

Happy, happy reading!

Best,

M. K.

HEARTWARMING

A Family for the Rancher

—

M. K. Stelmack

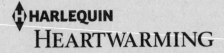

⊕ HARLEQUIN
HEARTWARMING

HARLEQUIN®
HEARTWARMING™

ISBN-13: 978-1-335-58485-4

A Family for the Rancher

Recycling programs for this product may not exist in your area.

Harlequin Enterprises ULC
22 Adelaide St. West, 41st Floor
Toronto, Ontario M5H 4E3, Canada
www.Harlequin.com

Printed in U.S.A.

M. K. Stelmack writes historical and contemporary fiction. She is the author of A True North Hero series—the third book of which was made into a movie—and The Montgomerys of Spirit Lake series with Harlequin Heartwarming. She lives in Alberta, Canada, close to a town the fictional Spirit Lake of her stories is patterned after.

Books by M. K. Stelmack

Harlequin Heartwarming

A True North Hero

A Roof Over Their Heads
Building a Family
Coming Home to You

The Montgomerys of Spirit Lake

All They Want for Christmas
Her Rodeo Rancher
Their Together Promise

Visit the Author Profile page
at Harlequin.com for more titles.

To my editor, Adrienne

Thanks for forcing me to write stories worthy of your tears.

CHAPTER ONE

STANDING ALONE, Mateo Pavlic looked across the heads of the fifty or so lunching after the celebration-of-life service to the Janssons, father and daughter. They sat, chatting with one of the Claverley boys Mateo had grown up with and his wife. Knut was doing most of the talking, which wasn't unusual. He had spoken at the open mic about Jakob Pavlic and somehow found enough kindhearted and funny stories about his recently departed friend to trigger tears and bowed heads from the assembled. If Mateo hadn't known Jakob like he did, he might've experienced a twinge of regret himself for the passing of the man everyone thought was his father.

Knut hadn't changed much in the dozen years Mateo had been away, but his daughter was definitely a changed woman. Haley Jansson still had thick red-brown hair and a quick smile. But she was pregnant. Very, very pregnant. Seated sideways to him, she reached down to discreetly tug at the hem of her maternity top straining over her baby bump on her petite frame. She must have felt his attention, because she glanced his way. Whatever she saw wiped the smile clear off her face.

Fair enough. She had good reason not to be happy with him.

"I'm sorry for your loss." It was Dave Claverley with his wife, Janet.

"Thank you for coming today." It was the one line Mateo could muster that wasn't false. He did appreciate the chance to shake hands and get hugs from the circle of neighbors he'd once thought to live out his days with. To Janet, he added, "I couldn't have pulled this off without you."

He might not have known about Jakob's passing and made the five-hour trip up from his boss's ranch in the Alberta Foothills if Jakob hadn't had Mateo still listed as next of kin. Along with his most recent address. Jakob had been keeping track of him. Rich, coming from the man who'd disowned him soon after he turned eighteen.

The duty of dealing with the dead fell to the next of kin, along with footing the bill, which had nearly cleaned out Mateo. It would've cost more if Janet hadn't reached out to him through the funeral home and invited him to use the country school that had been renovated for community events like weddings and…this.

"I wasn't alone," Janet said and gestured in the direction of where Haley had joined a bunch of women. "I had lots of help. There's loads of food. Make sure you dig in."

That was something he should probably be saying to the attendees, but he'd forgotten— and anyway, everyone seemed to know what to do on these occasions. Be sad and respectful for the first part, then eat and talk and even laugh for the rest. Grieve and then get on with life. Mateo had finished with the grieving part long ago. Jakob Pavlic's actual death from a heart attack eight days ago seemed redundant.

"Thank you, I will." A thought rippled mild panic through him. "What happens to the leftovers?"

"Whatever you like. The staff will package it up, and you can take it with you."

What would he do with broccoli and date

squares? "I don't want it. I'm leaving tomorrow."

"So soon?" Dave said. "I was hoping you'd come by. I hear you've seen a few good horses while you've been away, and I got some I want to show off."

Mateo was tempted to take him up on the offer. The Claverley cutting stock was making a bit of a name for itself, but these last few days stuck in a Spirit Lake hotel had about done him in.

"Perhaps next time," Mateo evaded. "My boss is already shorthanded."

"Who are you with?"

Mateo hesitated. He'd made it a point for more than a decade now not to release his exact whereabouts to anyone who might leak it back to Spirit Lake. He'd wanted a clean break. But now that Jakob Pavlic was gone, he no longer minded if connections were drawn between who he once was and who he'd become. "Hawk Blackstone."

Dave's eyebrows shot up as if Mateo had passed on the winning lottery numbers. He looked excited and cagey. The Blackstone Ranch might be a half-day's drive south, but it was known throughout the province for its quality cutting stock. Dave lowered his voice. "He still got his quarter horses?"

Barely. Mateo didn't know much about Hawk's finances, but his divorce was bleeding him dry. Crossing a horse pen the other week, Mateo had overheard Hawk on the phone say he'd consider any decent offer, his eye on the prize filly.

"He does," Mateo said.

Dave opened his mouth, but his wife touched his arm. "Mateo, do you want me to spread the word that people can help themselves to the leftovers?"

Relief swept through Mateo. "If you don't mind, that would be appreciated."

Janet cut away, leaving Dave alone to finish what he'd started. "Any two-year-olds he's willing to part with? I'm looking for a filly to train up."

"He has a filly," Mateo said cautiously. "You'd have to talk to him directly about selling her."

Another reason to hurry back. Mateo wanted to train the filly himself. He was sure that if Hawk could hold on to her for another year, Mateo could make her worth well into the five figures. Hawk could square away whatever was outstanding on the lawyer's bill and keep his twin toddlers in boots and beans. And it would go a long way to establishing Mateo's reputation as a trainer. He was getting tired of just being a hired hand.

Dave glanced over Mateo's shoulder. "I'll do that," he said quickly before raising his voice. "Knut, you shop off the same rack?"

Now that the two men stood side by side, Mateo noticed their same blue shirts with thin white pinstripes. "More like my daughter shops with your wife," Knut said.

"Great minds and all," Dave agreed, and might've added something more but for Knut's nod toward Mateo.

Dave got the hint. "Good to see you again, Mateo. Drop by if you have time. If not, have a good trip back."

He steered off, and Knut frowned at Mateo. "You leaving?"

"Tomorrow morning is the plan."

Knut's frown deepened. "Paul Chambers get in touch with you?"

Mateo remembered the name of Spirit Lake's better-known lawyer from when he'd still lived here. Jakob Pavlic had retained him when he and Mateo's mother had divorced. "No."

"He asked me—since me and Jakob were neighbors—to ask you to stop by his office. Your father had a will, and I'm thinking that since you're next of kin, there are matters to tie up."

Knut probably hated having this awkward conversation, and Mateo sympathized. It wasn't Knut's fault that Jakob had sold him five generations of Pavlic land—nearly a thousand acres—because his only son who had lived and breathed those six quarters didn't share a drop of his blood. Not that Knut had an inkling of that particular family secret. But now that Mateo thought about it, why wouldn't he know? Jakob and Knut had been childhood friends, just as he and Haley had been. And they'd stayed friends right to the end. Yeah, Knut might very well know.

And if he knew, did Haley? If she did, he'd feel like even more of an impostor. Digging through that deep mental pile, Mateo floundered for a reply. "Thanks for coming." Idiot response.

"Not at all," Knut said with equal politeness. "How are you doing?"

"Well, all things considered. And you?"

Knut shifted his weight from one leg to another. "Still on the right side of the grass." He paused. "Due for knee surgery at the end of May. As if things won't be busy enough for Haley."

"I saw," Mateo said.

Knut looked across the room to where she was laughing with Will Claverley and Krista. Will had introduced Mateo to his wife earlier, along with the toddler in his arms and their second child in Krista's arms. Haley was playing peekaboo with the baby. Why hadn't Haley's husband come today? Then again, it was the middle of March, and calving was in full swing. Another reason to get back. Hawk was dealing with three hundred cows, with only his rheumatic father to help.

"I suppose you can get help with the cattle," Mateo said neutrally.

"The cattle aren't the problem. It's Haley on her own with the baby."

Haley wasn't married?

"Dirtbag husband left after she told him she was pregnant. She signed the divorce papers last week."

Mateo felt the other man's anger as if it were his own. "Better off without him."

Knut snorted. "Her very words. She'll get through this. Not the first time a guy left her hanging."

He stared hard at Mateo. Was Knut implying that Mateo had abandoned her? There was some truth to that. The day Jakob Pavlic told Mateo he was no son of his was the last day he'd spoken to Haley. He had never attempted to keep in touch with any of his friends, but he came to regret cutting off Haley. As time passed, a phone call or social media message hadn't seemed right. He'd have to do it in person.

What was his excuse now? The unforgiving look she'd just given him. And the fact he was leaving again tomorrow. Why bring up old hurts?

"I'm sorry to hear about that." Mateo picked his words carefully. "But you're right. If there's anyone who can get through this, it's her."

"Yeah," Knut said. "That's what she thinks, too. She's giving me the eye. Time we head home. You get in touch with that Paul fellow, okay?"

"Sure," Mateo said, "I'll do that." He could finish up with the service in the next hour or two, drop by the lawyer's office before closing and be on the road first thing tomorrow morning.

MATEO FLIPPED THE two-page will back and forth and studied Jakob's signature. He recognized the sloping handwriting, but the words "To Mateo Pavlic" on this document made no sense.

Jakob Pavlic had left all his possessions to the son he'd told to get off his land. His three vintage cars, the ten acres he'd subdivided away from the land he'd sold to Knut, the house thereon and the contents therein, and the funds in his three bank accounts. Only the shares he had in the dealership would be rolled over to the remaining partner, as per a previous agreement.

"Are you sure?"

Paul Chambers tapped his copy of the will. "It's legal. There'll be an extra step to verify your identity before releasing assets."

Assets, as in money. "How much are in the accounts?" Hopefully, there'd be enough to pay off burial expenses and maybe even a little more.

Paul Chambers twisted his mouth downward in clear disapproval of Mateo's crassness. Let him think whatever.

"I couldn't tell you for sure. Enough for this process to go into probate."

A decent outlay, then. Eventually. "How long will it take?"

Down went the lawyer's mouth again. "Depends if there will be challenges to the will or not. Do you anticipate any?"

He thought of his mother. He'd called her last week to inform her of her former husband's passing, and she'd asked if he was going up to the funeral, as if he were only attending and not running the event, and then she'd gone on to talk about how she planned on driving down to Montana to the second home she shared with her current husband.

"Possibly my mother, but I doubt she would contest the will. She leads a pretty good life, as it stands."

"Any other relatives? Your father didn't mention any, but you'd be surprised how many read the probate notice and challenge it just to see how far they can go."

There were cousins scattered about in Saskatchewan, but they'd never kept in touch with the Alberta Pavlics. "As far as family goes, I'm it."

Jakob had probably willed it to him because there was no one else in the family. Except he wasn't Jakob's family. His one-time father had not ever attempted to reconcile with him. Why, then, had Jakob bequeathed his personal fortune to him?

Mateo zeroed in on the date of the will. Nearly five years ago. Disbelief and confusion blew away, replaced with the familiar rock of anger. Jakob had never intended to reach out to Mateo while he lived. Only in death, when pride didn't matter anymore.

Then again, as the saying went, don't look a gift horse in the mouth. Ten acres to call his own—a scrap of land compared to the nearly thousand acres Jakob had once promised him free and clear. Why had Jakob not sold that, too, and moved into town where the dealership was?

"Can I go to his place?"

Paul tapped the will with his pen. "You don't have title to it yet. That's its own headache, so my free legal advice is to not take up residence yet. Don't break in if it's locked."

As it turned out, the house was locked, but the key was kept exactly in its usual hiding place under the boot scraper.

A gravelly meow rolled up the stairs, and up trotted a ginger tom, big and muscled. He rubbed against Mateo's leg, rambling away with throaty meows and purrs.

Jakob kept a house cat? Janet hadn't mentioned it, but the animal obviously thought he belonged. Growing up, Mateo had always wanted an indoor cat, but Jakob had firmly said that cats belonged in the barn. The rule had clearly changed, proven when the cat strutted in ahead of Mateo.

That wasn't the only change. The interior of the ranch bungalow had taken on a decidedly masculine flavor. The peach walls of his mother's time had switched to a white-and-gray schema; and the renovated kitchen was in black, white and gray, with stainless steel appliances. Mateo could see how the look would appeal to car-crazed Jakob. It was constructed of the same materials and with the same sleekness as a car. He had stamped the place with an upscale, contemporary identity, a bit out of keeping with the rural setting.

Mateo felt a flicker of something for Jakob—not sympathy, but understanding. It couldn't have been easy to break from tradition to become his own person. Mateo idly opened a cupboard. The old, mismatched cookware had been replaced with heavy stainless steel. He went to shut the door, and it slid closed slowly. Dealing in cars had proved lucrative for Jakob Pavlic.

One of the cupboards held a bag of high-end organic cat food, and Mateo rattled kibble into a stainless steel cat bowl and poured water into the companion bowl. Mateo scratched the top of the cat's head. His left ear had a notch, probably a battle scar.

"You come with a name?"

His mouth full, the cat didn't reply.

As Mateo traveled from room to room, he got the sense that the place had been tidied. Jakob had suffered his heart attack in the middle of the night and had been rushed by ambulance to the hospital. Yet his bed was made, and there was no toothbrush in the adjoining bathroom. No garbage in the bathroom can or in the trash under the kitchen sink. Janet Claverley must've stopped in and not thought to mention it. The location of the key apparently wasn't much of a secret.

Out of habit and mild thirst, he opened the fridge. It had been cleaned right out, except for a small food platter from the service covered in tin foil. Janet again. But then his gaze fell on the jug of cranberry juice. He'd drunk a glass every day since he was a kid, craved it like many craved coffee. His father couldn't stand the stuff. No way would he have stocked it in his fridge. Only one person would've remembered his peculiar addiction. Haley.

It wasn't Janet after all.

He shook free the tin foil. Roast-beef-and-coleslaw sandwiches with a pecan-butter tart on the side. She also knew he used to eat those tarts by the dozen.

Haley hadn't forgotten him. This was her way of paying her condolences. First thing tomorrow, he'd swing by and thank her for the food. And, if he had the guts, apologize for freezing out his first friend. And his best.

He took the platter and a full glass of the tart juice to the bare dining room table. Minutes later, he was chewing the last mouthful and tapping up crumbs with a damp finger while the tom cat did his own cleanup job on his face and belly.

Mateo washed up and, acting on sheer muscle memory, was headed over to the back door by way of the kitchen when he stopped at what had been his mom's old sewing room. From the looks of the desk, padded chair and the four-drawer filing cabinet, Jakob had converted it into his office.

A computer with a fancy curved monitor sat squarely on the desk, along with a full-size office printer. A credenza supported trays and metal organizers of folders, papers and letters. Mateo was going to have to set time aside to deal with a whole lot of business. Sort, sell, donate or throw out. Every last little thing, from the pencils to the plates to the socks in the bedroom drawer.

Overwhelmed at the monumental task ahead, he dropped into the office chair. The momentum spun the chair sideways, and it butted up to the desk. He idly opened the top drawer. There were loyalty cards, sticky notes and two tickets to a car show in Calgary next month. Mateo flicked through the assorted pens on the tray. One from a tire-repair shop, one from the barber shop and a lemon-yellow one from a travel agency. In the end, Jakob had gone on a trip no one comes back from.

Mateo tossed the pen back, but it bounced off the drawer and rolled underneath the desk. To fish it out, he pushed the drawer tray farther along its track, revealing a list on a narrow strip of cardstock. A list of usernames and passwords. Including banks.

Well, well, well. Mateo powered up the computer only to be stumped by the access password. He tilted his head and the paper this way and that for a clue. There, in the top-right corner, was the word "Smokey," followed by the year of Mateo's birth. That was the name of Mateo's first horse bought as a foal the year he was born. Why had... Never mind. Mateo had long ago given up trying to figure out the ways of the man who had once been his father.

Mateo fell back in the office chair when he opened the first bank account. Jakob Pavlic might have sold off his family's legacy of land, but he'd turned it into his own kind of legacy. The amounts were smaller in the other two accounts but not by much. Providing probate went through without a hitch, Mateo stood to become a multi-millionaire.

Jakob Pavlic had given Mateo the means to change the direction of his own life, as he'd done for himself. The ginger cat jumped into Mateo's lap and took up that hunched squat known only to cats.

Stroking the thick fur, Mateo looked out the window. The falling daylight glinted off a newly constructed steel shed. Home of the vintage cars mentioned in the will, Mateo surmised. They would go straight to the auction block. Engineering feats of historical import they might be, but his interests lay in livestock and land.

Now he could secure his own land. Buy a section for sale around here. Or anywhere. Or… His gaze drifted beyond the shed to the trees and pastures beyond, to land that had once belonged to a Pavlic but was now owned and operated by Knut Jansson.

He could buy back the family land. He could finally take back what Jakob had robbed him of and become the sixth-generation Pavlic to operate the ranch. Continue the legacy.

He could have a place to call his own. He

could come home. Even if it was not by in-vitation.

Tomorrow, then, he would go to the Jans-sons with a word of thanks and an apology to Haley—and an offer to Knut.

NOW, WASN'T THAT just like a man? Never there when you need them. Never there when they promised they'd be there for you. For the third time in twenty minutes, Haley called her fa-ther and it automatically went to voice mail. Once again, she had to listen to his deep, roll-ing voice tell how he might be in the barn or out on a ride or not taking calls right now—and wasn't that obvious?—but that the caller could leave a message that he'd get around to picking up.

"Dad, it's me. I'll say it again—I'm in labor, for real. My water broke three hours ago, and I mean, broke like a burst water pipe." She contemplated the mop and pail she'd used to clean up the mess. "I'd really appreciate it if you could take a break from checking the cattle and run me to the hospital so I can get on with delivering you a grandkid."

As she ended the call, her abdominal mus-cles gave a terrific squeeze. A definite contraction. She looked at the clock stove to measure the time to the next one, as instructed by her midwife. She'd called Dinah when her water broke, but she was an hour's drive north, delivering a home birth. Of course, she would be. She'd said to keep in touch, as if they were occasional friends and she wasn't the one person Haley was depending on to help her bring new life into the world.

"You're two weeks ahead of schedule," she informed Bump. "I still have casseroles to make and… Oh, geez, the car seat."

Her sister had bought it during a whirlwind shopping trip three months ago. She'd blown up from her place in Calgary in the morning, took Haley on a three-hour shopping spree, dropped Haley and the loot off, and torn back to Calgary to catch a weekend meeting with her law office partners. She'd not even stopped to share a meal.

The day Haley intended to sort out the car seat was the day her father had come down the hall to tell her of Jakob's death. The first thing that had come out of her mouth was "Is Mateo coming home, then?"

As if it mattered. As if she didn't have enough to think about with cows calving all hours of the day and night, and her with all the agility of one. Did they get up three times a night to pee? But when her father confirmed the next day that Mateo was indeed coming, her stupid, lonesome teenage self wondered if he might stop by.

He hadn't, and why should he? He'd torn off twelve years ago as if on fire and changed his number after her second pathetic call. That she had felt his eyes on her during yesterday's service meant nothing.

In the nursery, a box cutter still rested on the car seat package from before. There was endless tape and Styrofoam and reams of plastic wrap. She ended up cutting through the box as though she were performing an emergency cesarean. She lay the package on its side and eased the seat out. Midwife to a car seat. There were plastic-wrapped straps and instructions in French and Spanish included, but none in English.

Her phone lit up, and she moved to where she'd left it on the changing table. But it was only a notification from the local baby store that breast pumps were 20 percent off today only. She'd meant to get one, too. Maybe she'd ask Krista to pick one up for her. Better yet, her friend could take her to the hospital. Krista had made her promise to tell her immediately when she went into labor and had promised Haley she'd drop everything and come with her into the delivery room.

Haley didn't want Krista there—didn't want anybody, for that matter. She and the baby could do this alone, barring the usual medical help. But a ride to the hospital would be nice, except her call to Krista also went to message.

Once again, as soon as she ended the call, her next full contraction came. Thirty-seven minutes from the first. And this one kinda hurt, even considering her usual high tolerance for pain. She called Dinah again.

"I'm finishing up here," the midwife said. "Get to the hospital and I'll meet you there. Or tell me now and I'll come to you."

Haley didn't want that. Mostly because she didn't want to clean up after a home birth. She called their hired hand next. Brock Holloway had eyed her growing belly over the months with pity and fascination like she had a tumor gone wild. But he would show up to help get her to the hospital. He, too, had gone silent.

Brock and her father must be having prob-

lems with a cow if neither were picking up
for this long. What do you know? The cows
were getting better treatment than she was.

She'd drive herself in. She wasn't calling
the ambulance. They'd charge five hundred
dollars. Let them be available for real emer-
gencies.

She had time anyway; the hospital was a
short half hour drive away. She'd throw a few
things in a bag, put the car seat in the back
of the twin cab with the buckles and straps
and instructions. She could figure it all out
in the hospital parking lot before going in.
If she ran out of time, she'd make her father
do it—suitable punishment for not answering his phone.

She had just set the car seat into the back
of the crew cab when the next contraction
had her clutching Bump. That couldn't have
been thirty-seven minutes. She pulled out her
phone. Thirty-one. Time to hustle.

A truck pulled into the lane and made its
leisurely way toward her through the slushy
melting snow. A truck she remembered from
more than twelve years ago, when it had been
far shinier.

Mateo.

He got out of the vehicle as if he had all the time in the world, took a good long gander around as if the Jansson homestead was a stop on some kind of tour. She slammed her door shut and came around the hood. "This is," she said, "about the worst-possible time for you to pay a visit. Dad's not here, the guy working for us can't be reached and I'm heading to the hospital."

"Why?"

She pointed to Bump. "Guess."

"Alone?"

"What does it look like to you?"

"I can give you a ride."

"You can't. I've got the car seat in this truck."

"I'll drive your truck, then."

"Then how will you get back?"

He took in a bit more of the Jansson ranch, as if she'd pointed out interesting aspects of the house and yard he should note before he finally looked back to her. "Haley, consider it as a way of thanking you for the supper last night."

Haley sucked in her breath. He had noticed. He had come back to his old home.

Mateo crossed to her and held out his hand.

There were calluses along the pads, and the thumb jutted out as she remembered. She'd never held his hand, even though they'd kissed.

"Keys?" he prompted.

Of course. She was as stupid as they come. Looking to hold a man's hand—the same man who'd treated their friendship like old chewing gum—while about to give birth to the child of a man who'd deserted her the day he discovered he was about to become a father. She sure knew how to pick them.

She slapped the keys into his hand. "Fine," she said and jerked open the passenger door. "Let's do this."

CHAPTER TWO

HALEY HAD INSISTED Mateo drop her off at the front doors of the hospital, and she'd take it from there. No way he'd let that happen. She'd had such a powerful contraction on the way to the hospital that she'd braced herself against the dashboard and breathed so deeply it had felt like she'd sucked up all the air in the cab. He'd floored it after that.

He commandeered an abandoned wheelchair at the hospital entrance, but she said that walking was better for moving the process along. He offered to carry her backpack, but she trucked on. They rode the elevator, and he held the doors open while she stopped to have labor pain on the threshold before they continued on to the nurses' station.

Leaning on the counter at the station, a gray-haired woman, muscled and tattooed, introduced herself as Dinah, the midwife. She looked at Haley expectantly.

"This is Mateo," Haley explained. "He's on his way out of town, so he dropped me off."

That wasn't the case at all—or at least, there were a few more steps involved. "I'm an old friend," he said to Dinah, "Is there any way I can help?"

"No," Haley said. "Thanks. We got this. If you want to do something, go install the car seat. I want it on the passenger—" She grasped the counter and went into her deep breathing, more like a thrumming moan. He didn't like the sound of it, and from the way the midwife thinned her lips, neither did she.

"All righty, you need to get yourself into a bed so I can check you." Dinah gave Mateo a quick head to toe. "Is this all you could find?"

"He's not coming in," Haley said.

Dinah snorted. "Then where's the backup you promised me?"

"I didn't promise you any," Haley said. "I told you that Krista might come, not that she would."

"You knew perfectly well that as a one-woman traveling show, backup is required, but we've not the time to prove me right," Dinah said. She pointed toward the delivery room. "Walk while you still can."

Mateo didn't know whether to stay or go and looked at the nurses, who reflected back his own uncertainty.

"Just go on," said one with bright purple hair and scrubs of penguins playing sports. "You can work the camera, if nothing else."

He compromised by pacing outside Haley's room. He could hear their muted voices, the squeak of sneakers, the hum of a bed being adjusted and then a moan from Haley as she entered another contraction. He stood outside, deep breathing alongside her. Silence edged in and then Haley's quiet voice: "Dinah, I can't do this."

Mateo pushed open the door. Haley was on the bed, pale and gripping the bedsheets. She turned to him. Hope sprang into her eyes, but she said nothing. He decided to twist the nurse's words just a little and addressed Dinah, seeing as how she seemed like an ally. "The nurses' station asked me to come in. They're shorthanded. If you needed help in here, then I'm to go get them."

Dinah spoke before Haley could. "Sink's over there. Scrub up well. She's already at eight centimeters, so we'll see some action soon here."

"What do you want me to do?"

"Give her sips of water between contractions and support her when she's having them. Other than that, keep quiet and out of the way."

That, he could do. He didn't know what to do about Haley's jerky breaths of panic. He bent closer. "Don't worry. You're in good hands. I pulled a couple dozen calves already this spring."

A corner of her mouth flicked upward. "You rub the cow's lower back while you were at it?"

"I might've, but none of them indicated any interest."

Haley leaned forward as much as her belly allowed. "Consider this an indication."

He obliged, and his hand had barely warmed on her spine before her entire frame convulsed and she announced, "Positions, everyone. It's happening."

Mateo glimpsed the baby before Haley did. A red, jerky-limbed body with a wet mat of hair. From the looks of it, a healthy boy. Mateo released a long exhale, only then realizing the hard tension in his muscles. The little guy was quickly swaddled and placed in Haley's waiting arms.

"Hello," she whispered. "Hello, welcome."

The baby's eyes sprang open, and he frowned at Haley.

She giggled. "Are you giving your mom 'tude already?"

"I wonder where he'd get that from?" Mateo said. He thought he'd spoken softly, but the baby gave a startle reflex, his tiny hands splaying out. Mateo didn't think. He held his finger out, and the baby grabbed on. A feeling of power and peace and absolute terror spread through him.

He could only imagine what Haley was experiencing. Her eyes were on him, and she smiled quietly. "Pretty cool, eh?"

He cleared his throat. "Yeah."

He wiggled his finger as if in a handshake. "Hello there. My name is Mateo. What's yours?"

There was a slight hesitation from Haley, and then she said, "Mateo, I'd like you to meet my son, Jonah Knut Jansson."

Mateo looked at her in surprise. "But that's—"

"Your middle name. I know. I've always liked that name—and it's not as if you're the only one who has it, you know. I'm not naming him after you, just so we're clear on that."

They hadn't seen each other in twelve years before today, so he believed her. Still. He thumbed baby Jonah's brand-new soft hand. Still.

CHAPTER THREE

ENTERING THE FARMHOUSE, it was hard for Haley to believe that she'd only been away since yesterday. Everything was still in its place—even the mop and pail in the kitchen—but it felt as if it were staged from a different time. She glanced over at the tiny being in the car seat her father held. That would be the reason.

Nothing would be the same again.

"Can you bring him into the kitchen?" Haley said over her shoulder as she led the way. "I will fix us sandwiches before he wakes."

"You'll do no such thing," her father said, setting down the car seat on the dining table. "Dinah said you're supposed to sleep when the baby sleeps, so get to it."

He was right, but there was so much to do, and she didn't feel at all sleepy. Jonah had slept for five straight hours last night, her alongside him for most of that. She was sore, yeah.

But she'd feel that way sitting, too. "I've got enough in my tank." She opened the fridge.

Knut shouldered her aside. "I went through this twice with your mother. I know exactly what to expect. You don't. At least go lie down on the couch."

First, she checked on Jonah. He was still sleeping, his fingers twitching. Was he dreaming of holding on to Mateo's finger? Mateo had looked at Jonah yesterday with the same pride and wonder she'd once hoped Trevor would have. If Mateo could view a baby who was not his own that way, he would make an awesome father. For all she knew, maybe he already was. He'd left the hospital as soon as her father came, and she didn't know if she'd see him again.

The back door opened and closed more quietly than in all the twenty-nine years she'd lived here. Brock slunk in and eyed the car seat like a ticking bomb.

"Come to see the latest Jansson?"

"Actually, I was just wondering," he whispered to her dad, "if you wanted me to give the cow her medicine and then let her out into one of the big pens? There's another cow that should go in."

Didn't that sound familiar? No sooner had Haley cleared the bed this morning than another deep-breathing mom-to-be-or-be-again was installed.

"You can," her father said, pulling out bread and random stuff from the fridge, "but you'll have to put her in the chute every time for her medicine."

Brock scratched the side of his neck. "I can give her a shot now, but, uh… Well, I got my first rodeo coming up in a week in Texas, and it's five days of driving."

Which meant he needed to leave now. "But we're in the middle of calving," she said.

Her father shook out bread slices onto the kitchen island and started to stack on one of everything he'd found in the fridge. "You sure you don't want to change your mind?"

Brock hung his head. "I get that I'm leaving you in the lurch, Knut. But I did talk to you about this last month."

Her father layered dill pickles onto a cold fried egg. "You did. Then calving hit, and there was Jakob, and it kind of slipped my mind."

"Slipped your mind?" Haley said. "I'm about to blow mine."

Jonah whimpered, and Brock hunched his

shoulders, prepared for fallout. She had only minutes to iron this out before Jonah went full throttle. Day one, and it was already time to dip into the emergency fund she'd set aside for Jonah. She turned to Brock. "Okay, how much?"

Brock shook his head. "It's not the money, Hal. I committed to the season."

A rodeo season lasted until at least September. No, no and no. "Do you know anyone who could replace you?"

"I have asked around, but it's calving season for everyone."

Jonah's whimpers had turned to little gaspy cries. Haley unbuckled the car seat straps and lifted him out. His little mouth immediately opened wide. She would have to feed him soon. Brock, meanwhile, edged closer to the door. "How about I go deal with the cows?"

He didn't wait for an answer before exiting out through the mudroom. There was a rap on the front door.

Mateo.

"Nothing for twelve years," Haley muttered, "and then not a day goes by."

"And wasn't that a good thing yesterday?" Knut flipped the top side of the bread down on three inches of foodstuff and pressed down.

"Come on in, Mateo," he called out loud enough to be heard and then lowered his voice when Mateo stepped inside. "Good timing. We were just having a bite to eat. Want one?"

Mateo did not grimace at the sandwich, but he did quickly say he'd just eaten. He turned to Haley. "You're home already?"

"They let me out for good behavior." She had to lift her voice to be heard above Jonah. "Listen, I'm going to have to deal with this guy."

Mateo got in her space, just like yesterday, and Haley felt herself go light-headed. At least she'd been in a bed before. Now she had to stand and take the fact that their faces were so close she could be a cat and rub cheeks with him. Rub cheeks? Her post-partum hormones had her bonding with the wrong new arrival. She tilted her head away to open up space between them.

Mateo did the whole stuck-out-finger trick, and Jonah's flailing hand caught hold. "There you go, buddy. Bring it down a notch or two. We heard you."

Jonah tilted his ear toward Mateo and quieted.

"There, that's better. Now you let Momsie get you sorted, deal?"

There Mateo went again, taking over. More annoying was how good he was at it. Now where was her feeding cover-up? "Dad, where did you put the diaper bag?"

The sandwich builder licked mayonnaise off this thumb. "What does it look like?"

"Really? It's like a big purse, like small luggage with a strap—you know."

"Could be still in the truck. Let me finish up here, and I'll go get it."

Her dad's idea of finishing up was to eat, wash up, watch videos and nap. "I'll go get it myself."

Mateo angled in front of her. "I can do that. I'll be faster."

"Good idea," her dad said. "Keys are in the usual spot."

It was a good thing he was fast, because Jonah hit the panic button as soon as the back door closed on Mateo, and no amount of jiggling and cooing cut it. She could feel her nerves fraying. Her dad was right. She should've rested. She sought the couch when Mateo brought her bag faster than she thought possible.

"You need anything else?"

"No thanks." Jonah wailing in one arm,

she tried to tug open the diaper bag with the other.

"Here. I got him," Mateo said. He brought his face close again, his hands slipped under hers, and the pass off was complete.

"Be careful. You have to watch the neck," Haley said, but Mateo already had Jonah's head cupped in one hand and his bum in the other. Mateo did have him.

How? He interpreted her look correctly. "I did diaper duty and night shifts with twins a couple years back." He dipped and swayed Jonah.

Hawk's kids. The Janssons and Blackstones were family friends, so she knew of the twins, but their names escaped her. So Mateo was not a father, then. But that didn't mean he wasn't a parent to someone else's children. Anyway, who cared? She extracted the long sling. She'd not practiced using it before, and after one look at its bulk, she tossed it aside. "Hand him over. Time to see if I remember what Dinah showed me."

Mateo discreetly retreated to the kitchen while Haley and Jonah worked out a good latch. As Jonah settled in, Haley could focus on other matters. Like the lack of help.

Not that her dad seemed concerned. She could see into the kitchen to where he and Mateo sat together at the island. Her dad was powering through his behemoth sandwich, his leg with the bad knee extended. Mateo sat in half-profile to her, talking quietly. He kept his voice down, probably out of respect for her and because that was who Mateo was. But her father carried on as if Mateo stood halfway across a pasture—is he going deaf?—so she easily followed their conversation about the price of fertilizer and cattle, and how hot and dry and cold and wet it was all over. Her dad loved nothing more than a good catchup of news, and Mateo could provide twelve years' worth.

She absorbed Mateo's every word, too. She'd no idea he'd spent a full three years working for Hawk Blackstone. Haley didn't think it a coincidence that the Southern Alberta rancher's reputation for quality cutting horse stock had soared in the past three years. Mateo had always had a knack around horses. She glanced down at Jonah. For any living being. Except her. He had barreled away from her like from a tornado.

And now he was back, chatting away as

if he were an ordinary neighbor. *Get to the point, Mateo.*

Finally, her arms aching from holding Jonah exactly right to maintain the latch and tiredness dragging her eyes shut, she'd had enough. "Mateo. What did you come over for?"

Her dad's shoulders sank at Haley's rudeness.

Mateo turned to face her. "I have a reason, true. I can talk with Knut outside and leave you alone."

He was the master at leaving her alone. It was on the tip of her tongue to inform him that she was as much in charge of the ranch as her dad, but then Mateo's reason might not have anything to do with the ranch and everything to do with the passing of his dad. Their fathers had been the best of friends. Just like she and Mateo had once been. She dipped her head to hide the swell of old sadness for their broken friendship.

"You do that," she said. "Jonah and I could do with a little peace and quiet."

"Sorry about that," Knut said as they made their way across the barnyard to the calving sheds. Dodging puddles and slick spots,

Mateo wished he had his lined rubber boots on instead of his good pair of boots. "She's got enough to handle with the new baby, and now she's all het up about Brock leaving today."

Mateo didn't blame her. She was out of commission for the time being, and Knut had his bum knee. "You don't have anyone to replace him?"

"Not yet." Knut squinted. "Looks like Brock's bringing in a couple of cows now."

It definitely looked that way. And from the way the cows stopped and started, probably absorbing contractions, none too soon. Knut grunted. "It'll be another busy day."

Now hardly seemed the right moment to make his offer, just as it hadn't seemed appropriate back in the house with Haley outright wondering the reason for his visit. At least he'd tamed Jonah's crying, though from the way Haley had tilted herself away from him, he was certainly not wanted. He might as well make himself useful if he hoped to get Knut's attention on him and not a cow.

"How about I help out here today?" Mateo said. "After, we can talk."

"Oh, I don't want to put you out. You got a pile of driving ahead of you. What's on your mind?" But even as Knut said it, his eye strayed to the calving sheds.

"I'm wondering if you've got an extra pair of boots and coveralls? Don't want you to come up with yet another excuse for why you won't accept my help."

In the end, Brock handed his own coveralls over to Mateo before shaking Knut's hand. Knut watched Brock head over to his truck. "I guess that's the last I'll see of him for a few months. Good worker."

Mateo sensed Knut regarded Brock Holloway as more than a good worker. "Will he come back in the fall?"

"Hard to tell with him. He's got itchy feet." Knut shrugged. "I hope so. He adds to the place."

Knut didn't expand. Did Haley view Brock as more than just a seasonal worker, too?

"This one's good on her own," Knut said, referring to one of the two cows Brock had brought in. "She'll be wanting out as soon as she gets the calf cleaned up."

Kind of like Haley. Not a comparison she'd likely appreciate, though it was a compliment. Haley never did like the indoors much. Baby

Jonah would not run short of fresh air and sunshine.

"The other's a heifer," Knut said. Enough said right there. If a cow had any trouble calving, it was usually with their first. Sure enough, this one looked panicky, with wide eyes and heavy breathing. Mateo pushed another unwanted comparison to Haley from yesterday out of his mind.

Three hours later, with a little pulling on Mateo's part, the heifer dropped a healthy black calf. Meanwhile, the veteran cow had calved, cleaned up her new bull calf and left for the pasture. Knut had walked four more in, all used to this particular spring routine. The exercise had hit Knut, though, and he limped, favoring his bad knee.

"I think we can let them be," Knut said. "We've done enough." He pointed with his head to the first heifer. "Let's see if she can figure out how to get it to suckle."

He leaned against a nearby fence, away from the east wind. The wind here in Central Alberta wasn't as bad as the howlers in Southern Alberta, but cold wind was cold anywhere. Mateo picked his place beside Knut and interpreted the lull as Knut's invitation for him to state his business.

"I went to see the lawyer the other day. A good thing, too. Turns out that Jakob left me practically everything." If Knut noticed Mateo referred to the man whom everyone thought of as his father by his first name, he didn't show it. He merely gave a nod of acknowledgment. Mateo wondered again if Jakob had confided Mateo's true status to Knut.

"It'll come out to a fair amount in cash alone." Mateo drew a breath and let it spill out. "Enough to make you an offer on the land you bought from...us."

Knut shot Mateo a sharp look. Then he looked away, studied the blue sky and the muddy ground. "All six quarters?"

Mateo hadn't considered the possibility of splitting the thousand acres up, and he didn't now. "Yep, all six."

Knut pulled his ear. "How much you thinking?"

Mateo named a rough figure.

"That's fair. Not saying I'm agreeing, but you're in the range that shows we can do business."

Mateo suppressed a smile. Knut Jansson hadn't succeeded at ranching by making bad deals. The fact he hadn't turned Mateo down flat out meant there was a chance.

"I don't want it to seem like I'm taking advantage of you being shorthanded, but this would give you cash in the door."

Knut straightened, sore knee and all. "I got cash."

Wrong move. Mateo backpedaled. "I didn't mean it that way. Sorry. I guess I was thinking overall. Not you, but with Haley and the baby… This'll give her options. There's all those expenses…" Mateo trailed off, not sure how to carry on, especially under Knut's scowl.

"What do you mean with Haley and the baby?"

Mateo could feel the thin ice he was treading on crack. "I don't want to interfere. Haley's capable and all, but right now, she can't be both a mother and a farmer. Hard to be in two places at once."

Knut grunted. "You got the grit to tell Haley that?"

"I… Well… Uh—"

"Exactly. The thing is, the land is technically in my name, but Haley runs it as she sees fit. That heifer there is hers. So is that cow we brought in. We pasture both her cattle and mine on the land you want. Now, I'm not opposed to selling the land back to you— with Haley's approval. And I'm telling you right now, she's not inclined to give up one square inch."

Disappointment choked Mateo. With Knut, it would've been a straight business deal, but Haley… With her, it always had been a whole lot more.

Knut poked his head around the shed. "Look at that."

Mateo joined Knut. There was the heifer with her newborn calf suckling at her bag, its hooves planted in the straw, its tail swinging for sheer joy.

"Haley would get a kick out of this," Mateo said. Now why had he said that, as if he had private admission to Haley's feelings? He could feel Knut's eyes on him.

"She would," Knut agreed. "I got chores to do. Maybe you could go to the house and tell her about the heifer. Tell her your idea and see what she says. I might be wrong."

They both knew they weren't. Still, he had to give it a shot. He owed himself that much, and he'd like to see Haley and Jonah one more time, even if it was only to say goodbye.

INTO HALEY'S DREAM of Jonah burping up bits of Knut's sandwich crept an intruder. He stood over them and rubbed his forehead. He padded away but didn't leave entirely. She could sense him hovering. Weird, and as she formed that thought, the dream disappeared and she woke with a start.

Mateo was standing at the edge of the living room. She shot upright from where she was lying on the couch.

He raised his hands in apology. "I'm sorry, Haley. I didn't mean to wake you. I was just going to leave."

Leave? The room, the house, the property? "You woke me up to tell me you're going? I could've figured that out on my own." She had the satisfaction of seeing him squirm.

"I know, but Knut… Your dad sent me in. He, uh, wanted you to know that the heifer calved and she's good. The calf is up and nursing."

"Bella?"

"If she's all black, that would be the one."

"That would be one of a dozen," Haley

said. "Still, that's good." She looked at her phone. She'd slept for nearly two hours. That would carry her through whatever night Jonah treated her to, but it also meant she was two hours behind on her day jobs.

She flipped back her throw and pushed herself to her feet. "You want coffee? Something to eat?"

"No, no," he said. "You rest." He took in the empty car seat, and she answered his unspoken question.

"Down the hall, in Grace's old bedroom. I converted it into a nursery."

She shuffled toward the coffee maker, but Mateo beat her to it. He swung open the cupboard above the maker. "Yep. Same place. How about you take care of you, and I'll make the coffee."

Embarrassment curled her toes. "You're saying I stink?"

"I'm saying that I can make coffee while you do things I can't do."

Getting a shower in now made sense, given she didn't know when she'd fit the next one in-between diaper changes, feedings, calving and—oh, yeah—hiring help.

She hated turning to Mateo for anything,

but hey, after helping her give birth yesterday, he wouldn't bat an eye at this ask. "You wouldn't happen to know anybody to replace Brock?"

Mateo had his back to her as he spooned ground coffee into the top of the maker. "Not offhand. Let me think on it."

In other words, no. Never mind, he wasn't here to solve her problems. Except that in the short time he'd reappeared, he had been doing nothing but that. "Sure. I'll be back. Pour yourself a cup. If you're not taking it black anymore, cream's in the door of the fridge."

She wasted no time in the shower, though her body begged her for a bath. Nope, in her next life. Basic hygiene was her new daily goal. She coiled her long, damp hair into a messy bun. It would take the rest of the day to dry. She should opt for a short "Mom" hairstyle. Another thing she should have had ready before Jonah arrived.

In the hallway, she paused outside the nursery. Silence. He'd been sleeping a long time. What if he was dead? Suffocated under the blanket. His little heart stopped. She sucked in her breath. Paranoia was no way to mother.

She forced herself to step away. *Newbie mom, you could always check the monitor you set up in the living room first.*

In the kitchen, she discovered her maternal instincts weren't totally off. Mateo had Jonah slung in one arm while he was flipping an omelet.

"Careful. You'll splatter hot oil on him." Haley reached to rescue Jonah, but his eyes were closed, his face smooshed against Mateo's arm. "Why did you get him up when he was sleeping?"

Mateo looked sheepish. "I heard him on the monitor when you were in the shower, so I went into his room. He was awake, and I didn't want him to cry and get you out of the shower. By the time I brought him here, he'd fallen asleep again. It seemed easier to hang on to him rather than put him back in the crib."

Taking care of her baby and cooking. This was too much. "Here, give him to me." But when Haley slipped her hands underneath him, Jonah gave a little cry and snuggled closer to Mateo. Great. Her own baby preferred a stranger to her.

Mateo eyed her, probably noting her sour face. "Eat while you can."

"Might as well. Fuel the pumps. Since that's all I am to him." She sounded petty, and his polite silence told her as much.

Only when she was seated at the island with her coffee and a fluffy, golden omelet did Mateo, leaning on the counter opposite, say, "Jonah is one day old. He doesn't know how to pick favorites."

"I know that. It's just that—" She broke off to gather her thoughts. She stuffed egg, cheese and broccoli bits into her mouth. It was delicious. "Thanks," she said, though she wasn't sure if it was for the food or his assurance. "It's just that I don't want him getting used to you being around. Any minute now, you'll be out of here."

He gazed down at Jonah, who made little smacking noises in his sleep. He'd probably prefer Mateo's cuisine to her milk offering.

"Maybe not," he said.

Haley paused, egg dangling from her fork. "What are you saying?"

"We could be neighbors again."

"You're…coming back?"

"I was thinking on it. I was left the house

and the acreage. And a good amount of money. Enough to buy back all six quarters from your dad. If you agree."

She stared at him, and he met her eyes levelly, his hands interlaced under Jonah like a businessman at a boardroom table.

"So that is why you came over yesterday?"

"And to thank you, Haley. But yeah."

She was so stupid. Of course the only reason any man showed interest in her well-being was to take her land. She tamped down her anger. "Well, the answer is a flat no, Mateo. I'm all Jonah has, and I intend to give him a good life, which means making the most out of the Pavlic land."

Mateo nodded and tucked Jonah's arm back under his blankie. "I don't blame you. I'd say the same thing if I were in your shoes." He gave her a small smile. "But I had to give it a shot."

"Yeah," she conceded. "And since we're switching shoes, I don't blame you for asking, either."

He looked out the kitchen window to the row of lilacs, still leafless in the early spring. She and Mateo had played underneath them, worming their way through the trails. "I'd like to make another offer."

"Forget it. I'm not selling Jonah until he's at least halterbroken."

"How about taking me on as your hired hand? For the short term. Say six weeks or so."

For the second time in as many minutes, she froze with her fork halfway to mouth. "But—but what about Blackstone?"

"I'd have to make phone calls, for sure. There's a chance I could find Hawk someone, and I could stay here. Before I do all that, I want to hear from you first."

Mateo here every day, working with her cattle, coming in for noon meals, holding Jonah while she showered. No, she mentally shook herself free of that last thought. "Did you talk to Dad about your bright idea?"

"No. I just thought of it now while you were in the shower. But it'll give him a chance to rest up his knee."

Mateo had noticed. Haley couldn't wait for the operation, even if it meant a minimum six-week post-surgery recovery period. She hated seeing her dad in constant pain. And apparently, so did Mateo.

"I don't know if we can pay you as much as Blackstone does."

"If I can afford to buy a thousand acres, I'm not in it for the money." He looked at her, the focus of his blue-green eyes square on her. She'd never forgotten the brilliance of his eyes. "I think it's my way of apologizing to you, Haley. When I left years ago, you called me, and I cut you off. I wanted a clean break, but it was cruel of me. I realized how wrong it was, but owning up to you in person would've meant coming back here, and I was still too angry for that. I placed my anger above the hurt I caused you. So I guess I'm apologizing for what I did and how I made you feel."

Mateo had tapped into her deepest feelings about that miserable time.

He'd come storming over with news about how Jakob was selling the land and how he was taking off. He'd left, just like that. She'd called after him, asking where he was going. His last words before tearing up rubber were, "Anywhere but here."

He had meant it. Hurt didn't begin to cover the tears in her pillow, the friendly badgering of people asking if she'd heard from Mateo, the constant checking of messages only for him to finally change his number without forwarding her the new one. Ever since she'd learned a week ago he was coming back, those old feelings had started to churn away. Now they were caught in the emotional upsweep of mothering hormones. If she didn't accept his apology now, he would know how much it had mattered.

She affected a puzzled frown. "Yeah, I did wonder what was up. But don't worry. It's all good. You don't have to give up your life because of something small a dozen years ago."

"It's bothered me, Haley. More as time's gone on. So you'd be doing me a favor if you let me stay for a bit."

Jonah wriggled and emitted a waking whimper, a small fist bursting free of his blanket. "You're up," Mateo said to Haley and came around the island to hand Jonah off.

She reached for her baby, but Mateo held on. "What do you say?"

It was probably because they were nearly cheek to cheek again, but it no longer made sense to push him away. She and her dad were desperate, and Mateo would be perfect. "All right. You're hired."

CHAPTER FOUR

MATEO DID THE fastest bit of talking in his life during the next hour as he sat in his truck outside the Jansson house with the heater running at half power. Haley was right. It was time he gave up on the old girl, but he'd had her since high school. Once he got his hands on some cash, maybe he would.

He persuaded his contact to help Hawk out, starting in a couple of days. Then he bit the bullet and called Hawk. The man he'd known since they were kids had given Mateo time off out of common decency, with the understanding that he'd return as soon as possible. And sending along a substitute had its own problems if he didn't work out.

"I've worked with this guy," Mateo assured Hawk. "I totally vouch for him."

He could hear Hawk's sigh. "All right. I'll take your word for it. He any good at horse training?"

"No. Just a cattle man."

"That's that, then."

There was a note of finality in Hawk's voice. Mateo asked, even though he wasn't sure he wanted the answer, "You selling the filly?"

"I don't have much of a choice now," Hawk said. "I was hard-pressed to keep her in the first place, but now that you've moved on and I don't have the time, there's no reason."

"I'm just here until May," Mateo said. "Both of us will have more time, then."

There was a pause. Mateo recognized that bit of silence from whenever Hawk was preparing to deliver bad news, but his next words seemed easy enough. "So you and the Janssons are neighbors again?"

Knut's wife had been fast friends with Hawk's mother before she passed. During visits to each other's ranches, the kids had hung out together, but Hawk and Grace had usually split off from Mateo and Haley.

Hawk cleared his throat. "I remember one time Grace and I were trying to shake Haley off our tail. She finally yelled out in the general direction of the bales we were hiding behind that she didn't care. She was going over to see you, who she liked a whole lot better than any of us anyway."

Mateo made a poor attempt at an easy laugh. "I don't think she'd say that now."

"I don't know her mind, but I bet you're not just there to help out. You're there to help yourself. You're going after Haley, aren't you?"

Not Haley, but her land. He'd told her that he accepted her refusal, but even as he'd said it, his mind had scrambled for another way in. "I don't have any intentions that way."

"Then you aren't done lying to yourself," Hawk said. "I dare you to tell me that again in two months."

Mateo hadn't told Hawk about the inheritance or his desire to buy the land, but Hawk deserved to know something of Mateo's plans. "I should tell you that the two months is for my time here. After that, I plan to move on to…other opportunities." If he could somehow persuade Haley to change her mind.

"Huh. They involve Haley?"

"They might, if it all works out. But not the way you're thinking."

"Right," Hawk said. "I got another call coming in. I think it's that buddy of yours. Call me when you're ready to admit the truth."

Mateo let his now former boss think what he wanted and met up with Knut forking hay into the bull pen.

Mateo took hold of a second pitchfork. "I might as well take over here, seeing as I'm your new hire."

Knut leaned on his long-handled fork. "You don't say."

There was a faint challenge to the older man's stance that had Mateo scrambling. "That is, if it's all right with you. Haley did ask what you thought of the idea, but I said I wanted to ask her first."

"I don't mind you working here. I am a little surprised she didn't chase you off the place when you brought up buying the quarters."

Mateo spread the hay this way and that, that way and this. "That was a no go. I might ask again, though."

Knut stood there like a Viking warrior with his spear. If they were going to work together, Mateo had better own up.

"I told Haley that I haven't been much of a friend over the past years. I'm trying to make up for it now."

"You're trying to butter her up before you make another offer."

"I'm not buttering her—" Mateo winced at the image created. "I do want to help her—and you—out. I don't even care if I get paid or not."

"That's because you feel guilty for still angling for the land when she just refused you."

Mateo turned away to compose his thoughts. The bull in the pen was peaceably munching on the hay, his mild eyes riveted on them, like a moviegoer with popcorn. Mateo set aside his fork and reached through the fence slats to scratch the coarsehair on the huge head. The Black Angus halted his chewing and leaned into the sensation. Mateo tried again. "You said it yourself. She's in no mood right now to consider my offer. And the fact is, you two need help now. There's nothing wrong with giving her a bit of breathing space. And there's nothing wrong with me showing a little patience."

Knut lowered himself onto an overturned metal trough, stretching out his leg. How often did the man give his knee these little breaks during the long work days?

"You'll only make it worse. You stay on

and then ask her again, she'll see you as mercenary. That you were pretending to help out when your real intention was to go after her land. And then she'll see you out the door on the toe of her boot. And she'll be none too happy with me, either."

Mateo didn't want to cause a rift between father and daughter. His gaze drifted over to the calving pens as he searched his mind for a work-around.

Knut made a disgusted noise. "I'm at fault here. I should've moved faster on getting a replacement. I meant to make calls, and then everything happened with Jakob. I mean, your dad."

Mateo caught the slip. It could be that Knut was used to referring to his lifelong friend by his first name. It could also be that Knut was aware of Mateo's biological status but was keeping that knowledge to himself, maybe fulfilling a promise to Jakob. Yes, it could be that Knut had his own secrets. And if he had secrets, then Mateo had a right to his own, too.

Mateo gave the bull a final quick scratch and picked up his pitchfork again. "I'll tell you what. Six weeks will take us through most of the calving, and Haley will be more sorted with Jonah. I'll have a timeline about when the funds will be released by then, too. I'll ask again. And…" Mateo hesitated before continuing. "If she kicks me out then… I guess I had it coming."

Haley would recover soon enough from any sense of betrayal. She hadn't seemed too fussed when he'd brought up leaving her a dozen years ago. His own guilt had probably made him misinterpret her coldness toward him. She was just being her usual outspoken self, coupled with the more pressing matter of becoming a mother.

Knut shifted on his cold metal seat. "You would have it coming, and I hate to see her upset."

Mateo's mind flashed to little Jonah, so warm and trusting in his arms. His hackles would go up if anyone upset Jonah, and he'd only known the boy for one day, not for nearly thirty years. It couldn't have been easy for Knut to watch his daughter suffer because of her scum husband. "I understand. I'll stick to my word."

"All right, then. Six weeks and not a day

more." He looked toward the house. "I'm going inside to see how my grandson's doing."

Mateo was more than happy for the change in topic. "He's doing well. Bright, alert. He grabbed hold of my finger, and there was power in his grip."

Knut gave Mateo a long, speculative look. *What?* Haley's father nodded and opened the gate. After he closed it behind him, he called over his shoulder, "Check the cattle and the cow's due for another dose of medicine. After that, carry on."

Mateo took it as a compliment that the older rancher trusted him to know what all that entailed.

"Now, JONAH, this cow is my favorite." Haley rubbed the Black Angus between the ears. "Jonah, meet Bella. Bella, look I had a baby, too."

Bella snuffled Haley's sling. Cozied inside, three-week-old Jonah widened his eyes at the unusual noise. "You think that's strange? Wait until you see what made that noise." Haley tilted Jonah up so he could see Bella. More the other way around, since Jonah's range of vision still didn't extend much beyond her and whoever else was holding him, which typically was—

"Careful she doesn't bunt him."

Mateo.

At Mateo's voice, Bella reversed so fast she popped her own calf off her udder. The calf, an exact replica of her mama, trotted after her to latch on again.

"I've known her all her life. She's good."

"Not saying she'd do it purposely, but it wouldn't be exactly the best introduction to cattle."

Haley gave Mateo a second look. His eyes were on Jonah. Ever since he'd started working here, it seemed his attention swung to Jonah like metal to a magnet. She was simply the thing that fed and dressed her son. How much was Mateo here for her and how much he was here to soak up Jonah? "How do you know I haven't been out here before?"

Mateo dragged his gaze to hers and gave her a dry look. "There's not much that goes on out here I don't know about."

He had a point. He practically lived and breathed these cattle. In fact, he'd temporarily moved into Brock's old quarters attached to the house via a carport. From the nursery window at night, she would watch Mateo leave with a flashlight to check on the cows. It had given her an odd feeling of companionship and also relief to know that all was in hand.

A feeling she shouldn't get used to at all.

"Anything I should know about?" she asked.

He gave her a guarded look and glanced away. Her question had been innocent, but he acted as if she'd caught him stealing supplies.

"You mean about the cattle?"

"What else would I be asking about?"

He indicated the five-gallon pails full of chopped grain in his hands. "I mixed selenium in with vitamin powder for a few that are bagging. Knut said they go all weak after calving."

He hadn't directly answered her question, but she'd give him the benefit of the doubt. "Which ones? You can't go by what Dad says. He always cheaps out on the mix, and then they get sick and we're out here giving them a shot."

Mateo was eyeing Bella, whose neck was outstretched to Jonah again, sniffing. "Come with me. I'll show you."

They headed to an open part of the feed pasture, their pace slowed by Mateo with the full chop pails and by Haley stepping carefully so she didn't stumble with Jonah. Just the three of them out on a walk. How sweet, how temporary, how stupid.

Haley redirected her mental energies to the cows they were approaching. "Where's Georgia?"

"A couple thousand miles south of here," Mateo deadpanned.

"Funny," Haley said. "She hasn't calved, I know that." Mateo filled in the digital records she made a point of scrolling through every day. "You got to watch her like a hawk. She's a weird one. Every other cow goes off to calf, and she walks right into the middle of the herd to drop hers. Has she bagged?"

"Seeing as how I still don't know which Black Angus among the one hundred fifty Black Angus you're talking about, I can't tell you. What's her number?"

Mateo turned three rubber tubs right side up and shook grain into each of them. A half dozen pregnant cows made their ponderous way forward. Haley could relate. Except they had an excuse. She was no longer pregnant, just fat.

Haley began to rattle off Georgia's ear-tag number. "No wait, it ends in eight-four. No, six-four." What! She knew the tag numbers like store clerks knew produce codes. Post-partum, sleep-deprived brain. "I know what she looks like. She'll be over there with the main bunch."

She pivoted in that direction. Empty five-gallon pails clanged to the ground, and Mateo appeared in front of her. He had a habit of getting in the way. "Not with Jonah. All you need is one cow to step sideways or to swing her head or—"

"If you want to hold him, say so."

Mateo cracked a slow smile. "That obvious?"

"Like a horse in a pigpen." She handed over Jonah's warm bundled self and tossed the sling over Mateo's head. The pink-and-yellow splash of color livened his appearance. She expected him to toss it right back, but to her surprise, he looped it this way and that. Within moments, he had Jonah snugged tightly against him, as if he'd been doing it all his life.

He shrugged at her expression. "I've watched you, and I've tied a few knots before."

Three weeks. Three weeks was all it had taken for him to come back into her life and completely upend it. No, he'd made it better. Even though her girlfriends, Dana and Krista, had cautioned her about how exhausting babies were, she hadn't realized how bone-deep it went. Mateo had taken his sweet time coming home, but he'd come when she needed him the most. She ought to show a bit of gratitude for his pink-slung presence, for however long it lasted.

She shoved her hands in her jacket. Things cooled off fast when there wasn't ten pounds of baby strapped to your front. "Mateo, I just wanted to say that it's been…good having you here. I know I wouldn't be able to get what little sleep I have been getting if you weren't handling all this. Dad helps, but the last few years, we've grown to count on having an extra hand.

"I'm not saying this to make you stay longer than we agreed, and I know you're trying to make up for what you think is a past mistake, but I guess I'm trying to tell you that we're good. What you're doing now more than makes up for it. Okay?"

Mateo had adjusted Jonah's tuque while

she'd rattled on. He raised his eyes to her, and there it was again—the same look of guilt. Call it hypertension from being sleep-deprived, but she couldn't let it go on. "Are you hiding something from me?"

"No," he said quickly. "Other than the fact that doing this, working here, it's not the big sacrifice you seem to think it is." He stripped off his workman's glove and stroked Jonah's cheek. "There's an upside."

Mateo had taken to Jonah as if he were his son. And there had once been a time when she'd hoped for a moment like this. An ordinary dream in which Mateo was holding a baby—their baby.

Dream on, girl. For all she knew, he already was seeing someone. She hardly knew anything about his personal life, even as he'd been privy to all of hers.

Then again, it was none of her business, and in the end, it didn't matter. He'd drive off in his rust bucket in another month or so, leaving behind her and Jonah. At least this time, it would be on good terms.

MATEO WAS HIDING in the horse barn. On the surface, it looked as if he was brushing down

Haley's horse, Canuck Luck. He'd saddled the mare up and taken her for a quick ride. Rides usually helped to collect his thoughts, but he figured he could cross the country and back again before he was ready to face Haley.

Knut was right to say that the six-week delay in making a second play for Haley's land would only worsen matters. Today marked six weeks to the day, something that Knut had reminded him as soon as he'd emerged from his bunk quarters that morning. As if he could forget. It had hung over his head like a noose the past week. He'd rehearsed lines while shaving, and twice he'd almost mustered up enough courage to bring it up while they were checking cattle.

He had ridden Canuck Luck over the land he wanted for his own. Brome grass had lent a green haze over the warming hay land. He'd taken the mare into last year's wheat stubble. If it were up to him, he'd plant oats for greenfeed. There hadn't been much snow this past winter, and his gut told him it would be an unusually dry summer. Next year, he'd seed it to pasture for the horses and cattle he would buy the year after that. The years had unrolled in his imagination. In the end, riding the land had only riled his thoughts worse because he wanted it all the more.

"If I can only convince Haley," he muttered to Canuck Luck as he brushed her withers. Convince her to sell the quarters in a way that didn't stomp on her growing trust in him. He wanted the land and he wanted Haley in his life. He stood to lose both.

The mare's ears tipped forward, and Haley stepped into the barn, weighted down with the baby sling. Fussing cries rose from inside the cloth folds.

His feet were moving before his brain kicked in. He handed the brush to Haley and scooped out Jonah, hitching him high into the crook of his arm. The raised position gave Jonah a sight line on the action. Haley tossed him the sling, but he looped it on the hook for the reins. It felt better to have Jonah tucked close. "Look at you, buddy. All bright eyes. Come to help out?"

"If you teach him time first. He's supposed to be getting his afternoon nap in, but he was arching his back on the mattress as if it was poking him. I finally gave up and decided to take us for a walk." Haley applied the brush to the sorrel's flanks. This had come to be their usual routine. She'd come with Jonah whenever she could to wherever he was, and they'd switch places. It suited them both; Haley had a break from Jonah, and Mateo... Well, he got to hold a little guy he was getting far too attached to.

"You rode her?" Haley asked him.

"Yeah. She has good instincts."

"She is a beaut, isn't she? I picked her up about a year ago. Before Jonah. I probably wouldn't have bought her if I'd known he was coming. Maintaining her in the style to which she has become accustomed won't be easy. You're not in the market for a horse, are you?"

He detected a line of seriousness underneath her joking question. If she was rethinking her assets, could it also extend to the land? "No use taking a horse if I have no land to put her on."

"You have ten acres."

And a house that didn't feel like his own. He checked in to feed the cat and sort through the mail, but he stayed the night in the Jansson bunkhouse. With calving mostly over, he'd have to find a way to get used to the four walls he'd grown up in. Now was the time to ask her about the land again. Jonah squirmed in his arms, to look straight up at him and then smiled, a real one that rounded his cheeks.

"Hey, did you see that? He smiled. He actually smiled at me."

Haley examined him, tipping her head so close wisps of hair brushed his chin. "Oh, that. It could be gas. He drank a ton and then wouldn't burp."

Mateo flipped Jonah over his shoulder and tapped him twice. Jonah emitted a huge belch that had Canuck Luck twitching her ears. "There, buddy. How about that?"

Jonah smiled, a real one. At him. An emotion, strange and powerful, surged through Mateo. The general pleasure he'd felt around other babies was nothing compared to this feeling of tender ferocity for Jonah. "See? It is a smile."

Haley shrugged. "So he thinks you're the best. What else is new?"

"You're not jealous, are you?" He didn't want her to be, but neither could he deny his pride in the special bond between him and Jonah. It was something like the relationship between him and Hawk's filly, instinctive and natural. Like that, but way more.

Haley gave a vigorous brush to the mare's hindquarters. "Of course I am. I'm with him day and night, and he cries when I hold him and is all giggles when you do. And you'll be gone any day now, and he'll be stuck with me."

Now. Say it. "I don't have to go."

Haley froze, the brush suspended in her grip. "What are you saying?"

"I was thinking…now that you've had time to think about it, maybe you'd like to reconsider my offer about selling the land."

Haley paled. Her lips trembled and she bit them so hard he worried she'd draw blood. She looked hurt, but then she raised her head and he saw angry, flashing eyes. "These past six weeks have been all about you getting your hands on the land I already told you I'm not selling?" She spoke in a low, dangerous voice. All his rehearsed lines flew from his head.

"No! Not all of it. I didn't want to give up, and you needed help, so…it seemed like the right thing to do."

"The right thing to do, sure. You made it all up, didn't you? That whole apology for ditching our friendship."

Knut had warned him she might feel this way, and fragments of his careful arguments floated back to him. "That's not it at all. That was the reason I didn't ask again right away. Because I wanted that apology to count for something. I wanted it to be more than words."

She glared at him over the roan-colored back of her mare. "You wanted it to be a way in. A way to soften me up and then hit me with the offer. You wanted to show me how I couldn't do this by myself without your help. And then you'd sweep in with your offer, and I'd see you as my savior. Is that it?"

He was losing her trust. If he could lay it out rationally, show her that he'd done some good. "You already do see me as that, Haley. Remember out there, a few weeks back with the cattle, you said I was a lifesaver. That you couldn't have got through calving this year without me. And it's not going to get any easier."

"I'll hire help. You are replaceable." Haley spoke through clenched teeth. "The land isn't. You only want it to get back at your dad. He sold it out from underneath you, and now you want it for yourself."

There was something to what she said, yet hearing it from her, he realized there was more. It wasn't just about past hurts but the unknown possibilities it could give him. And her. "I can't force you to believe me, Haley. But I am serious about the offer. About two months from now, I'll get paid out my inheritance. I can pay your dad in full. That'll be a tidy sum for you…and Jonah. For the future."

If possible, she flared up even more at his last words. "I do nothing but think of the future." She pointed to Jonah. "His. The 'little buddy' you pretend to like so much. If you did care—if you really understood the value of the land, of me and him—you wouldn't have dared make your offer."

She stepped close, toe-to-toe. "I'd like my son back, please." Her voice was cold, hard.

He didn't delay responding to her request. He'd screwed up, blown away what little trust he'd gained. She nestled Jonah against her shoulder, and his cheek scrunched against the soft padding of her jacket. Mateo felt the empty space against his arm as if it were its own kind of weight.

"Haley, I—"

"Go," she growled. "Now. And don't come back."

"Look, at least let me stay until you get—"

"Go. Now."

On the way to his truck, Mateo met Knut coming out of the house. Knut took one look at him and sighed. The two men didn't exchange a word as they passed by each other with their heads down.

CHAPTER FIVE

SUPPER THAT NIGHT was a silent affair. Just the clink and scrape of cutlery as Haley and her dad plowed through overdone meatloaf, underdone boiled potatoes and half-done cauliflower. Haley had choked down bites of the latter before she remembered that cruciferous veggies made Jonah backfire like Mat—like somebody's old truck.

She pushed away her plate. "Not my best meal, I admit, but we've lived off each other's cooking for years now. We'll survive."

Her dad crunched down on the meatloaf. "Odds narrow daily." His chewing turned thoughtful. "Mateo cooked up a lasagna last week as good as you get at a restaurant."

Better. He'd come in with grocery bags one day and put it together while she and Jonah napped. She'd woken up to its mouthwatering smell. He'd even come in from his chores to take it out of the oven on time. Now the memory churned her stomach, because his meals had just been a ploy to trick her into giving up the land.

"Let's face it. The only way we're getting food that good again is if we actually go to a restaurant. No use pining for the past, Dad."

He made a face as if he might contradict her, but he kept his mouth shut. Wise move.

For him, maybe. But she'd bottled enough in. She glanced at the monitor. Jonah had conked out an hour ago, having missed his afternoon nap. That meant she was in for a long night, but right now, she could have it out with her dad.

"You think I should have sold him the land."

Her dad swallowed, which took a couple of tries. "I think you could've listened to what he had to say."

"He could've listened to what I told him. He spent the past six weeks sucking up to us so he could make us feel weak and then take us down."

"I don't feel weak around him."

Implying she did. "You should. Six weeks, and you're sore for his cooking. Yes, he helped during an important time, but it's not as if we didn't pay him. We don't owe him anything."

She stabbed a potato with her fork and bit down. Ugh. She scraped back her chair and took both their plates. "I'm nuking the potatoes."

"The meatloaf—"

"I'll trim off the crispy bits."

The microwave humming, Haley tried again. "Look, Dad, I know you've got nothing against Mateo. He was your best friend's son. You probably feel responsible for him, in a way. But all I see is a selfish manipulator." She whacked the blackened edges off the meatloaf and scraped them into the garbage. She hated throwing away even a mouthful of beef. A steer had died for it. Lado used to eat up the scraps, but he'd passed last summer. She'd lost a husband and the dog in the same month. She missed the dog.

Her dad sat back in his chair. "This has little to do with the land, does it?"

Haley kept her focus on sliding the meatloaf back on their plates. "I don't know what you're talking about."

"Yes, you do. You're still mad at him for not keeping in touch."

"I am not. I wouldn't give him the emotional real estate."

"I think you have. About six quarters of real estate."

The microwave beeped, and Haley spun around to attend, which neatly turned her back on her dad and his barbs. She decided to ignore his comment. "Do you think I should sell the land? And don't say that it's up to me. I know that. I want your opinion."

She set the plates down in front of them again. Knut took up his fork and knife in preparation for round two. "You sell, and you'll have quite a bit of cash, even after the tax collector takes their pound of flesh. Cash means you can do whatever you want."

She didn't need cash. On top of what flowed into her regular account, she had twenty grand socked away for an emergency.

Her dad was aware enough of her solid finances to add, "But if what you want is to stay put, then don't sell."

"I want to stay put." It was what she'd wanted to do since she was a girl. It was others leaving that she had a hard time dealing with. Like Mateo—and then not a year later, her mother. Her sister had already gone off to university when their mother passed. Now Grace bombed in and out of their lives every few months or so. She kept promising to visit her new nephew, but Haley wasn't holding her breath.

"Well, then," her dad said, loading up on a steaming pile of potato. "I guess you made the right decision."

He spoke in a careful, neutral tone, which immediately made her doubt herself. She popped hot potato in her mouth and immediately danced it around on her tongue to cool it off. She bit down and tasted the bitter edge of raw tuber.

She made a face but smoothed it when Knut raised an eyebrow. He wasn't the only one who could pull off the careful, neutral act.

FOR THE NEXT WEEK, Mateo woke on his own at two in the morning ready to check the cows, only to remember he was in his—Jakob's— bed and Haley had fired him. He'd force himself back to sleep, and then he'd wake at quarter to six, ready to check them again. By then, it was close enough to dawn for him to fire up his dad's stainless steel espresso machine and pour himself a cup of something he'd have to pay quadruple the price for at a boutique coffee shop. Mateo preferred clunking around with the old-fashioned coffee maker. Like the one that sat on the Janssons' counter.

He completed odd jobs around the place. Fertilized and cut the lawn, repaired the fence around the acreage, cleaned windows while listening to grain and cattle reports and also checked real estate listings for local land for sale. There was a quarter or two here or there—nothing like the spread next to him. Knut had been right to jump on Jakob's offer. Land didn't change hands often.

He went to the shed-cum-garage and contemplated selling Jakob's three cars. Maybe to the partner Jakob had willed his shares in the dealership to, but that didn't feel right, so he closed the door and left. The ginger tom agreed to the name of Dodge, and they celebrated over canned tuna.

He could go back to Hawk's. Put house, acreage, cars up for sale and call it quits. Except in his heart of hearts, he didn't want to go. This place was his, even if it was only because Jakob had had no one else to pass it on to. Haley also kept him rooted here. He suspected she assumed he'd run again. He had to prove her wrong, if only for his own sake of worth.

He happened to be driving along the Jansson fence line when he noticed low-lying barbed wire. Jakob had stored wire cutters and staples in the shed, and so it didn't cost Mateo anything to tighten the wire. The next day, he thought he might as well check the entire length of the section, and he discovered a rotting gate post. Since he was going into town anyway, he picked up a new one, along with cement mix.

Once he replaced that post, it wasn't much to bump his truck across Jansson wheat stubble to the fence on the other side of the field, the one that divided the grain field from the summer pasture. It had to be strong to keep the cattle out of the crop, and from the looks of the odd leaning post and sagging wire, it wasn't. Mateo remembered pounding some of the posts in with Jakob. He'd argued with him about not putting in the fence and letting the whole half section be for pasture. But Jakob had wanted to turn one quarter into grain. "Wheat doesn't make you get up in the dead of night," he'd said. Mateo had thought

Jakob was lazy, but it was just that his heart wasn't in it.

Fixing the fence would take a few days, but it was work he could do undetected. He was sure that even other neighbors couldn't spot him behind the band of trees that ran along the bordering roads, but on the third day, Knut drove up in his farm truck with posts loaded in the back.

Knut stepped out of the truck and surveyed the fence line. "You've been busy."

Since he hadn't pointed out Mateo's obvious trespassing, Mateo stuck to the topic at hand. "Mostly tightening wire. There's a fair bit of work on the gate to do. A post has to get changed out."

"Two."

Mateo knew the second one he was talking about. "Post's good. Cement didn't take right. Dig that out, pour in new cement, and it'll hold."

Knut grunted. "Trevor balled that up."

Haley's ex. Mateo had spent many an idle moment wondering how bright, independent Haley had ended up with someone who by all accounts was shiftless and incompetent, but he wouldn't gossip with Knut. "Not exactly his wheelhouse, I guess. This kind of life isn't for everyone." Mateo's gaze strayed back in the direction of Jakob's acreage.

When he turned back to Knut, the man was studying him.

"You talking about Jakob?" Knut asked.

Mateo leaned on a sturdy post. He'd not had a proper conversation with anyone in nearly two weeks. He'd considered taking Dave Claverley up on his offer to look at his horse stock, but Krista was good friends with Haley, and the women had no doubt talked about the underhanded hired help. He figured both he and Dave could do without the awkwardness. During all that alone time, he'd brewed a good deal about Jakob Pavlic, and now was as good a time as any to bring it up.

"I am," Mateo said. "He and I didn't part on the best of terms, and I spent the whole time blaming him. But I came back and saw the life he'd made for himself. It couldn't have been easy to change direction and go after what he wanted. I always thought selling the land was an act of vengeance, but it took courage. I'll give him that."

Knut leaned on his truck box, a signal that he, too, was up for talking. That, and he was probably giving his knee a rest. "I got to tell you that when Jakob came to me about selling the land, I tried to talk him out of it. I didn't want him to throw it all away without thinking it through. I brought up you and the whole line of Pavlics that came before him. But the more we talked, the more I saw that he had thought about it for a long time, and the upset with your mother just gave him the push."

The upset with his mother. That hardly described the glass-shattering fight that had taken place. Mateo had pulled up to the house after finishing his last high school exam. They'd been so deep into it they hadn't heard him arrive, and Mateo had stood outside the back door and heard every last single word. Jakob's shouts of betrayal, his mother's screams of defiance, the ugliness on both sides, the lifetime of bitterness and festering resentment. Mateo's lifetime.

He looked Knut in the eye. "Did Jakob tell you everything behind that fight with Mom?"

Knut gave a single nod. "He told me you weren't his son by blood." His pale-blue eyes bore into Mateo. "And that's the first time that piece of information has passed my lips since Jakob told me."

Meaning Haley didn't know. Meaning she still believed that he and Jakob had had a fight over the land, such a bad fight that Jakob had kicked him out and Mateo had only been too happy to leave. It's why she believed that he only wanted the land to get back at Jakob.

"I appreciate that, Knut."

"I promised Jakob." Haley's father paused. "It might be easier all the way around if you shared with your former good friend now the way Jakob did with me."

Once again meaning Haley. It might soften her anger—or make her feel even more manipulated. "I suppose I could try."

"It might be more to the point than fixing the fence for her. No good the secret lasting another decade."

"We didn't exactly part on the best of terms this time, either."

"You regretted that the first time it happened. You want to make the same mistake again?"

He didn't, but… "I haven't changed my mind about the land. I still want to buy it."

"Then I suggest you propose a new deal she might consider." Knut pushed himself away from the truck. "In the meantime, there are posts to pound."

"I got it. You rest your knee."

Knut flicked a smile. "I missed your help."

Had his daughter? There was only one way to find out, and that was to meet with her. It gave him one more chance to set things right between them. Yes, he wanted the land, but he also wanted his old and good friend back.

ONE MORE THING. That was all this day had been for Haley. Just one thing after another. She'd boiled the eggs dry, the smoke detector her first clue. Jonah had shrieked for a half hour after in response to the alarm. Jonah had shrieked again when a calf shoved his wet nose into the stroller while she wedged a stone out of the hoof of another calf.

When she'd come out to take Jonah for his checkup, the front tire was low, and she had to pump it up with the air compressor, which put her behind schedule by a quarter hour. While buckling Jonah in, she'd leaned over to tighten the seat harness, and her phone slid from her pocket and bonked Jonah on the head. More shrieks. She'd arrived late at the doctor's, certain from the swelling bruise she'd injured her son's brain.

And on it went. Jonah had shrieked all the way home at the sun angling into his eyes, the haskap bushes were backordered and a carton of eggs fell out of the grocery bag right on the threshold while she was wrestling Jonah, herself and a grocery bag back inside the house.

She was mopping up eggs with paper towels when Jonah shrieked again from his car seat beside her.

"What now?" Haley said crossly. He was indeed shrieking. With laughter.

There was the scuffing of a boot on a step. Even without looking over her shoulder, she knew that one more thing had arrived.

"Hey, buddy, good to see you, too." Mateo squatted down by the car seat and held out a finger by way of greeting. Jonah clutched it as if it were the last line cast to a drowning victim. "You got a bit of a shiner there."

Haley tossed gloopy egg into a bowl. She didn't have to justify the accident to him. The doctor had said Jonah was fine, and that was good enough.

Mateo didn't seem to expect an explanation. He listened to Jonah's version of events.

"Oh," Mateo said when there was pause in Jonah's cooing. "I should see the other guy."

Jonah explained more.

"Twice your age, you say? Nearly six months and a full twenty pounds?"

Jonah demonstrated with kicks and punches.

"Yep, he didn't stand a chance."

From the corner of her eye, Haley noticed Jonah arch his back. He wanted to be picked up, and not by her. Mateo had noticed, too. "I could, buddy, but you should probably ask your mother first."

"As if I have any say in the matter," Haley snapped. She dropped the tenth and final broken egg into the bowl.

"I wouldn't be asking if I didn't think you had one," Mateo said. Ugh. He looked so calm in his clean T-shirt and jeans. His brown boots, belt and hat all matched. Calm and way too good-looking.

She ought to order him off the property, but that would make her just plain mean. "Take him," she said. He was probably only here to see Jonah, anyway. She gathered up the rest of the grocery bags from the truck, and when she returned, Mateo had disappeared Jonah into the house.

She heard them in Jonah's room. And from the banter, she surmised that Mateo was changing Jonah. Not here a quarter hour, and he was already behaving as if he'd never left.

Because she was letting him. *Pull yourself together, girl. Refuse whatever he's here for. Stay strong.* She unpacked the groceries and wondered if there was enough propane to fire up the barbecue. She could do with a thick, juicy burger. She opened the fridge and checked on the package of ground beef. Mostly defrosted. There, one good thing.

"You keep cereal in the fridge?"

Haley pretended not to hear. She removed the tall box that her dead brain had shelved there and put it into the cupboard. Then she turned to face the bane of her life. The one holding her happy son. He'd changed not only Jonah's diaper but his outfit as well. He was now wearing a blue-and-brown onesie. The two of them were a matching set. Except Jonah's hair was damp and stuck up on end.

"I wiped his head down," Mateo said. "Cooled him right off."

Stay strong. "Why are you here?"

Mateo shifted Jonah in his arms. "Knut—

your dad—suggested I talk to you about coming up with a new deal."

Ever since their supper conversation, her dad had stayed mum on the subject, but last night, he'd said that Mateo had showed up and helped with the fencing. He'd then asked how the hiring of a new hand was going. It wasn't, as he well knew.

"I'm still not selling."

"I hear you're still hiring."

"I'm not hiring you."

"Okay." Mateo seemed to have expected that answer. "How about a partnership instead?"

"No."

"You haven't heard the terms."

She crossed her arms and waited.

"I work for free. For a year, with an option to renew. In return, I get half of whatever you sell by way of livestock and grain in the next year. You sell yearlings, I get half. You sell this year's calves when they're two-year-olds, I get half. You sell a truckload of wheat, I get half."

"You living in the bunkhouse or at your place?"

"At my place. Come calving next spring, we can make other arrangements if need be."

"This'll cost me more than just hiring help."

"And why haven't you got anyone, then?"

Because a good ranch hand was hard to find. And a good one was essential this year while her attention was on trying not to kill Jonah from maternal ineptitude. "It hasn't even been a month. I'll get one soon enough."

"Haley." A single word of reproach. "You're being stubborn. And unfair to your dad."

He was right, but she didn't like the idea of a partnership. "You're trying to weasel your way in to get your hooks into the land."

Mateo ruffled Jonah's sparse hair, and Jonah flopped out his arm and chilled. "I admit that I still want the land. It's an open offer. But here's my thinking. I can harangue you for something you will not give, and neither of us will get what we're after. Or I can offer something you do need in exchange for me getting something I want."

"And how does half of the sales get you something of the land?"

He looked out at the lilacs now in full purply bloom. "Because I can still walk the land that once belonged to my family, still plant the crops, cut the hay." He pivoted his beautiful blue-green eyes to her.

C'mon, Haley, hold out.

"I can still have that old dream of mine to carry on with the land. Even if it means sharing in the decisions with you. Even if it's not mine in name."

She caved like dirt under water. "You promise not to bring up the subject of selling again?"

"Yes."

That was quick. Too quick. "And not to my dad, either."

"I promise."

She spread her hands wide. "Fine. You have a deal."

Mateo set his hat on the island. "I have other conditions."

Haley recrossed her arms.

"Probate cleared. I plan to buy one of Hawk's cutting fillies. I'd like to use your stock for training, and I'd like to stable her here. In return, you will get half of all proceeds, whether I sell her or show her."

"How will I know what you make if you show her?"

"You will have to trust me."

She tightened her crossed arms. "Meaning I will have to take what you give. But you know what, fine. It's not as if it will cost me or Dad anything. You cover feed and vet bills, right?"

"Right."

"I want our deal papered."

"Agreed." He hesitated, his eyes on Jonah. "One more thing."

"That pretty much describes my day. Fire away."

Mateo ran a finger down Jonah's soft cheek. "I want—I guess you could say I want visitation rights."

"You want to be his father?"

"I honestly don't know what I want. You said I was pretending with him. That's not true. I only know that I've missed Jonah these past weeks."

She couldn't deny the bond between them. It was a rare thing. But it wouldn't be permanent. "You'll leave, probably in a year, and I'll have to get Jonah through it when his little heart breaks." Hers would do a little cracking, too.

"I don't intend on leaving."

"You mean you don't intend on leaving *again*." She hadn't meant to, but her old anger had slipped in. Humiliation crept in, too, because now he knew how much his leaving had hurt.

He gave her a look of regret and sympathy. "Haley, I never meant—"

"Of course you never meant," she said. "But truth is, you demolished me when you left twelve years ago."

He flinched at her honesty. Well, there was more about to hit the fan.

"I don't know what that fight with your father was all about. I don't know what he could have done that was so bad you refused to come home except for his funeral. But I wasn't part of it. You took your anger out on me, too. And it hurt. It hurt that you didn't return my calls and then changed numbers. I was not a telemarketer or a bill collector. I was your best friend."

He had bowed his head over Jonah while she let fly, but now he lifted his eyes to hers. "Okay," he said softly. "Okay."

"Don't try to sweeten me up. We're partners, okay? As for you and Jonah, I'm not going to do what you did and make my son pay for my anger. You can see him whenever it works out."

"Thanks," he said. He looked relieved, yet regret still played across his face. "I wish you'd told me how you really felt about me leaving when I brought it up right at the start."

"Don't you dare twist this into my fault. I didn't bring it up because I didn't want my old hurts getting in the way of what was supposed to be a short time together."

"And I get that. But had I known, I might have gone about making the offer on the land differently. I would've known how much anger you hold against me."

If only it had been that. She was angry because of all the other emotions he'd churned up. They had once gossiped together like old hens, laughed until their sides hurt, raced their horses, stuck up for each other when a teacher or parent laid down an unfair rule. Him leaving had hurt so much because once upon a time, she had loved him. Like a friend, of course. Their one kiss hadn't changed their status.

"Now you know," she said. "Now you know how your apology is only a start." Her voice trembled. If she released her feelings, he would see how weak for him she was. She gripped the counter to ground herself.

Mateo opened his mouth to speak, but praise Pete, in walked her dad.

He took in the two of them and the tension that was probably buzzing thicker than flies. She might as well clear the air. "Mateo and I have come up with a business plan. He'll work here in exchange for a share of profits. There are some other conditions."

Her dad's gaze drifted over to the empty supper table. "Any of them involve cooking?"

CHAPTER SIX

RISKY BUSINESS REFUSED to load. The filly had been skittish around trailers ever since her first ride in one done to get the yearling used to trailering. There'd been a flash thunderstorm, with hail crashing on the roof. Mateo had pulled over and talked to the filly, ice chunks clattering on the trailer roof. It's when he'd come up with the show name that Hawk thought appropriate, given the filly's spirited nature.

Now, a year later, Mateo had tried every trick and technique he knew. He'd parked the Jansson trailer in the corral to get her curious about the big, shiny box on wheels. He'd left all exits wide open. Risky B had given it the side-eye and then stayed away. He'd worked her to move forward to the back end of the trailer. Then she crowded Mateo to get away.

Mateo stood alone in the trailer, stomping and scuffing around to assure Risky Business that there was nothing to worry about. She watched from a safe distance and only approached when Mateo left the noisy death trap.

"I guess we should've practiced this with her beforehand," Hawk said from the corral fence. "I didn't think I'd be moving her this soon."

Mateo bumped his hat up. "Didn't think so, either. I was hoping you wouldn't have to sell her, so I guess I put it off. But now that I'm the buyer, I wish I hadn't delayed."

"Want me to have a go at it?"

"She'll have to deal with me eventually. Now is as good a time as any."

"You're welcome to stay the night. Leave the trailer here, and we'll try again in the morning. It'll be suppertime in another couple of hours, anyway. And driving in the dark with a loaded trailer isn't the best. Especially with Risky B. Especially with that truck."

Truth. Except Mateo was itching to get back to the Janssons' to show off the filly to Haley. He'd told her he'd be back tonight, and he didn't want to break his word only five days into their new deal. "I'll keep at her for the time being."

Hawk looked to the hills. Mateo knew for a fact it was a good place to rest the eyes when the brain was on fire. "How's it working out with Haley?"

Hawk was calling the bet he'd placed two months ago when Mateo had given his notice. "We're good business partners."

"That all?"

"We haven't had that conversation."

"I'll bet. You're still playing an angle, still looking for a way in."

"I'd like us to be friends. The way we were."

Hawk grunted. "No going back to the good old days."

Haley had said as much, said she was his best friend. He needed to face the fact that whatever he and Haley had now in their new partnership was a horse of a different color from their teenage friendship.

Hawk pushed off the fence and rolled his shoulders. "I'll leave you to it." He regarded the filly. "Only…don't ask for too much, too fast."

Mateo assumed Hawk was talking about Risky B, but thoughts of Haley intruded. He'd showed up early, worked late, coordinated his time with Jonah so she could have breaks. He had cooked an extra lasagna at his place last night, so all she had to do tonight was warm up the dish. In return, she'd been polite but didn't engage. She didn't trust him.

Was he pushing her the same way he was on Risky B's case? He dropped his butt onto the end of the trailer and stretched his legs out. He raised his eyes to the surrounding Foothills. The high sun of the day had edged over now and was tipping softness onto the ridges. There'd be a good sunset tonight, full of color but short compared to the long sprawl of light at the Janssons'.

He and Haley had taken long sunset rides back when they were teenagers. It was during one of those rides that he'd kissed her. The first girl he'd ever kissed. It had only ever happened once, but he hadn't had another more beautiful than that first one. He'd been fifteen and had thought about kissing her since he was eleven. Four years he'd waited.

It might take that long to build her trust again. Was their new partnership worth it? *Yes*. Funny how he'd lived a dozen years without her, and the instant she was back in his life, he couldn't stand to be separated from her. That's how someone who wanted more than friendship would behave.

Was he that someone? He turned so his back rested against the side of the opening and his legs were stretched out. The shade relaxed his eyes. He'd rest awhile, have a think.

He heard Risky B approach. Her hooves tapped the dirt, and she snuffled gingerly about his head. Mateo didn't move. "I should've told you how much I missed you first," he said quietly. "Hung out with you, gone for a ride. Instead, I tried to load you up and take you away."

He lifted his hat, and there was Risky Business's long head moving in, her nostrils soft on Mateo's face. Her idea of a kiss. Mateo rubbed the side of her head. "Sorry," he said, "for not respecting your feelings."

The filly had a go at grazing on Mateo's hair.

"Go on with you." Mateo pushed her away and sat up. "All right, then. We'll go for a ride."

He stood and walked to the cab of the truck. He'd call Haley and tell her that it didn't look good for him getting back that night. He was reaching for his phone when the trailer shuddered.

He came round the back to find the filly with her front hoof on the trailer bed. Mateo scooted around to the side door and stepped into the trailer to face the filly. He picked up her dangling reins and waited. Risky B nosed his boot.

"Yep, same pair I had on down there."

Mateo casually edged a couple more short steps into the trailer. Risky wouldn't like the unevenness of her stance and would move forward or backward soon enough.

The filly chose forward, and Mateo moved back. He rubbed Risky Business's head and neck. "There. That wasn't so bad. As you can see, there are exits on either side and to the back. Lots of headspace. The Janssons bought a quality trailer. And that's where you're going. To a real quality place. The owner's been around horses all his life. His daughter, too. You'll like her." He rubbed the filly around the ears. "A lot. And she's got a baby. Jonah. He's pretty important, but he's squeaky as all get out. Just like the twins."

He could try closing up the trailer, wait to make sure the filly didn't freak and then head out. He could keep his promise to Haley.

Or maybe he could give her some space.

Maybe he could stop trying to make it happen. Whatever that "it" was. "I know you can go forward, Risky." He touched his hand to the filly's shoulder. "How about reverse?"

The filly obligingly stepped backward, hesitated at the drop-off and then descended the rest of the way. She tossed her head. "Yeah, yeah," Mateo said. "I kept at you to go in and then I changed my mind."

He pulled the phone from the back pocket of his jeans and called Haley. She answered on the fifth ring. One more, and it would've gone to voice mail, as it had a few times in the past week. He'd wondered if she'd done it purposely.

"Hey." It was her customary greeting. He liked that it wasn't the typical hello, as if they were at a different level. Or maybe she couldn't be bothered to spare him the extra syllable.

"I got the filly loaded, but it wasn't easy. I thought I'd better give her more time, get her more comfortable."

"Okay."

"Hawk offered for me to stay the night and start out tomorrow morning."

"Makes sense."

"Everything…okay?"

"Yep, all good."

"Okay, I'll see you tomorrow, then?" Shoot. It'd come out more like a question than the offhand statement he was aiming for.

"See you tomorrow," she said. That might've been the end of it, except she sighed, long and slow, as if she'd been holding her breath for the entire conversation. "I appreciate you calling to let me know your change in plans. It means…a lot."

He fought to keep it casual. "Sure, no worries."

But after the call, he gave the air a fist pump. Five hours and three hundred miles apart, he'd come closer to her than for all his trying in the past two months. "Come on, girl. Let's ride."

"She's gorgeous."

Haley had caught a glimpse of the filly from the kitchen window when Mateo unloaded her at noon. But a presurgical appointment for her dad followed by a routine checkup for Jonah had kept her from taking a closer look.

The second Jonah closed his eyes, she was out the door, leaving her dad inside with the baby monitor and his phone within reach. She found the filly in the corral abutting the stables. Mateo was leaning on the railing and turned at Haley's comment.

"That, she is."

Haley stepped up on the bottom railing to be level with Mateo. On the short side, she was always looking to compensate. Across the corral, Risky Business sized up Haley and returned to her contemplation of the green pastures.

"You're not riding her?"

"Not today. Not a good idea to ask too much, too soon."

He hadn't applied that philosophy to her. He'd come straight out of the gate with a big ask from her, and she was pretty sure he had set the bar high for the horse, too. "What's your plan? And don't tell me you don't have one."

Mateo rubbed his chin. He hadn't shaved today. The rasp of his stubble sounded like walking through long, dry grass. Where snakes and mosquitoes hung out.

"I'll let her get used to the place, put her in with your mare in the pasture there. Start with light training. Stops and turns, and then crank it up slowly from there."

"That'll take all summer. You'll run out of time to enter her into shows."

"That's fine. No rush."

"So I won't see a penny off her."

"Likely not this year."

At least he was honest. "I guess wheat will be the sole cash crop this year. Will you start seeding soon?" By this time last year, the wheat had been in the ground for a week. She'd driven tractor herself with Trevor running the sprayer, which had turned out not to be helpful at all. He'd seemed scared of equipment.

Mateo made the walk-in-grass sound on his chin again. "Have you thought about greenfeed instead?"

"Greenfeed? Why?"

"There's an auction out west. Fifty yearlings are up. Black Angus. If we keep them over winter, we'll need feed."

"We already got three quarters of hay. That'll be enough feed."

Mateo kept his eyes on the filly. "We haven't got the rain we should've. Bales will be down this year."

"It's still the middle of May. Too early to tell. I've never known when it hasn't rained in time."

"I've been on plenty of places where it hasn't."

"Yeah, but we're talking about here. And you know as well as I do that it always rains. We usually end up with too much at the wrong time, and then we can't get the crop off."

"That's the way it's been in the past, but not if we have more cattle."

Why was Mateo being so obstinate? "It's not an either-or question. We can have both cattle and wheat. Both will get us good prices. Wheat especially. A shortage overseas is predicted."

"There'll be a shortage right here when there's no rain."

"It'll rain," she ground out. "And if doesn't, we'll buy hay."

"From who? Everyone will be buying, and we'll lose our margins on the cattle." He shook his head. "We can't have cattle if we don't have more feed. Which means greenfeed. Barley or oats."

Was that the choice he was giving her? She was willing to compromise, but he just wanted to ram his plan down her throat. "I choose wheat."

He turned to face her and said mildly, "Okay. How are you getting that planted?"

"I thought we decide together what we do with the Pavlic land and then you work it."

From across the corral, Risky B whinnied, probably in reaction to their rising voices. *Her* rising voice. Mateo was keeping his usual cool.

He climbed over the railing, dropped to the ground and gave a low whistle. "Hey, girl. I told you about Haley. Come meet her."

Man and horse stared across the corral at each other. Haley remembered and took out an apple from the pocket of her hoodie. Behind Mateo's back, she held it up to the filly.

Risky B hoofed it over, and Mateo took hold of her halter. He turned to Haley. She popped the apple away in time. "See? Don't ask too much, and you get even more."

Haley let Mateo have this small win. She was after bigger game. She withdrew the apple, and Risky B left Mateo for her. Good girl. "I advocate bribery to win friends and influence horses."

Mateo seemed about to deliver a comeback, but then he shook his head and gave a long, slow smile of concession. "All right. What's your plan?"

She frankly hadn't a clue. She'd never had to compromise with her dad. He'd given her free run of the Pavlic land, mostly to avoid confrontations like the one she was now having with Mateo. She hadn't expected him to contradict her decisions. If she couldn't have her way, he wasn't getting his, either. "Let's compromise. Half the quarter to wheat. Half to greenfeed. I bought the seed for the wheat. You buy the seed for the greenfeed."

He stared. "You serious?"

"Why not? We'll both get some of what we want. As you say, don't ask for too much, too soon."

Mateo rested his hand on Risky B's shoulder and gazed over her withers to the rolling land beyond. The sun was setting, and the sky was painted in purples and oranges. He gave Risky B one long pet from her withers all the way to her haunches.

"Okay," he said. "Half and half."

He sounded resigned, as if he were getting half of nothing. Well, he'd suggested the partnership with her. Now he was getting a taste of what it meant to deal with someone who knew their own mind.

HER DAD'S KNEE surgery went well enough. He returned home with ice packs and excruciatingly detailed instructions that confined him within the four walls. For a man who solely saw the house as a place to sleep and eat, it was not going well.

After his second day back, Haley called Grace and told her to hustle her butt to the ranch and help with their dad, because she was about to commit patricide, and then Grace would have to raise her nephew on her own—the nephew she hadn't bothered to come see in the two and a half months of his existence. Haley also mentioned that just because Grace was some big-time city lawyer didn't mean she should expect Haley to handle all the responsibility for their father. Grace arrived bright and early the next morning.

Breakfast over, Haley could hear her father and sister now. Their bickering voices drifted down the hallway to the back porch, where Haley was lacing up her work boots.

"Let's get out of here," she said to Jonah, dropping him into his front-facing backpack. He was still a bit small for it, and she had to bolster him up with a little blankie, but he liked the forward view and babbled about everything.

"Shall we go see the new horse?"

Jonah kicked and squealed. It was what

Haley had felt like doing when she first saw Risky B. The filly projected intelligence, spirit and power.

She'd told Mateo as much, and he'd agreed. Then he'd tickled Jonah under the chin and left to do whatever he had planned. Not that she blamed him. Calving might be over, but now there was seeding and cattle checks and machinery repairs and equine care and the several million chores that took up a day.

Mateo was keeping his end of the bargain. She had no complaints. Only ever since he'd returned from Blackstone, he'd seemed distant. And she wasn't sure if she liked that or not. He didn't appear to be hiding anything from her, but she'd been fooled once before.

She rounded the corner of the horse barn to find Mateo in the adjoining pen, training the filly. He'd ordered in truckloads of fine sand to cover the pen in a good half foot of softness, just like in real show pens. No expense spared.

He looked over his shoulder at them and then turned back to Risky B. Their presence might distract the filly, and Haley moved to slip away. That's when Jonah let loose a very distracting squeal. Haley turned back to the corral, and Jonah reverted to burbling.

Huh. She and the filly were both getting trained. Mateo was working on getting stops and drawbacks, important for keeping on a cow. It was a thing of beauty to just watch Mateo. His posture was relaxed but concentrated, and Risky B responded to the tension on the reins.

Jonah must've thought so, too, because he let loose a long, undulating call she'd never heard before. Risky B swung her head and sidestepped.

"Sorry," Haley said. "We'll leave."

"Hold up," Mateo said, dismounting. "She might as well get used to him."

He led the filly over, and she stuck her head out toward Jonah. Haley rubbed her nose, angling Jonah away from any accidental contact.

"Hawk's twins were walking when she came, so she's fairly used to their noises."

"It's okay for Jonah to be around horses but not cattle."

"Not horses in general. But Risky B's different. Later, it'll be good for her to learn to stay focused no matter what's going on. Babies come to shows." He patted the horse's neck. "That's enough of a break. Back to it."

There he was, withdrawing from her again. "Do you need any help?"

Mateo looked at Jonah strapped to her. "How do you figure you could?"

"I don't know. It's just that you are having to do everything, and we're supposed to be partners. I don't feel as if I'm pulling my weight."

"Your labor wasn't part of the deal."

"Still, I've got more of a routine going with Jonah now. And he likes coming outside, anyway."

Mateo smiled. "You're trying to get away from your dad and Grace."

"Can you blame me?"

"Nope. Them two get along as well as they ever did."

"Dad's always been disappointed she moved away, and she's always been disappointed he can't accept her decision."

"So you're the good daughter."

"I'm the one who stayed, that's all." Haley immediately regretted saying that, because Mateo must think she was bringing up the whole business of his leaving again. And she wasn't. Blowing up at him had helped her, but now she wondered if he was trying to remove himself from any more blasts. She didn't want him to look at her and feel guilt. She wanted him to see her, to be with her, to work with her as good partners did.

"Anyway, I'd like to help. Even if it's just brushing her down afterwards to free you up for other jobs."

Mateo didn't answer right away. He contemplated the corral railings and the pens beyond. It was that same wide-ranging survey of the place he'd done on the first day he showed up. Sizing things up. "Thing is," he said slowly, "I don't have a flag line set up to get her tracking."

He had a problem, and he was asking her for a solution. "Dave Claverley's probably got one. I could ask to borrow it, if you want."

Mateo lifted his baseball cap off by the beak, scratched his forehead and set it back down. "Yeah, I don't know that I want Dave involved."

"He's the competition."

"There's that, and I might've turned him away from buying Risky B earlier. It might look as if I bought her out from under him."

"Which you did."

"It wasn't my intention. I spoke to him before I came into the money, and I only wanted to return to Hawk's and train her myself."

"So if I go over there and ask for the pulley, that'll be rubbing salt in the wound. Does he know you bought her?"

"I drove past their place with the loaded trailer last week, and I know Dave called Knut after his surgery to see how he was doing. I can't see your dad not telling him."

"Okay, then. We buy a new one."

"I buy a new one."

Enough. "Look, Mateo. We agreed we'd split profits from the shows. You bought the horse. The least I can do is pony up for some equipment."

Mateo looked here and there, no doubt thinking up another excuse. She stamped her foot in irritation. "Stop freezing me out. You can't do everything by yourself. And you don't need to."

He brought his gaze back to hers. "I've been saying the same thing to you for the past two months, but have you listened?"

There he was, turning things back on her. "Then you really should take your own advice."

His eyes widened in disbelief. Yes, he had a point, but if he pushed her to explain why she'd resisted accepting his help, she would have to admit that a personal edge had crept into their business partnership. She liked hanging out with him, but if he discovered her interest in him, he'd have her at an advantage. She could see herself getting talked into making decisions that weren't in her best interest.

Her misfire of a marriage to Trevor had been a lesson well learned. He had sweet-talked her into committing to a life together, and when he'd discovered she didn't come with property, he'd abandoned her and their unborn child.

Mateo wanted her property, too, but not at the price of becoming romantically involved, it seemed. If they were ever meant to be together, it would've happened a long time ago, after their first kiss. Clearly, Mateo had never felt the chemistry she had.

To prove his disinterest to herself, she asked, "You seeing anyone?"

She expected him to tell her to mind her own business. That would've been her response if he'd asked. Instead, Mateo turned away and rubbed Risky B's neck. "Not yet, no."

An answer that begged another question. "That makes it sound as if you've got someone in mind."

He kicked at the sand. "The question's kind of personal, Haley."

There was a time when he would've told her personal things.

"I'm heading into town. You want me to pick you up anything while I'm there?"

He sure could pivot a conversation. "You're not going there to buy a pulley before I can, are you?"

"No."

"Good. I don't need you to get me anything."

"All righty, then. I'll see you later." He turned the filly toward the barn.

"I can brush her down," Haley called after him.

"It's my turn," Mateo said without breaking stride.

Now, wasn't that a clever way of putting her off? She had pushed into private territory, and he'd turned tail. She only had herself to blame.

Jonah kicked and punched at the sight of the retreating man and horse. "I hear ya, Jonah. I kinda want to follow them, too."

CHAPTER SEVEN

EVERYTHING SHONE IN the showroom at the dealership—shone so much that Mateo considered putting his shades back on. The tall bank of windows, the rubbed-down new trucks and cars, the reception desk. All in black and white and gray. Like the house. Mateo wondered if Jakob had just sent the interior decorators over to the ranch house after finishing up here.

"Good morning! Can I help you?" The young woman behind the desk was dressed in gray. Company colors.

"I'm in the market for a truck. I was told this was the place to come." Every radio station, every online marketplace, every farmer at Tim Hortons he'd taken an informal survey of had urged him to go to Spirit Lake Motors.

"Certainly." She turned to the bank of sales offices. All five looked to be busy. "If you can wait, I'll have someone help you straight away."

He hoped it wouldn't take too long. He already knew what he wanted. He caught himself looking more at the place than any specific vehicle. Rows of vehicles circled the building, all makes and models. It was the middle of the week, and prospective buyers were out there with salesmen. Jakob hadn't built this business alone, but he had been part of something bigger than himself.

Heels clipped from behind. "Hello, sorry to keep you waiting."

Mateo turned. A petite, mature, dark-eyed woman smiled up at him. She was dressed in casual wear, unlike everyone else, but her jewelry and hair gave the sense that it was part of her well-groomed appearance.

She stuck out her hand. "I'm Crystal."

He gave her his hand but not his name. It didn't feel right anyway, as if he was name-dropping in order to get a better deal. "Crystal, I'm in the market for a truck."

She took his cue and got down to business. "What did you have in mind?"

"I'd like you to give me what you can for that—" he pointed out the window to his truck "—and put me into something like that." He pointed to the fully loaded crew-cab showroom model. Crystal glanced at the top-of-the-line truck, but her attention veered back to his old truck.

"Are you sure you want to sell that?"

"It's got close to four hundred thousand miles on it. The brakes need replacing, and the transmission is due. I'm sure."

Crystal walked over to the windows to get a closer look. Her expression softened. "It's a classic in its own right. The year after they made that, the whole assembly line was changed, and they started rolling out crap."

"It has served me well, I admit. But I have to upgrade. There are no anchors for a car seat, and even if there was, I don't trust the truck not to break down with the baby."

"Ah." Crystal's eyes crinkled at the sides with grandmotherly lines. "You're a father."

Mateo's insides flipped at her mild declaration, surprised at how much he didn't mind her assumption. "No. My friend has a baby."

Mateo let her draw her own conclusions. Most people did, anyway. She pivoted to the vehicle he'd pointed to earlier. "This one would fit the bill."

She began her spiel. "I know the specs," he interrupted. "Any chance I can test-drive one?"

She blinked. "Certainly." Spirit Lake Motors' standard response. "Let me get plates, and we'll take one out."

Mateo had forgotten that salespeople liked to ride with the prospective buyer to impress them with all the details. He would've preferred to put the truck through its paces alone, but there it was.

Instead of trying to sell him on the truck, Crystal was quiet, twisting a ruby ring on her right hand. Mateo had curved through the town and had opened it up on the highway when she really spoke. "I know who you are. I attended your father's funeral."

Mateo shot her another look, trying to place her. "I'm sorry, a lot of people there." And every spare glance had gone to Haley.

"Yes. He was my business partner."

Right. Like Haley and him. Crystal would've received his shares through the will. "I see."

"We were also…more than business partners."

Mateo kept his eyes on the road. Unlike Haley and him.

"We didn't make a big production of it. The staff might've known, but we liked our privacy. He talked about you."

The speedometer showed him twenty clicks above the posted limit, and he'd hardly applied the gas pedal. "That right?" Mateo said.

"He showed me pictures of you. You and the truck the day he gave it to you. He said you would've probably preferred a horse, but a truck would get you farther."

"Yep, the truck took me far from here." Even he could hear his edge of sarcasm.

"But only in one direction, right?"

Mateo deliberately made an abrupt right. He really didn't want to get into it with Jakob's girlfriend, but she was needling him. "You only got one side of the story. He turfed me out. He disowned me. And in the ten-plus years I was gone, he didn't try to track me down or reach out to me. He got on with his life, which I guess included a love life. I came back, and I can see how hard he worked to get that life, but he made it very clear that he didn't want me part of it."

"He was angry and hurt. With your mother."

"But he took it out on me." Just as he'd taken it out on Haley. Inexcusable of them both.

"He did. Uh, Mateo, just so you know, cops like to hide on the other side of this hill."

Forty clicks over the limit. He backed off on the gas. More than that, he swung into an approach leading into a hayfield. He wasn't fit to be on the road right now, and the wide spread of green calmed him.

"As you can see, the brakes work well," Crystal commented mildly.

"I'll take it," Mateo said. "And I'll pay in cash. And yes, it'll be Jakob's money."

"It may interest you to know that he was excited to get this truck model in. He considered buying it for himself."

"Full circle. I guess he will buy my second truck, too."

"Doesn't quite make up for the past, though?"

"He never apologized. Never once tried to." He turned to her. "Did he tell you everything? About how I was another man's kid?"

She rolled the ruby ring. A gift from Jakob?

"He did. He regretted his anger but not his decision to sell. He said the Pavlic legacy ended with him because you weren't blood. He said you would have to start over with your own legacy."

A legacy Mateo believed started with re-taking the old Pavlic land. But since it had to be shared with Haley, any new legacy had to take her into account. How much could they build together?

Their partnership seemed to work best when he kept her at arm's length. But it wore on him. This morning with Risky B, he'd had to rein in hard from spilling everything on his mind, from buying a truck to how Dodge seemed off his tuna. She'd asked if he was dating. Did that mean she cared about his love life, or was she just curious? Her question only brought to the fore how alone he was and how he was still attracted to her.

"So he left me money to make it happen."

"I think he planned on getting it to you sooner."

"He was going to get in touch with me?"

She tipped her head to the side. "He knew that you were down at the Blackstone Ranch. I guess he thought there'd be more time." She turned away to look out the passenger window. "We all did," she added, her voice trembling.

They sat together in the cab of the vehicle Jakob had taken a fancy to.

Crystal took several deep, shaky breaths and wiped tears from her eyes. "I never used to carry tissues. Now I go through half a pack a day."

"It's okay. I wish I could cry," Mateo confessed.

"That man could always make me cry. Mostly from laughing. But once, he told me that his biggest regret was telling you that you weren't to call him 'Dad' anymore."

"'Better yet,'" Mateo quoted, "'don't call me at all.' And I never did."

"Yes," Crystal whispered. "He told me that part, too. We all regret words we've said."

Mateo thought of all the years of silence he'd maintained with Haley. How they'd missed out on a partnership and whatever else might've happened. Time for him to make a U-turn with Haley. "Or not said," he added.

The trip back to the dealership was silent, but when they pulled up, Mateo said on impulse, "Jakob's vintage cars are parked out at his place. They're yours, if you want them."

She shook her head. "No, he gave them to you."

"He did. And now I'd like to give them to you. They are a gift from me. You can see the value in them that I can't. I honestly don't know why he willed them to me in the first place."

Crystal shrugged. "Maybe he thought you'd look at them and fall in love the way he did."

"If I fall in love, it won't be with a car," Mateo said and thought again of Haley.

"All right, I'll take them. How about we do an exchange? The cars for the truck?"

Mateo considered her offer. "No. I want them to be a gift. Not from Jakob to you. But from me to you. You gave me a bit of peace and understanding. That's worth three shiny old cars to me."

Crystal looked out across the dealership, where she and Jakob had worked together during the day and gone home from together afterward. "Fair enough," she whispered.

"I am sorry for your loss," he said and meant it.

"Thank you." She drew a couple of deep breaths and then turned to him, her voice once more professional and upbeat. "Now, let's put this truck in your name."

"You bought a car seat?" The apparatus in the back seat of Mateo's new crew cab seemed weirdly alien. "But this is your… Your castle on wheels. Why?"

Mateo had invited her and Jonah out to check out his new truck, and she was kind of pleased that he'd specifically wanted to share his big, bright toy with them, but this… This was significant. This meant he viewed them as part of his daily life, as people he'd be going places with.

"And every castle needs its throne," he said and came in close to lift Jonah from her arms. She held her breath, still not used to him getting right in her space. "C'mon, King Jonah, tell me what you think."

Her son would happily go along with anything Mateo proposed. She was the parent. She was the one who needed to figure out for Jonah's sake where all this was headed.

"It converts into a booster seat," Mateo said as he clicked and adjusted straps.

Haley felt all kinds of fluttery at that. "But…why are you doing all this?"

"Shoot. I forgot a sunscreen for the window." Mateo cocked Jonah's cap to block out the evening light. "There, that'll do until I get to town again."

He shut the back door and opened the front passenger side. "Hop in."

She didn't budge. "You're ignoring me again."

"Sure am. Because I'm not getting into a conversation with your dad and sister watching us from the front window."

Haley turned to see her dad and Grace were side by side on the sofa, taking in the drama outside. Grace actually had the gall to give a little wave. Haley hopped in.

The outing lasted for a mile. Mateo pulled into Jakob's yard. Correction, his own yard.

"Last time I was here was the day before Jonah was born," she said.

To bring over leftovers from Jakob's celebration of life. It had been her idea. She'd noticed that Mateo hadn't eaten and then had left early. Back then, she'd justified her food delivery and tidying as a kind of charity, but Mateo had interpreted it as something more. It had been enough to bring him over the next day. Things had certainly picked up speed since then.

Mateo lifted Jonah out and carried him to the house. "I guess we're going inside," she said to herself, trotting after two of the most aggravating males in her life. Her sister could deal with the third.

A ginger tom darted inside ahead of her. "A cat ran in," Haley called.

"That's Dodge," Mateo called from the kitchen. "He was here before I came."

Inside, Haley couldn't help feeling she was underdressed in her jeans and shirt. Jakob's chrome-and-gray palette had always struck her as cold and formal. She would have gone for warm tones, switched out the chrome for wood. Still, it was a masculine schema, and Mateo suited the kitchen well.

He opened a cupboard chockablock with tins of cat food and set one into the automatic can opener. "Those there when you came, too?" she said above the buzz of the machine.

"I added to it, but yeah. He had a cat in his life." "He" meaning "Jakob." Mateo couldn't even say "Dad"?

He opened the stainless steel fridge. "Want anything?"

Haley came alongside to peek inside the glowing white interior. "Definitely fuller than last time I was here. It's now a beverage dispensary. I'll have a can of carbonated water. Root beer flavor."

"I mostly sleep here. I usually have my meals over at your place. Doesn't make sense to buy stuff for it to rot." Mateo reached for her request along with a real beer for himself with one hand, Jonah in his other.

Trevor had given the same argument for moving into the Jansson ranch before they were married. She wondered if it had all been part of Trevor's plan to wear her down into marriage. What were Mateo's designs for her?

At least he had his own place. He was offering her help and wealth. And a car seat.

"I thought about having people over for a barbecue," he said. "I have my eye on this grill. There's already a cement pad set up for one outside."

"If you're cooking, we're coming."

"I'd like that," Mateo said simply. "This place could do with... With..."

"Color."

"Yeah. Color and people. Everything here seems so new. I swear I can still smell the paint. Come."

Mateo made for the living room, where there was an enormous curved black leather sofa complete with cupholders. It was the kind that could seat him and two hundred of his closest friends and family. Mateo sat, slotted his beer into a cupholder, unlatched Jonah from the car seat and then sat back with Jonah lounging against his chest. Mateo pushed a button, and up flipped a footrest. Man with baby and beer. He looked…at home.

Haley squelched down on a seat a little out of arm's length away. The sofa was cold but soft. "I should give you a throw. Grace quilted up a bunch. Compensating for abandoning me in my hour of need."

Mateo gave her one of his straight-on looks. "You weren't abandoned."

It demanded work, but Haley didn't look away. "About that. What's with the car seat? I can't help but think you're sweetening me up for another deal."

Mateo brought his beer to his mouth, and Jonah swung for the bottle and missed. "I met Crystal at the dealership."

"Mateo," Haley ground out in exasperation. A straight answer from him was like getting a bull up a chute backward.

"Did you know she and Jakob were together?"

"Uh, well… They came over for supper a few times." A few *dozen* times, but Haley figured the frequency didn't matter so much to Mateo as the substance. "They didn't make a big deal of it, so we didn't, either. Dad and I got the feeling that they wanted to keep their relationship low-key, so we respected that."

Mateo brought his bottle within reach of Jonah who tested his fingertips on the cool, hard surface. "Sounds much like she said. They were business partners, and they didn't want their private life spilling into their workday."

Haley got the flutters again. No, way more than the flutters. A whole flapping flock. Why was Mateo bringing all this up? Was he proposing a relationship? They hadn't even held hands or kissed or…anything.

But he had become like a father to her son.

"Are you using Jonah to get in good with me?"

He gusted out a sigh. "I'd hoped you'd know me better than to think I'd use a baby to manipulate you."

She had made a nasty accusation. Fear of betrayal painted her thoughts as cold and sterile as Jakob's kitchen. "I am sorry. That was low. I guess I don't know where we stand.

You were gone for years, and now… Well, look at you. Look at us."

His face softened. "Yeah, if you'd asked me three months ago if I'd be driving around a new truck with a car seat and be happy about it, I would have got a gut ache from laughing so hard."

Happy about it. "And now?"

"Crystal told me something that Jakob said."

"Mateo!"

"Hold on, there's a point to all this. She said that Jakob regretted the fight between us, but he didn't regret selling the land. He said it made sense that I start a new legacy instead of continuing an old one. And he was right. I should start a brand-new one…with you."

The flock lifted off. Haley breathed in. "We already have an agreement. Am I missing something, Mateo?"

"I'd like to amend the agreement. Make it long-term, more than a year. We can still have termination clauses and all, but I'd like us to be full business partners like Jakob and Crystal were."

Since he was avoiding the obvious, she wouldn't. "They were more than business partners."

"They started as business partners."

"I have just come off a horrible marriage where I can't remember us having one honest conversation, except our last one. So talk. Tell me what you want."

Mateo took to looking about.

"I swear, Mateo—"

"I wasn't Jakob's son."

Well, that settled the flock down fast.

"He found out that day. On my last day of high school, Mom told Jakob that she wanted a divorce because she'd only married him to give her and me security until I was of age."

"Ouch."

"Yeah, talk about the last conversation being the only honest one. I walked in on it, and Jakob delivered the news like a punch. He said we were both out of his life. He said it was a good thing the land was in his name, because neither of us were getting one square inch. Mom said she didn't care. That's when Jakob totally lost it. He told the both of us to get out. Mom was already packed and loaded. She said she'd call me and drove off. And so did I."

"To me." He had come to her in his distress, but she hadn't been enough to keep him.

"I didn't mean to, actually. I came over so much I automatically turned in. You were there on the front porch with a pop and a book."

"Studying for a biology final."

"You remember?"

"The day's burned into my memory."

"Yeah, mine too." When Mateo lifted his beer and drained it, Jonah opened his mouth in a broad hint. "Not for another eighteen years, buddy."

"Here, give him this." Haley fished in her bag for a pacifier and leaned over to slip it into Jonah's eager mouth. She was in Mateo's space, and she didn't retreat.

"I told you what he said about the land, but I should've told you about me," he said softly.

"Did you ever find out who your real father is?"

Mateo smoothed back Jonah's dark hair until it stood on end. She'd seen him do that a few times, smooth it back and then just watch it settle, like meditating on a shaken snow globe.

"I asked Mom, and she told me. She said he lived south of Calgary and gave me his number. She said he was a one-week fling that had consequences. I drove out there not long after the blowup. He was a cook at an Italian restaurant, of all things. I went in, ordered a meal, ate it and left. I never met him. I told myself I could always go back. I never did. The longer I stayed away, easier it became."

"Like with me."

"No. I stayed away from my biological father because he isn't important. I stayed away from you—and Jakob—because you and him were important. It would hurt too much to meet up with him, and I knew it would hurt you if I showed up out of the blue after all the years had gone by. Problem was, I should've told you from the start about what happened. What mattered, what *always* mattered, was that we could talk to each other. What mattered was that I didn't tell you the truth."

His confession winded her. "I could've told you right then and there not to let the drama with your family damage us, instead of you taking a decade to figure that out."

"Yeah, what a waste of time. All I thought about was how I was nothing. All my plans were gone."

"And now?"

"And now, I've got them back. And you're part of them. And that's a good thing."

He dodged better than a chased rabbit. "And us?" she asked. "Not as business partners but as us. You and me. Be honest and please, be quick."

He turned to her, and his cheek rested against the pillowed top of the sofa. Without thinking, she laid her cheek against her own cushion and faced him.

"Haley," he said, "you've given me all I could hope for by letting me be here with you and Jonah. If you ever want to give me more, I'd like that very much. But right now, I'm a contented man."

For the first time in a long time, maybe since she'd discovered she was pregnant, Haley felt a rush of excitement and possibility. And then, almost immediately, apprehension. She'd given too much of herself away to Trevor, and she might be falling into the same trap here. Mateo said he'd let her set the pace, but he'd asked for the partnership, and tonight he suggested making it permanent. They had separate residences, but their lives—meals, chores, Jonah—were twisted together. He might be contented, but for how long?

And if he made a move, would she have the willpower to resist him?

"Thanks for your honesty," she said. She believed him. It was her own mind and heart she couldn't get a clear reading on.

IN THE END, their agreement to extend their arrangement was more a meeting of the minds than anything hard and fast, a few more lines added onto the present clauses. Haley supposed that was for the best as she waved goodbye to Mateo from the porch of the house.

Inside, Grace sat alone on the couch before a stretch of papers.

"Dad in bed?"

"For now."

"You sound like me with Jonah," Haley said. "Except you at least got him in bed. I fed Jonah over at Mateo's, but I have to change him before bed."

Grace pulled a sour face. "You nursed in front of Mateo?"

"I'm discreet. It isn't the first time. If I had to run off every time Jonah was hungry, we'd get nothing done."

"Just seems a little personal."

"Nothing he hasn't seen since the day the

kid was born." Haley spread out diaper paraphernalia from a shelf on the bookstand with
Jonah on the change mat as the final piece.

"I mean, given the history between you
two."

"What history? We don't have a history."

"You two never spent a day apart since the
day Mateo walked here on his own when he
was four to play with you."

"We were friends. Nothing more."

Grace leaned over the coffee table, her eyes
sharp and gleeful. "Not ever?"

"I feel sorry for your opposition. They probably confess to mass murder to avoid dealing
with you."

"You're not answering the question."

Like Mateo ducking her question earlier.
"We kissed once when we were like, eleven
or twelve. We wanted to see what the big deal
was. And we both agreed it wasn't anything."

Grace tapped her stylus on the side of her
pad. Even wearing sweats and a T-shirt, she
came off as intimidating and capable. Everything a big sister should be. "What about if
he kissed you now?"

Haley tucked Jonah's legs back into his onesie and started in on the snaps. "What about you mind your own business?"

Grace gave a little triumphant hum. "Thought so."

Her sister knew nothing about babies or men. Haley swaddled Jonah, following Mateo's trick of leaving his arms free. Jonah kept an eye out for things to grab. "Here. You hold him until he gets sleepy. Then put him in the crib. I've got dishes to do."

"Get into the twenty-first century and buy a dishwasher. I've got work to do that can't be replicated."

"Like snuggling with your only nephew." Haley didn't give Grace a chance to object again and slipped Jonah into her arms.

Grace stayed rigid and then slowly relaxed. "Hey, time for sleep, 'kay?"

Jonah reached up and latched his fingers into her hair. "Ow. Haley, how do I...?"

"You'll figure it out," Haley said and scooted into the kitchen. Grace was leaving tomorrow. It would be good for Auntie to have alone time with Jonah. And it would be good to have some alone time herself.

Hands immersed in soapy water, her reflection caught in the window overlooking the darkened yard, Haley permitted herself to give full thought to Mateo's proposal tonight. Not the business partnership but the relationship.

Common sense screamed at her that a relationship with Mateo was a no-fly zone. Had she not just gotten herself out of one manipulative relationship where a man had said all the right things until she'd refused him the only thing he wanted—her land? Why jump into another, especially with a man who had said right out of the starting gate that he wanted the same thing?

Because it's Mateo.

Grace had only touched on the depth of the friendship between Haley and Mateo. They had grown up together, like two stalks vining around each other, sharing fries and secrets. And first kisses.

It wasn't when they were eleven or twelve, an age where it could be seen as innocent. It was later, when Mateo was almost fifteen and she was about to turn fourteen. They were riding together along the fence line in July, stopping now and then to graze on saskatoon berries, hands and lips staining blue.

They had talked about an upcoming summer party. A girl Mateo had had his eye on was going. Haley had teased him, trying just as Grace had, to gauge how deep Mateo's interest went. He had remained frustratingly noncommittal.

As they were walking to find more berries, their horses' reins in hand, Haley had pushed for information. "Are you going to kiss her?"

Mateo had looked at the ground. "I don't know how to."

Haley had laughed. "How can you not know how to kiss?"

Mateo had given her a look tinged with annoyance and embarrassment, and Haley realized that he really might not know. His parents were standoffish with him, and he was an only child. He never kissed.

"I mean, I know in theory," he'd muttered.

He looked so sad and hurt that Haley wanted to help him. In a rush she later could never quite regret, she said, "I'll show you. It's easy."

Mateo came to a full stop. "You're kidding?"

"No."

"When?"

Swept up in his eagerness, Haley had said, "Now is as good a time as any."

She took off her cowboy hat and kissed him on the cheek. It was a quick peck, the good-night kind she gave her parents. Mateo had startled and touched the spot. Catching himself, he flushed.

"Is it…my turn?"

She'd offered her cheek, and he reciprocated with a peck. "A little hard," Haley evaluated.

"Oh."

"Do you want to try again? On the other cheek?"

"Okay."

He was much better the second time. The brush of his lips had sent a little tremble through her insides, something that had never happened before with any of her other kisses. *So this is what it's like to kiss a boy.*

For the first time in their lives, awkwardness fell between them. Mateo had looked off across the rows of cut hay, and Haley looked at Mateo in a way she hadn't ever before.

Mateo had turned to her and said, "Should we try on the lips?"

He wanted to kiss her—*really* kiss her. "I—I haven't kissed on the lips."

"Me neither." He gave a shy grin. "Obviously."

"Okay," she'd said. "I guess if we mess it up, only we'll know."

Except they didn't. They aced that first kiss. It had tasted of berries and them.

They pulled apart, and reality set in. They had crossed a line, and Haley got scared. She didn't want to lose their easy friendship. She was still thirteen. His friendship meant more than the door the kiss had opened.

Fighting to keep her voice casual, she'd said, "I guess that was okay."

Mateo had dropped his hands from her waist and picked up his horse's reins, "Yeah, it was okay." He looked across the land. "Thanks."

Haley picked up her reins. "You're welcome." She swung up into the saddle. "Come on. We better head back."

They'd had no reason to return, but Mateo seemed to accept the excuse. They rode back, and when they parted for their homes, their goodbyes were as casual and easy as they'd always been.

Tonight, she had pressed again, and Mateo had expressed his interest. She was back to the same dilemma. Should she swap friendship for a romance? Or more precisely, a business partnership for a romance? What if he left again? What if this was all part of a plan to take over her land, as it had been with Trevor? She had been devastated when Mateo had broken off their friendship. What if they got married, and he took her for everything—

A touch fell on her shoulder, and she whirled around, soap bubbles flying everywhere.

Grace squawked. "You soaked me." She rubbed at the teeny-weeny wet spots on her shirt with a hand towel.

"Yes, drama queen," Haley said.

"Anyway, I came to tell you that I put Jonah in his crib. He opened his eyes and then closed them again, so hopefully, he's gone back to sleep."

"Look at you," Haley said. "A natural."

"No way. It's on you to continue the line."

"One. I have one. That's enough."

"Not if Mateo has his way."

"He's my business partner."

"Cause a 'business partner' would install a car seat in his brand-spanking-new truck."

"I'm not getting into it with you. I'm tired, and you have an early start yourself." Haley pulled the sink plug to underscore her point. She wiped her hands on the towel Grace was dabbing herself with. "Good night."

And then—call it muscle memory—she leaned over and kissed her sister on the cheek.

Grace pulled a face. "What was that for?"

Haley switched on the overnight light and flicked off the overhead ones. In the soft glow of the room, she explained, "Just keeping in practice."

CHAPTER EIGHT

DARK CLOUDS HAD gathered the next morning when Mateo reached the end of his driveway. The rain would be good for the wheat and oats he'd seeded weeks ago. He'd catch up on yard work, maybe duck in and hang out with Haley and Jonah a bit. No doubt she'd rub it in about the rain. No matter so long as they got a soaker.

He prepared to turn left and saw a vehicle approach. Grace's car, better suited for the city than these gravel roads. Haley had mentioned she was heading back to the city today. Just as well. He and Grace had never gotten along. She had always poked him about one thing or another when they were growing up. He'd tolerated it well enough because she was Haley's sister and he'd not wanted to put Haley in the middle of a fight.

He expected to lift his hand in greeting as

Grace barreled past, but she parked instead, blocking the driveway. Guess they were talking.

They stepped out of their vehicles at the same time, and Grace rounded the hood of her sleek gray ride. Mateo let Grace take the lead. She usually did.

"We didn't get a chance to talk," Grace said, coming to join him at the front of his truck. She gave a low whistle. "Nice."

"Yep."

"But a gas-guzzler."

And there was the first poke. "I can afford it."

She looked past him to the house and buildings. "I suppose you can. I guess you can afford a lot of things now."

"I suppose you're right."

Grace tilted her head. "I'm sorry, you seem a little short. Did you have somewhere more important to be?"

Second poke. Mateo looked deliberately over to the Jansson ranch. "Actually, yes."

"Then, I'll get to the point."

Mateo waited.

"Haley told me about the business arrangement you have with her. I read over the papers. It's solid enough."

He wondered if Haley had talked about the amendment they'd agreed to last night. He trusted Haley to be discreet. Even as a teenager, she had kept his secrets...*their* secrets. But Grace was in the business of uncovering the truth to better the position of her client. Who in this case was Haley.

"The termination clause seems fair. Sixty days' notice of labor. Haley gets to do what she wants with the cattle if you bail and vice versa. You have no claims on the land."

He'd still have no claim on the land, but they would share cattle revenue. "I already know this, Grace. I helped draw up the terms."

"I want you to feel assured that I'd read it. And I will read all future legal documents between you and any of the Janssons."

"Go right ahead. I'm sure they'll appreciate your input."

She placed her foot on the front bumper. It would leave a smudge, maybe even a scratch if her boot held gravel. Which she knew full well. Jakob would have blown a gasket.

"The thing is," she continued, "I can watch over Haley's legal affairs but not her heart."

And here we go. He could feel his temper rise.

"You left without a word to her a dozen

years ago, and now you're back with a whole lot of money, and suddenly you're all in with Haley. All sweet with her and Jonah."

"Leave Jonah out of it."

"No, I won't, because he also stands to lose if you leave again. So what are your intentions?"

"How's that your business?"

"Because this is my sister and my nephew and yes, my dad. Because Haley just came off a marriage where the guy used her for what he could get and then left her. And I made sure it was with empty pockets and forever." She scraped off her boot and got in his face. "I'll make sure you end up the loser if you break her heart again."

Again? Haley had told him how much he'd hurt her, but as friends. A broken heart implied Haley had felt more than friendship. His mind flashed to last night when he'd offered himself up. She had smiled and turned to Jonah, had not committed one way or another. He hadn't pushed. She had good reason to hesitate.

"If I hurt Haley again, you go ahead and do that."

She straightened and studied him. "We understand each other."

They did because they both cared about the same person. Except Grace thought she had the edge over him. "We both want what's best for Haley. You think that because she's your sister, you're closer to her. The thing is, I grew up with Haley, too. I would argue I spent more hours together with Haley than you did."

She dared to look insulted. "Blood runs thicker and all that."

"I know how that works—and let me tell you, it doesn't. Nobody is going to tell me that I don't love Jonah as much as you or Knut. Maybe only Haley could possibly love him more."

There, he'd said it. He'd said the word "love" to the one person who would probably mock him for it. Instead, she stood there and let him have his say.

"I regret those years we had apart. She knows it. But I'm here right now. I'm making up for it the best way I know how. And if you hadn't parked your car in front of me, I'd be there right now. Time you got out of my way so I can go take care of your family."

Of all things, a smile glimmered across Grace's features. "I will. Now that I know they're in good hands."

She turned to leave, but Mateo called, "Wait."

He opened the door to his truck and drew out a cleaning rag. "Wipe off my truck."

And she did, grinning.

A WEEK LATER Knut took a tumble down the front porch steps and tore up his recovering knee, so Haley spent the day with Jonah in the emergency room, texting updates to Mateo. Actually, Mateo did more of the updating, as he kept her posted on his various activities, including a short video of Risky B running the flag.

Wish I could've been there. Beats sitting in a hospital. It smells funny.

We live on a farm with a baby. You should be used to funny smells.

Finally, she was allowed to see her dad.

"Sorry," he said, groggy from painkillers. "I should've listened."

She adjusted Jonah in her arms and bent

to kiss her dad's cheek. "The first right thing you've said in a while."

He lifted a finger in argument, though it hung at half-mast. "I was right to be moving around, but apparently, there's a method to it."

"Next time I tell you to do something, admit I'm right and do whatever I say."

"I guess it's over to you and Mateo for the summer while I get myself sorted out."

You and Mateo. Her dad linked them casually together. It made sense. They were business partners, but Knut would require extra care now, and she guessed that would be up to her, but she didn't want to give up on helping Mateo train Risky B.

"You look a bit put out," her dad ventured.

She was, but she couldn't hold on to her anger when he had so quickly owned up to his blame. She had collapsed like a shot duck when Mateo apologized, too. The two men had her heart wrapped around their little fingers, and they just knew how to squeeze it, which left her exposed to their schemes, the small ones and those the size of six quarters. She really needed to stand her ground, slick and rocky as it was.

"I am. As if I don't have enough to do, now I'll be taking care of you."

"I'll get myself a nurse."

It turned out there were no nurses to be had, other than a twice-weekly drop-in home aide to provide personal hygiene and a medicine review.

"I can shave myself," her dad said, "and count my own pills."

"It's a little more than that. She'll check your—"

"I can take care of myself. I have been ever since your mother passed."

Haley gave him a look.

Knut sighed. "With your help."

There was movement at the drawn curtain, and Mateo entered, carrying three bright helium-filled balloons. "Balloons!" Knut grumbled. "What am I? Six?"

"No confusion there," Mateo said. "They are not for you. Somebody—" he smiled at Jonah "—is three months old today."

Jonah's own mother had forgotten the mini-milestone. The birthday boy went wild with joy at the splash of color in the dull setting, kicking and waving at the balloons.

"He can't have them," Haley said. "There are all sorts of horror stories about them."

"Got it. That's why he gets this instead." Mateo produced a teething toy, and not just a simple ring but the champion of all toys complete with a tiny mirror. Jonah's greedy hands latched on to it, and he immediately bit down. She had wondered if his recent drooling meant he was teething. Mateo had not only seen but also acted. He was turning up the heat on her already-melting heart. Any more and she'd have to report to the hospital desk for an emergency replacement.

"Say 'thanks,'" Haley prompted, channeling her appreciation through Jonah. Coward. She raised her eyes to Mateo's. "I apologize for his rudeness. Thanks."

Mateo set the weighted balloons on the food tray and took Jonah from her. Haley had gotten so used to this invasion of space that she only got a wee breathless now. In fact, when the transfer loosened Jonah's hold on the teether, she leaned past Mateo's shoulder to make the adjustment without a second thought. She might have stayed that close had she not caught her dad's considering gaze.

"Don't you all look the picture of a happy family," he said.

Haley widened the gap. "The painkillers are causing hallucinations."

He settled back in his pillows. "You're probably right. Whatever you say."

Sweetly tossing her words back in her face. She could feel Mateo's eyes tracking them, no doubt pretending he didn't know what was going on. They were in total cahoots.

She got down to business. "Dad's out of commission for the rest of the summer. Which means that between swapping out ice packs and running him in for physio, I'm going to be even more useless to you than I have been, Mateo. Are you up for the extra work, or should we try again to look for help?"

Mateo studied her dad like he was a sick cow in the field. "He'll come around soon enough. No sense paying out full-time for what'll be temporary. If we're stuck, we can call Will or Dave."

"Dave will find out about Risky B."

Mateo exchanged looks with Knut. Those two. "Why do I feel like I'm out of the loop?" she asked.

"There's no secret," Mateo said. "Dave came

over when you were in town the other day, and I told him about another horse Hawk has. We're all good."

She crossed her arms. A tiny secret he brushed away with logic, making her seem shrewish.

"I'm sorry I didn't mention it, Haley."

She dropped her hands. "Fine. Fine, fine, fine. You get more than horses to fall in line, don't you?"

Mateo gave her a slow smile. "I hope so," he said softly, as if it were just the two of them alone, like back on his couch, when he'd told her that he wanted a romance with her. Wanted it very much.

Her dad cleared his throat. "Don't let me keep you two from the good work of running my ranch."

Haley snorted. "As if." They all knew that Knut held the ranch on paper only. Goodwill, ambition, hard work and something that looked a lot like love kept the ranch going. She looked at Jonah sitting noisy and content in Mateo's arms. Mateo was already showing her son all of that.

And her, too. He'd made a romance with him sound like a deal she could no longer ignore. Just as smooth-talking Trevor had. No. Mateo was different. He didn't run from responsibility. He threw it a birthday party. She didn't have to give her heart to Mateo, but she could give him—give them all—a chance.

THE ONE GOOD thing about working from dawn to dusk in June was how many hours there were to get things done. Mateo found his first coffee of the morning came earlier every day, and when the day's work was done after supper, he headed for the stables to train Risky B.

He could have eased up on the schedule since the filly wouldn't be ready to compete this summer, but it was an excuse to get one-on-one time with Haley. She'd get Jonah down and her father iced, with his phone beside him, and then join Mateo at the corral to run the flag.

Haley used a remote to zip the flag along the line, and with every session, the filly improved. Tonight, for instance, she started to sit back before he pulled on the reins in reaction to Haley snapping the flag to a stop.

"Come back halfway," Mateo said. "And hold it there."

Haley obeyed.

Mateo held Risky B to the spot, even though he could feel her pent-up tension. She was ready for the flag to dart in either direction, but she had to learn patience and attention. As he had to with Haley. In the two weeks since he'd indicated his romantic interest in her, she'd not indicated which way she wanted to go. She was the flag, and he twisted and turned to keep up. When a few beats had passed, he said, "Turn on her left foot again."

The flag didn't move. He looked over at Haley. She grinned. "I think she needs to learn to watch and wait."

His thoughts, but he was the trainer. "I'm on that," he said. "I want to keep her engaged."

"Not if you keep telling her what's going to happen next."

"She doesn't know."

"Are you kidding? She listens to every word you say."

"Something you seem incapable of."

Haley crossed her arms. "I propose a new exercise."

Why wasn't he surprised? Nothing stayed in place for long with Haley. Except their present relationship, which he dared not push into something more for fear she'd upend their whole arrangement. Besides, their lives were already so entwined. Much more and they might as well be walking down the aisle.

Holy… Had he just considered marriage when they hadn't even gone on a date?

"Aren't you two waiting nicely."

Was that a flirt or a goad? It was hard to tell the difference with her. He was in the mood for the former. "Anything for you, darlin'." He laid on the twang to leave an opening for her to interpret it as sarcasm or more flirting.

"I thought we could step up the game."

He liked the sound of that. "Okay."

"I work the flag by myself. You and Risky B follow."

Mateo rested his wrists on the pommel. "You'd like that, wouldn't you? Calling the shots?"

"No more than the next girl."

Definitely flirting. He'd play along. "All righty, then. Let's do this, sweetheart."

At that campy endearment, the flag shot off. He and Risky B gave it their all to get even with the flag over the new few lengths, and then she threw in short waits to give the horse a tiny breather. Or to keep him on edge.

The filly was learning to anticipate Haley's next trick. A deep sense of pure fun grew within, and he glanced over at Haley. She wore a face-splitting grin. She jerked the line, and Risky B initiated the turn. It was Mateo adjusting now.

After a few more rounds, Mateo decided it was best they call it a night.

"Time to stop," Haley ordered.

He'd let her have this last one. He swung off Risky B as Haley approached. She rubbed the filly's neck. "Good girl. Who's the smartest thing on four legs?"

"She'd beat out plenty of two-leggers," Mateo said, pulling off his riding gloves.

"Two-leggers? Is that even a word?"

"You can say anything so long as the other person knows what you're talking about." He took Risky B's reins, which brought him in close to Haley. She stiffened, as she always did when he took Jonah from her arms. It was an instinctive distrust he couldn't figure out how to break through.

"True," she said, falling into step beside him as he led Risky B back to the stables. Usually, she cut away at this point to return to the house, and he'd go back to his place to fill Dodge's bowl and go to bed. He itched to take her hand. "With some people, you can have entire conversations without having to say a word."

Did she mean that? Were they in the middle of some unspoken conversation? "I tend to do better when the odd word or two is inserted," he said.

Risky B's hooves clicked on the hard floor as they entered the stables. Mateo lined her up while Haley set up the lead lines. No words necessary. Mateo was uncinching the saddle when Haley next spoke.

"I got a few words for you, then."

It was Mateo's turn to hold his breath. He prepared for a blast.

Instead, she seemed hesitant, shy. "So tomorrow's Father's Day. A while back, Krista invited my dad and me over for a big barbecue at the Claverleys'. Every dad in the district will be there. Krista started it when Will became a dad, and she'll probably keep on doing it when he's a great-granddad." She picked up a brush and started on Risky B's flanks.

"Anyway," she said over the withers, "Dad

can't go now, and I know you're busy, but I was wondering…if…" She bit her lip.

"I can hold down the fort if you want to go."

She scraped her lip with her teeth. "That's not what I'm asking."

He dropped the saddle onto the railing and waited.

She trailed the brush lightly down Risky B's back, so lightly the horse shivered. "I was wondering if you'd like to come along…with me and Jonah."

He couldn't have heard right. "But it's for Father's Day."

"I know."

"But everyone'll think—"

She looked him in the eye. "I know."

He watched Haley slowly brush the filly. All he could manage was to stand and watch as he absorbed the message behind her words. She was prepared to make a community declaration that Mateo was her son's father figure. "Those are sure some few words."

She sighed. "It isn't any more than everyone can see for themselves. Any more than I can see. You are so good with Jonah. I couldn't have hoped for a better father for him. I lucked out with you. I couldn't ever see myself with a guy that I couldn't also see as a dad to Jonah. And I can see myself with you."

Three blinding realizations shot into Mateo's brain. First, Haley was asking him out on a date. Second, she was doing it because she saw him as good father material and not just as a good husband. Third, here was his chance to prove he could be both.

"Okay," he said, playing it cool. "I'd like to come. Thanks for the invite."

CHAPTER NINE

HALEY FORGOT THAT she hadn't brought just a date to the barbecue. She'd brought Mateo, a neighbor to all here and son to Jakob Pavlic, whose family had ranched in the district for the past five generations.

That became apparent when they rolled in with his new truck. Vehicles from all over the district were parked around the house, with men clustered at Will Claverley's truck. As soon as Mateo parked, men drifted over and settled there like crows on a fence. Comments flew, and Mateo fielded them as he opened the back door of the crew cab and unlatched Jonah.

"I can take him," Haley said quietly beside him. "You visit."

"I got him," Mateo said. "I'll bring him over when he's hungry."

That left Haley holding the diaper bag. She joined the all-female crew on the back deck of the Claverley ranch house. Nearly every woman she'd known in her life was gathered on the deck here. Babies and kids wove up and around like puppies. It was a living scrapbook, packed with memories and possibilities.

Haley dropped into an empty chair under a shady umbrella. Janet Claverley immediately offered her an array of nonalcoholic drinks.

"Go for the punch," Krista said. "I made it myself. You drink it, and Jonah will start popping muscles. Accounts for two more pounds on her this week." She pointed to Cassie, decked out in a pink polka-dot sun hat and sundress. Haley thanked her stars for Jonah's gender. It strained her fashion sense to get him into clean duds, much less coordinated ones. Besides, Jonah looked handsome in anything.

"It's pond scum," Dana said. "It tastes like moldy pineapple and grass clippings." Krista and Dana were sisters-in-law, both from families of sisters. They gave each other grief all day long.

"As long as it's cold, I'm good," Haley said.

"I'll get it. I have to see if Ella's up from her nap, anyway." Krista plopped Cassie onto

Haley's lap and skipped off. She wore a blue polka-dot sundress, and her curly ponytail swung behind her.

"Doesn't she just make you want to puke?" Dana asked.

Haley laughed along with everyone else, but guilt shortened it. When Trevor had abandoned her, Krista had showed up nearly every day, even though she was pregnant with Cassie and had a toddler, a husband and a business. She had still chiseled out time in her day to be a shoulder to cry on. Haley hated how much eye water she'd leaked over a man who Krista repeatedly kept saying didn't deserve her.

She searched for a change in topic. "Has anyone found a good baby carrier? I'm looking for one that'll easily adjust for men and women."

"You can have mine," Dana said. "But the shade got destroyed."

"You'll need a shade of some kind," Janet chimed in. "It's turning out to be one hot summer."

It was. Mateo's prediction seemed to be correct. The last noticeable rain was more than two weeks ago, when Grace left for Calgary, and that had amounted to a short inch. Mateo had reported that the wheat and oats had sprouted, but she had not gone out there herself. The road to town lay in the opposite direction, but that was no excuse.

"Did Keith use it much?" Haley asked, referring to Dana's husband.

"All the time. The twins loved it. But it's only a one-seater. They liked the view, but I think they mostly liked hanging with Keith."

"Same here," Haley said, bouncing Cassie on her lap. What an inane remark, and the blank stares of the females reflected their own confusion. "I mean, the same with Jonah and Mateo. He just wants to be with him all the time."

"You mean, Jonah wants to be with Mateo all the time?" Janet asked.

"Both ways. I swear, Mateo would pack him around all day if he could."

"Take it if you can get it," Janet said. "Dave wanted to help, but he has more of a knack for horses."

"Mateo has a knack for both," Haley said. She could hear the bragging in her voice. Knowing glances were being exchanged like secret notes among the half-dozen females.

Did they think she and Mateo were in a relationship? The only one excluded from the exchange was Dave's mother. As the eldest there, she had claimed the softest and shadiest seat. White-haired and wearing a cardigan even in the heat, she had hardly seemed to be following the conversation.

"Mateo? Jakob's boy?" she piped up.

"That's the one," Janet said.

"He's back?" Dave's mother asked.

"Yes, remember we—" Janet broke off. Haley had heard from her dad that Dave's mother suffered from memory loss. "Yes, he's back. He lives at Jakob's place and works at the Janssons' with Knut and Haley."

With, not *for*. News of their business partnership had spread, probably with help from her dad. She liked how it sounded. It also made sense in the minds of the neighbors that the son of Jakob Pavlic would be no less than a partner in a ranch.

"Oh, good. I always liked that boy. Hardworking and polite. Always feeding cats. Jakob will be glad to have him around the place again."

Awkward silence fell as Krista stepped back onto the deck with a pitcher of grass clippings and a sleepy toddler. Haley jumped up with Cassie to lighten her load, Dana made a remark that had the sisters-in-law playfully spatting at each other and the conversation righted itself.

Still, Haley found herself distracted by the remarks of the elderly Mrs. Claverley. She had given Mateo flack for the way he'd left all those years ago. She'd lost her trust in him, but the neighbors hadn't. They had concluded that whatever the reason for his long absence, it was all for the good.

Their goodwill rankled. They saw Mateo as an equal, but did they see her as one? Did they see her as Haley Jansson, not just as Knut's daughter? It was no secret that up until this year, she'd operated half the farm as she saw fit; it was also no secret that she had lived under her father's roof since the day she was born. All well and good to talk about going it alone, but she never had, and her partnership with Mateo was further proof. Dating him was an admission she needed a man.

Her determination to go it alone had begun to crumble the day Mateo drove her to the hospital. She'd come to depend on him to take care of the land, her son and her own happiness. At each step of the way, she'd called it something else—a temporary hiring, a business partnership, a friendship, a romantic attraction, a chance to build a life together. But really, it was a habit. A habit of giving herself away. One only she could break.

Krista touched her arm. "Everything okay?"

Haley held out Cassie to Krista. "Jonah's due for a feeding. I'm going to get him."

The men had drifted down to the barn. She caught sight of a brightly colored shirt or two at the entrance. The barn was like their man cave. She would intrude, pick up Jonah and return.

As she rounded the corner to the barn, she heard Mateo's voice. "Haley and I couldn't decide."

She stopped, curious.

"Flip a coin." That sounded like Howie. He ranched by himself. No coins involved there.

"It doesn't work that way with us."

"You can't run an operation that way." Howie again. He was giving Mateo the gears about the wheat and oats. "Some things have to be decided one way or another. All in or all out."

Mateo had said the same thing practically

word for word. Did nobody understand the meaning of compromise? And of course, Howie hadn't questioned her about the field because he assumed that the man made the decisions.

She took a deep breath and entered the barn as if she hadn't broken stride. In the airy dimness, the men were circled in camping chairs around a cooler of drinks like around a fire. Jonah was chilling in the crook of Mateo's arm.

All eyes swiveled to her. "Hey there," she said. "My turn with Jonah."

Howie looked between them. "You got him split the same way between the two of you? Big black strip up the middle of his back?"

Haley had no idea what strip he was referring to. She reached down for Jonah, and her eyes met Mateo's. Something flickered across his features, and she could tell he knew she'd overheard the conversation. She was pretty much an open book he could thumb through any time.

"Way it works with Krista and me," Will said, coming to their rescue. "Especially at bedtime. Kid roping should be a rodeo event."

But Haley wasn't about to let Howie off the

hook. With Jonah tucked against her, extra warm from nestling against Mateo's arm, she turned to Howie.

"You figure you know how a partnership works, Howie. But you work by yourself, live by yourself, eat and clean your clothes by yourself. You live on your terms. Good for you. But Mateo and I have a partnership. An equal one. That means we meet each other halfway. We don't leave our decisions up to a coin toss. There's no win or lose. There's just going forward."

She glanced down at Mateo, expecting a look of pride or at least, agreement. Instead, he looked down at the barn floor, the back of his neck flushed as if…embarrassed. The rest of the men looked as uncomfortable as the women had when Dave's mother made her sideways remark.

Well, let them think what they wanted. Truth tended to make people twitch in their seats.

"Good day, gentlemen," she said and carried off her son.

THAT EVENING, she discovered what Howie meant by the black strip. When Mateo had said he'd catch a ride back with Will, she'd driven back in his truck with Jonah to check on her dad. Then she'd transferred the car seat into the beater farm truck and bounced her and Jonah across the pastureland to the seeded quarter. There it was. To the right, the wheat was edging close to six inches. To the left was a shorter mat of oats that had been planted two weeks later. Down the center, straight off from the gate where she was parked, was a fallowed strip as wide as the cultivator. It stretched a half mile, the full length of the quarter.

It made sense that Mateo had separated the crops for ease of cutting and to make turning equipment simpler. She hadn't realized how conspicuous it would appear to anyone driving by. It looked odd, but it might be what it took for the district to recognize that a new kind of partnership had rolled into town.

Into town? "You know what I mean," she said to Jonah secured to the bench seat beside her. "You're going to grow up knowing what a strong mama looks like."

He grinned.

"Hey, how about we tear up a strip? No objections? Let's do this."

She opened the gate, drove the truck onto the top of the black strip and closed the gate behind her. Then she threw the truck into low gear and let her rip. At one point, she checked the rearview mirror. A gray cloud billowed out behind. Jonah was wide-eyed, and vibrations poured from his mouth in a throaty stream.

Second to marrying Trevor, it was the most pointless thing she'd done in her life. At the end of the quarter, she rattled over the pipes of the cattle gate and braked at the graveled road.

On the other side of the road was the Pavlic place. And there at the top of the lane stood Mateo, hands on his hips, hat pushed back, watching her performance. Was he still embarrassed? He'd kept clear of her during the rest of the barbecue, as if worried she might go off on somebody again. Like him.

Well, she wasn't going to let him hide away. If he had a problem with her, best he not run.

She gunned across the road and up the lane, pulling to a stop in front of Mateo.

He frowned through the windshield. "You brought Jonah."

"He's in there tighter than a screw in wood."

Of course Mateo had to worry about Jonah. "You know, you can trust that I won't bust up our kid."

Our kid. Wow. It was one thing to declare to Mateo that he treated Jonah like a son. Another to make the leap that Jonah was theirs, to talk about him the way Will and Krista could about their little girls. That was crossing their partnership over a line she'd only tiptoed along up until now.

If Mateo had noticed the slip, he didn't let on. He opened the passenger door and lifted Jonah into his arms.

She might as well bring up the black-striped elephant in the field. "I finally get what Howie was talking about."

"It wasn't a secret," he said. "I just…didn't care to bring it up."

"Because it's a sore point," she said. "It's us telling the neighbors that we do things differently."

Mateo brushed Jonah's fine hair back. Haley took a deep breath, like when she'd stepped into the barn earlier. "You ever wonder why I married Trevor?"

Mateo's eyes were still on their field across the road. "It's none of my business."

"You're right about that, but I bet you're curious."

He drew his gaze back to hers. "And I bet you're going to tell me."

"I am, because then you might understand why I said what I did today. Long story short. We both got duped. He had no family—no parents, brothers or sisters. He's an orphan, and I felt sorry for him. I wanted him to have a family, a real home. He didn't see a home. He saw an opportunity. He didn't realize the land wasn't in my name, that I only operate it even though I refer to it as my land. He married me thinking that because I operated the land, even called it mine. The truth came out eight months later when I told him I was pregnant. He told me he never intended to partner with me to farm the quarters. He wanted to sell it all along and figured he could charm me into signing on the dotted line. He said I could get my dad to put it up for sale or he was leaving. You can guess my answer."

"When he left, it felt as if I'd failed, despite Grace, Dad and Krista telling me that it was the best thing for me. We'd all been duped, and no one likes to be taken for a fool."

Mateo's mouth thinned. "I know the feeling all too well."

"What do you mean by that?"

"What did you mean by your little performance today?" Jonah arched his back, and Mateo set him against his shoulder.

"My 'performance'? You mean how I made it clear to everyone how our partnership works?"

"I think you made that very clear." Sarcasm etched his voice.

Why was he so upset at her for standing up to Howie? Haley pressed her fingers to her temple. She wasn't going to let this devolve into an argument. They were partners. Partners discussed their opposing viewpoints. This was the same as their differing views on the quarter, and they'd resolved that. They'd resolve whatever this was.

"Okay, I accept responsibility here. I tend to make more of things than is actually there. My marriage, for instance. I had to commit all the way. Turn it into a whole family-farm thing. I did it again when I pushed you to tell me if our partnership was more than business. I couldn't visualize it any other way. Telling Howie off made me realize I don't need to give away myself. I can go halfway and not push for a commitment from either of us."

Jonah gave a little squeak, and Mateo switched him back to his first position. Jonah still fussed, and Mateo threw a jiggle into it. Haley had never seen Jonah fuss with Mateo before, but he was doing exactly what he did when Haley held him and was stressed or tired. "Are you saying you don't want a relationship with me?"

Haley wavered, hated that she hesitated. She plunged on. "Yes, I want a relationship with you but not if it means risking our present partnership. The business end and your relationship with Jonah. We've got a good thing going here, already."

Mateo gestured with his free arm to the field. "You call that a 'good thing'? Do you really not see what everyone else sees? What Howie sees?"

"I bet you're going to tell me," she said, purposely echoing his earlier words.

"You look at that field and see compromise. Everyone else sees two people who can't get along. They see a line in the land between two ways of thinking."

"Let them think what they want. They will, anyway."

"What about me? Do you care what I think?"

"Of course I do. But we talked about it, and you agreed. If you were so opposed to it, why didn't you fight me on it?"

"Because I didn't want to push you away. Because our partnership was just business at that point. But then you invited me to the Father's Day barbecue. That was big, Haley. I thought it meant that if you trusted me with your son, you trusted me, period."

She swallowed. "I'm sorry, but I've learned my lesson."

"What you've learned is to spill your old grudge onto me. I'm not Trevor."

"I know who you are. You're my partner." She felt compelled to add, "We're equal partners."

He made a scoffing noise, and his breath ruffled Jonah's hair. "You want to prove to everybody how you're my equal in the partnership. Did you ever think that maybe I've got something to prove, too?"

"You've nothing to prove. Dave's mother remembers you as this polite, hardworking cat feeder. Remembers you when she forgot her own son's name tonight." She sighed. "The district already considers you as someone capable. You've nothing to prove to anybody."

He shook his head. "I once thought I had something to prove to you. I thought this partnership was a way to show you that you could trust me. But you've turned it into a competition about who is more capable. You want your independence, fine. But I want my own kind of legacy. I thought I could build one with you, but I can't if I'm fighting you every step of the way."

There was a finality in his voice that scared her. "It's just one point of contention. We're good with other things. Like Risky B."

"So long as you get to pull the strings."

"Somebody has to. That's the way it works."

"Wasn't that Howie's point?"

She had an answer for that. She just needed a moment to think it through.

Mateo didn't seem to care to wait. "You weren't wrong to commit all the way. Trevor was wrong to be careless with your trust."

He handed a wriggling, fretting Jonah over

to her. "I'm not good company right now. He's all yours."

He left her there and disappeared into the house, leaving Haley alone to buckle Jonah up and go back to her place.

She'd come to celebrate their partnership, and now she didn't even know if they still had one. Or if she even understood how one worked. She might have to go it alone—only this time, not by choice.

A SPECTACULAR ROSY sunrise was lost on Mateo as he made his way up the black strip on foot to the Jansson home. After he'd lent his truck to Haley at the barbecue, Will had driven him back. Mateo knew that he could call Haley for a ride, but he wasn't in any frame of mind to be in close quarters with her until he'd sorted himself out.

Nearly across the quarter following in Haley's tire tracks, Mateo was still in a whirl. Hope was the problem. He had hoped that Haley might let him into her life. He had avoided bringing up the divided field because he'd hoped she would change her thinking enough so that when she did see it, it would be obvious how she had to be more accommodating in their partnership.

He had hoped to keep the business end and his feelings in two different pens. Then he had hoped to open the gates between them and let them all mix freely. Hope had made him dream of a home and family. But he'd been kicked out of a family once. Why should it be any different this time?

Time to strike off in a new direction, go it alone. He bent through the strands of barbed wire as his phone rang. Hawk.

"Good to know I'm not the only one awake," Mateo said by way of opening.

"I've got kids that get the sun out of bed," Hawk said. "What's your excuse?"

Mateo hesitated on the edge of telling his old boss and now friend about his love woes. But newly divorced Hawk's input would probably not be the most uplifting input. He went for a semi-truth. "Out checking crops."

"Oh, yeah?" Like anyone who lived off the land, Hawk would welcome an on-the-ground weather report.

"Dry. Not burning yet. But we could do with a good four-inch soaker."

"The kind that comes down slow and steady

for three solid days until even your skin goes soft as flannel." Hawk's voice had gone dreamy.

Mateo continued his trek diagonally across the pasture that would bring him up behind the Jansson ranch. He had a half-mile to figure things out. First off, Hawk.

"Since I can't make 'er rain, what else can I do for you?" Mateo asked.

"Heard about the horse show over in Sundre?"

"I heard talk." Will and Dave Claverley had talked at the barbecue about entering the charity exhibition an hour's drive south, but Mateo had been too distracted by Haley's earlier set-to with Howie to give it his full attention.

"There's no money, but I thought of you and Risky B right away."

"She's not ready. I only had her with the calves last week, and no cutting. Just her getting used to them. I hadn't planned on showing her at all this summer."

"This isn't a competition. It would be a chance for her to get practice in a show pen without any pressure." Hawk paused. "It would be good for you, too. Get a little exposure for yourself."

Mateo stopped short in the middle of the pasture, and a dozen cows that had paid him no mind when he was walking now raised their heads from their early-morning grazing. This was it.

This was the new direction he'd decided on only moments before. The idea wasn't straight out of the blue. It was just moving up the timeline a bit. Waiting for good things to happen hadn't gotten him anywhere.

"I'll check it out. Thanks, Hawk. How are Amos and Saul?"

"Busy. Too busy to eat or sleep."

Mateo laughed. "Jonah's the same." He caught himself. He sounded as if he was talking about his own kid. He hurried on. "Everything going all right with the new guy? He working out?"

"He's good, but I might have to let him go." Hawk sighed. "It's not been my best year. I might sell the home quarter."

That piece of land had been in the Blackstone family for more than a hundred years. "That bad?"

"If it's dry up there, you can imagine what it's like here."

"You can't reduce the herd instead?"

"I might have to do both."

Mateo couldn't quite make himself commit just yet, but he did say, "I know a buyer here. Let me know if you decide to sell." He paused and ended sincerely, "I hope you don't."

"Yeah. Me too. Hope for the best, cope with the rest."

Mateo had already done plenty of that during the past three months. Hawk's call about the show had given him new energy, and he let it propel him straight up to the Janssons' back door and into the kitchen, where he ran smack-dab into reality in the form of Jonah in Haley's arms.

He wore a diaper and a smile that lit up his face at the sight of Mateo. He bore no grudge for Mateo's tense grip the night before but let off a happy squeal and reached for Mateo.

He couldn't go on like this. He couldn't continue with Jonah when his mother didn't want him. She had warned him what might happen, but he had given his heart over to the baby anyway. And now…

He looked in desperation at Haley. Her lips flattened.

"Haley, we need a different arrangement."

Jonah bucked in Haley's arms, eager to go to the man who never refused him. "Okay," she said, "but now's not the time."

He gave a quick nod, reversed direction and kept going despite Jonah's howls of protest.

CHAPTER TEN

IT WAS THAT evening before Haley caught up with Mateo. He was out with Risky B in the small pasture. He didn't appear to be doing anything in particular with the filly except walking her among the cattle. But every now and then, he'd bring her around to face a calf.

He hadn't mentioned anything about working Risky B with livestock. In fact, when she had asked about it, he'd said it was too early for that. Something must've changed his mind.

She considered waiting for him to return to the stables, but waiting wasn't her thing. Mateo had spotted her a ways off but kept working Risky B until Haley drew closer.

"This is new," she said, patting Risky B's neck. The filly snuffled her pocket, and Haley gave up the apple.

"I prefer if you hold off with the treats until I'm done training."

His shortness was also new. But perhaps not unexpected. Her stomach had been in knots all day anticipating this conversation. "Sorry I couldn't meet with you until now. Jonah was a hot handful today. He's definitely teething. Drooling worse than me over ice cream."

Her weak joke didn't even draw so much as a glimmer of a smile from Mateo. He swung off Risky B. "That's okay." He didn't comment about Jonah, like he usually did.

Jonah had made adorable chatter this afternoon after his nap, and she'd forwarded a video of it to Mateo as per normal. He hadn't texted back.

"You wanted to talk?" she asked.

"I've entered Risky B into a show at the end of July in Sundre."

She felt like he was dodging the big question, like he had when he talked about his dad. "But you said you weren't going to have her compete this summer."

"I know what I said. I changed my mind."

"Just about Risky B?"

He looked her in the eye. "I want out of our agreement."

She'd half expected that announcement all

day, and yet his declaration still winded her. "I guess that can be arranged."

"It can be. You put in more exits in the two pages than holes in a sieve."

She couldn't let that one slide. "And yet who's the one backing out?"

He straightened, ready to fire back, and then he clamped his lips together. He looked away, and Haley patted the other side of Risky B's neck. The filly's bulk went a long way to block her view of Mateo. And just as importantly, his view of her. She didn't want him to see her hurt.

"We both know neither of us are ever going to get what we want from our partnership." He spoke slowly, rationally, a man with a grip on his emotions. Even as hers threatened to blow away like straw in the wind.

"I never promised you anything."

"I never said you broke any terms. I'm saying I want out."

"And we both know the reason you want out is because I won't date you."

In two quick steps, Mateo came around Risky B's head to face her. "You're right. I thought I could take it slow, prove myself to you, give you every reason to let me into your life. But you don't want me. Fine, only I'm not waiting around, hoping you'll change your mind."

"It's not that I don't want you."

"Then why won't you fight for us?"

Because he was handsome. Because he could stand independently from her. Because he had a vision for a future that matched hers. Because he cared for her son. Because he had come back when she most needed him.

Because he was too perfect. And perfection didn't last. She had to prove she could stand on her own when the bad times hit.

"Because what if it doesn't work out? Already Jonah is in withdrawal from—"

"Don't. Don't drag Jonah into this." His sudden fierceness shocked Haley. Shocked Risky B, too, for she whinnied. Mateo rubbed her jawline, and she immediately settled. Simply observing his touch soothed Haley's nerves, too.

"You're right. This is about us. I guess when it comes to dating, my heart just isn't into it."

"Haley Jane Jansson. Birthday's November sixth. Favorite school subject was biology. Ate a grasshopper leg when she was eight on a dare. Hates Brussels sprouts but cooks them for her dad's birthday because he loves them. Favorite pie is saskatoon-and-rhubarb."

She blinked.

"Yeah, Haley. I know you better than anyone. I could even give your family a run for their money. So I know when you're lying."

"But—"

"But you're too stubborn to admit it. Let me tell you the reason, and you tell me if I'm wrong." He came alongside her, so close she had to tip up her chin to see him. She was tempted to take a step away, but she stood her ground. "It's the same reason you go all stiff whenever I take Jonah from your arms. You don't trust me."

He'd made that accusation last night, and she'd not denied it. Now was not the time to admit her stupid attraction to him accounted for her tightening up. Better he mistook it for distrust, better than appearing weak and opening herself up to him manipulating her feelings. "Right again. I don't trust you. And why should I? You turned your back on me once before and—"

"You forgave me, Haley. Do you know what forgiveness is? It means accepting and moving on. You haven't moved on, which means you haven't forgiven me. There is nothing that I can do to change the past. And that suits you just fine because then you don't have to do anything about the present." This time, Mateo anticipated Risky B's nervousness and released the reins. The filly wandered off, nose to the grass, to give the arguing humans space.

And boy, did she want to argue. "The present is that you want out of an agreement we just made. So yeah, I don't trust that you won't bail at the first sign of trouble, because you just did."

"That's because—" He broke off. "We're going in circles. I want out. There's nothing to stop it from happening. Are we done here?"

Done and done. And yet… "You still have sixty days. And the agreement said you could train Risky B here. Where will you go?"

"I'll ask Will."

"But you would have to load her up every day to train her here, and she doesn't like the trailer as it is."

"It'll be good practice."

"But you don't have a trailer."

"I'll buy one."

"You had all that sand hauled in."

"I'll haul in more at Will's."

"Look, why don't you keep her here? She hasn't been here a month. Moving her all around again will throw off her training."

Mateo considered the grazing filly. Haley pressed the point.

"Stay at least until after the show."

"Fine," he said abruptly. "In return, I'll keep up my end of the bargain and work until the crops are in or until you find a replacement."

"Deal." She had bought time. For what, she didn't know. All she knew was that she couldn't stand to have whatever they'd built end so soon. She still wanted it all.

Mateo took up Risky B's reins and swung into the saddle. "One more thing."

"Yeah?"

"I saw your Jonah text. I thought about replying. A lot. But—" He straightened. "You two are a package. And if there's no future for you and me, then there's none for him and me, either."

Their first two deals had tied them together but this one would leave them little more than strangers. She swallowed past the sudden lump in her throat. She tried to say the words, but nothing came out. Even on her second try, it came out as little more than a whisper. "I understand."

Mateo nodded once and quickly turned Risky B back to the stables. Haley watched them among the backdrop of the slow-moving, grazing cattle. A calf approached, but when Haley reached out her hand, it skittered away. Scared, like her.

HALEY PLUNKED A plate of scrambled eggs in front of her dad. "Breakfast is served."

Her dad eyed the yellow mass that was crispy in parts. "You couldn't have negotiated a better deal with Mateo? A half dozen calves in return for breakfast?"

"You don't like it, cook it yourself." Haley was bluffing. They both knew that the only thing worse than her cooking was her dad's.

"I don't know why things had to change at all," her dad grumbled, as he had every morning since the new deal had gone into effect nearly two weeks ago.

"That would be a question for Mateo," she said, taking a seat before her own clump of eggs. She picked up her fork and sawed away.

"Since the therapist won't allow me anywhere where the ground isn't like a golfing green, I can't go to him. And since he's not coming here anymore, I guess it's a question for you."

"And I told you I don't have the answer. Can we move on?"

Her dad usually did take the hint, but not today. "I don't know why you still hold a grudge against him."

"I don't. He wants more out of the partnership than I'm willing to give. That's it."

"What's wrong with him? He's a far sight better than that ex of yours."

"He is." She took in a mouthful of rubbery eggs.

"And he's good with Jonah. You don't often get men happy to raise another man's kid."

Haley wasn't in the mood to contest her father's old-fashioned views.

"Where's the little guy, anyway?"

"Sleeping in, after being up half the night complaining about his teeth."

Her dad grunted. "I can relate." He moved his eggs around and finally pushed away his entire plate. He really was put out if he was turning away good food. Well, food. "You should mend fences. It's not too late."

"Dad, you're the one holding a grudge against me. You blame me because you want your cook back."

Her dad's bright blue eyes flashed like summer lightning. "What I want is your mother back, alive and well and cooking breakfast for all of us."

Haley stared. In the ten years since their mother had passed, it had been taboo for Haley and Grace to talk about her in front of their dad. Such a look of pain and regret would cross his face when they did that they'd learned to exchange memories out of his earshot. She wasn't the only one who couldn't let go of the past, but out of respect, she kept her thoughts to herself.

"Since she's not," he went on, "I only wish for you and Grace to get yourselves set up with your own families."

Another old-fashioned view, this one borne of love and worry. "I get it, Dad. Just... Now's not the right time. Maybe later."

"Don't put me off like I'm a kid asking for candy. You don't put off something good for later. Because good things are snatched up. And that boy is a good thing."

"Dad, you liked Trevor, too, no matter what

you say about him now. And look how he turned out. How do you know that Mateo will be any different? He's been gone since high school. He could've changed."

"I admit, I did like Trevor, but I didn't know him well. I've known Mateo since the day he was born. You're hunting for excuses, Hal."

"I'm not. And I'm sorry I'm messing with your master plan to marry Grace and me off, but I don't owe you that."

Her dad took a gulp of coffee. "Not me, but you do owe your son. He and Mateo got along like father and son."

Haley shook her fork at him. "I don't like that part any more than you do. None of us do, so don't—" She lowered her fork. "Don't, Dad. Just don't."

Her dad's hand, thick and calloused from decades of work, covered her fisted hand. "Okay, I won't. I just want you happy. Like every parent wants for their baby, big or small."

"But, Dad, how can I be happy if I'm under someone else's control?"

Her dad frowned. "Is that the way you think it works?"

"How else? How did you and Mom make it work? Did she just go along with everything you said?"

Her dad snorted and patted her hand before withdrawing his. "Hardly. Seemed like every day we were hammering something out."

"But what if you two couldn't agree? What then? Who had the final say?"

"You don't go into it looking to win or lose. There's always something bigger at stake. The problem itself."

Like whether or not to plant wheat or oats. Like if there'd be a drought. She'd made it into a discussion about compromise rather than doing what was best. She'd manipulated Mateo's wish to avoid offending her and used it to succumb to her own insecurities. She'd been a crummy partner.

Her dad looked at her with the same hard sympathy as when he'd told her about the untreatable abscess in the mouth of her favorite cow years ago. "You have to figure out if you're happier with him than without. Then, even if you're giving up something, it's okay, because you still come away feeling—" a slow, fond smile of remembrance tugged at the corners of her dad's mouth "—like you're in a song."

Jonah's waking cries rolled down the hallway. "There's *his* song," Haley said, pushing away from the table.

She knew Jonah was not happier without Mateo. As for her, she missed him. That had always been her problem. She'd never felt complete unless she was with someone, but she'd always ended up emptier than ever. She didn't know how to trust Mateo and not fear losing herself. But for the sake of her son— no, for the sake of those she cared about, including herself—she should try to figure out a way to be not only an equal partner but also a fearless one.

FROM THE CORNER of his eye, Mateo caught sight of Haley approaching the corral where he was training Risky B. It was the most he'd seen of her three weeks into their new deal. While cutting hay, he'd see the farm truck cross into the pasture and Haley get out to check on the cattle. He'd worried about Jonah riding high in the backpack around the curious calves, but there was nothing he could say. Nothing he could say when she loaded a cow with a sore foot and took her to the vet on her own. He would've helped if she'd asked. But of course, she didn't.

He needed all the free time he could get, anyway. Risky B was sharp as a whip and got a kick out of her job, but she had a lot to learn about pacing and listening.

Right now, she had cut a calf from the bunch. The laziest, most relaxed yearling born on four legs. In the arena, a turnback rider would get the cow on the move again. Here, Mateo was on his own.

A sudden clap of a harness against the wooden railing shot the cow into action. Haley. Risky B's muscles bunched, and he practiced their turns, keeping her hooked on the calf. They went back and forth a few stretches, and the cow drew to a stop and glanced away, the signal for defeat. He let it trot back to the herd and then brought out a fresh one.

"Again," he barked to Haley, not even thinking. Again, there was a clap of leather and metal accompanied by a shout. The cow streaked back to the others, but Risky B cut him off, her haunches going deep into the powder-fine sand.

He didn't know how many more times he repeated the command to Haley as they worked different cows.

"Hey, Mateo," Haley finally said. "Maybe we should let up. She's getting tired."

Risky B had begun to flag. The timing on her turns had fallen, and her breathing came hard. "I'm working on endurance."

"What's in it for the cows? It's late, and they need their rest."

"They get their breaks. I can take over from here," he said. "Thanks for your help."

She didn't leave right away but instead continued to stand on the bottom railing, the extra six inches helping her to clear the top one. He'd teased her about her height when they were growing up, had called her Shortening just to rile her. She'd shriek at him, and he'd laugh until his gut hurt. Then she'd march off, and he'd call her back and promise not to say it again. Sometimes, if he hadn't riled her too much, she'd make a U-turn. But other times, she kept going, and then he'd wished he hadn't pushed her so far.

Too bad he couldn't invoke the immature term now to get her to move on.

"No problem," she said and hopped down.

Instead of leaving, she pulled the bar back on the gate and swung it open. The yearlings crowded out like school kids when the home-time buzzer rang.

Not a word, Mateo ordered himself. *Not a word.* He followed the cattle out on Risky B, turning her to the stabling barn. He'd take out his frustration when he brushed down the filly, giving her the best grooming of her life. And then he'd drive home to his showroom house, crack a beer and use Jakob's computer to finish off a spreadsheet on the pricing for an arena. He and Will were working out the details of a partnership in cutting horses, with the training arena at Mateo's acreage. Plenty enough work to distract himself from thoughts of Haley.

Except Haley trailed after him into the stables. She leaned against the open entrance as he hooked the guide reins onto Risky B and then took the saddle off her. When he took up a brush, so did Haley.

Even when she had helped with the flag pulley, she hadn't helped with the brushing down. She must have something to say.

The rasp of the bristles on Risky B, the crunch of her jaws on the oats, the tingle of the steel clasps on the reins and the shuffle of their boots on the wood floor were the only sounds. Haley's silence thundered around Mateo, and he stole a glance at her. She seemed absorbed in her task, a small daydreaming smile played on the edge of her full lips. The evening sun poured through and caught the rust-red glints in her hair, a match to Risky B's glistening coat.

What was she up to? Did she regret the end of their agreement? Was she aware that her presence had him strung tighter than barbed wire?

To create space between them, he swapped a brush out for a hoof pick and tapped Risky B on the lower leg. She obligingly lifted her hoof. Nothing there. He let her hoof drop, and there on the other side, Haley tapped the opposite leg and reached her hand out. Mateo passed over the pick. Haley took it and popped out a stone. She kept the pick and moved to the front hoof. Forgetting himself, Mateo followed up to the front hoof on his side, first removing the front leg wrap with a rasp of Velcro. A second rasp rose as Haley shed the wrap from her side. Risky B was clear on Haley's side, and she passed the pick under the filly's chest. Mateo checked the last hoof and wedged out a stone. An equal amount of work on both sides.

Haley brought a softer brush around to Risky's head. She broke her silence to sweet-talk the filly, telling her how proud she was of her, how she was more beautiful than a flower, how her eyes were yummy pieces of chocolate.

Haley reached up to brush the forelock, but Mateo bunted away her brush and took over. "My reach is better."

"Remember how you used to call me Shortening?"

He started. They were grooming the same horse, thinking the same thoughts. "For the record, you weren't fat then and you're not now."

"Yeah, I knew that then, and I know it now. But it has always mattered to me what you think."

He'd beg to differ. Instead, he bit his tongue, curious despite himself how she'd back up that claim.

"Crazy, right?" she said. "Given we shared the same thoughts on everything important."

Where was she going with all this? She

didn't wait for his answer, didn't seem to expect one. She put away the brush and sauntered off, humming.

It was all he could do not to call her back.

CHAPTER ELEVEN

"I THINK WE got the best seats in the house," Haley's dad said, stretching to look around the stands at the indoor agricultural facility in Sundre.

"Considering the show doesn't start for an hour, they should be," Haley said, arranging Jonah and his baby gear. Her dad had been chomping at the bit from the first rap on her bedroom door, a full half hour before the sun. His therapist had given him the go-ahead last week to go out and about, even drive on his own, and this show was his first chance to exercise his knee and his liberties.

He had even made breakfast so Haley could handle the outside morning chores while Mateo got Risky B loaded. Mateo had left early, and they wouldn't see him again until he was in the show pen, and then his focus would be on Risky B.

They hadn't brushed Risky B down together every night, and she hadn't made it out to see Mateo train every evening, but there had been a total of four times when they'd worked in silent harmony together, and she'd gone away ready to sing.

She wasn't sure what Mateo thought. At times, he looked surly; other times, distracted. Once or twice, he'd seemed at ease, which had given her hope that maybe they could find a way to a new kind of partnership. No, not partnership. A new way of being together that she herself didn't fully understand. He hadn't given any indication if he'd continue to board Risky B at the Janssons' or move her to the Claverleys' after today's show.

The stands slowly filled. Jonah had fallen asleep in his front carrier, his cheek mushed against her chest, his mouth yawned open. She hoped he would stay that way until after Risky B's performance. She wanted to give man and horse her full attention.

The announcer called for the show to start in ten minutes, and stragglers filed in.

"This is it," her dad whispered.

"Dad, it's an exhibition. No big deal."

He looked at her jittery leg.

"Okay, it's a little bit of a big deal."

The announcer gave a rundown of the events. Mateo was the first act. The headliners were saved for later. They ushered in a dozen yearlings, all black, twice the number the filly normally worked.

Or had Mateo upped the number during the times she hadn't been there? What did it matter, anyway? This was only for experience. Nothing was on the line. No win, no lose.

Mateo entered on Risky B. He had put on her regular saddle but had polished it to a gleam, and he must've shampooed her mane, because it flowed like she'd just stepped straight out of a salon. And Mateo...

He looked awesome. He wore dark boots and hat, and a deep blue shirt she'd never seen before. She'd also not seen him in his show chaps, either. He was the full package.

Mateo loped Risky B around the arena, giving her a feel for the space. "This is the first show for our filly here," the announcer explained. "How about we give her some gentle applause?"

Dutifully, everyone clapped. Risky B flicked her ears but took it all in stride. Good.

"Now, remember, folks—what you're seeing today is a novice horse. Risky Business is only past two and won't go on the circuit for another year or two. Her owner and rider, Mateo Pavlic, bought her from the Blackstone Ranch down in the Foothills, so while she has the genetics for cutting, she hasn't the experience."

Exactly. But still, Haley bridled at the cautionary words. Risky B knew her stuff. At the same time, Mateo reached over and patted Risky B on the neck, as if telling her the same thing.

They got down to work. Mateo spoke to one of the mounted herdholders and then walked Risky B into the herd. Half the herd cut in either direction, and Mateo held her to the group on the right. He rode her close as the herd peeled away down to two yearlings. One ducked out, and then it was Mateo, the filly and a cow. Mateo loosened the reins but still had Risky B under his control.

They were a team. Risky B head-to-head with the startled yearling, her haunches bearing down on the stop, and Mateo over the pommel, riding her to the same rhythm she rode the yearling. After a few short lengths of the corral, the yearling stopped and glanced away in surrender. Mateo pulled Risky B out of the run, and the yearling darted back to the herd amid short, appreciative applause.

Risky B and Mateo waded into the herd again and kept cutting until they were one-on-one with a white-faced black cow. They went through the same back-and-forth dance. The yearling broke away, and there was a disappointed gasp from the crowd, but Risky B wouldn't stand for. She broke into a fast gallop and cut the yearling off at the last moment, torquing hard to bring the yearling around into a face-off. The yearling caved and looked away. Mateo turned Risky B away, and the yearling cautiously rejoined the herd.

"Well, folks, the usual performance lasts for two cuts, but that was so good, how about we see one more?"

The crowd clapped in agreement while Mateo fell into conversation with one of the herdholders.

"No, Mateo," Haley whispered. "Don't do it. It's too much for her."

Her dad flexed his repaired knee. "Let Mateo make the call."

"But he's been pushing her too hard," she

said. "It's been so good up until now. I don't want it to crash for them."

"Have a little faith."

But her dad didn't know Mateo the way she did. He didn't know Mateo's hurts or dreams or his troubles.

Mateo moved Risky B deep into the herd and emerged with three that he and the filly narrowed down to one. This one was smaller and more scared. The straightest line back to the herd cut right through Mateo and Risky B, and the yearling followed that line at a dead run.

Faced with a charging calf, Risky B torqued hard, swung her forelegs and landed in a full stop. The yearling jerked to a stop but then started in a panicked runaway. Risky B followed hard after it. Another stop brought Risky B's haunches lower than Haley had ever seen her go. The cow seemed to lose steam, and Risky B paced it another length before it stopped and trotted away from the herd. Mateo turned Risky B away, and the yearling circled back to the herd.

A few stood to cheer the performance.

Haley was on her feet, too. Where her heart had plummeted to. For only she could see that as Risky B left the arena, her stride had shortened and her head was low.

Her first outing had been a spectacular success. She'd also suffered her first show injury.

THE VETERINARIAN ON-SITE said that it was a back injury, but an MRI would tell the real story. Mateo suspected he was right. The best-case scenario was full recovery after rest. The worst was an animal broken before her career got started.

Alone with Risky B in the stall, Mateo patted her neck. "You heard the doc. You'll have to put up your feet for a while."

"She'll be okay, then?"

Haley stood with Jonah in his carrier, his downy head pressed against her chest. Mateo turned away, uncomfortable. It was hard being in Jonah's presence without holding him. He felt much the same regarding the boy's mother.

"How did you know?"

"I could see she wasn't walking right when she left the arena."

He had felt the shift in Risky B when she'd come out of the last turn. There'd been a slowing down, a strain in her musculature. He had thought only he'd noticed.

"The vet here said she needs rest, which is what I figured."

Haley rubbed Risky B along the jawline. "You did awesome out there, girl. Too awesome. You could've let the last one go."

Risky B gave a little snort and tossed her head. Haley tilted away in time with Jonah.

"She's not herself," Mateo said. "She's sore, and that's made her grumpy. She's also coming off the high of her work, and the place is strange."

"So long as she lets Jonah sleep."

If Jonah was asleep, Mateo could keep away. Would Jonah still recognize him, anyway? It had been a month since he'd last talked to him, carried him. A month where he'd distracted himself from the little guy by channeling everything into Risky B, and look how that had turned out.

He'd messed up. "You were right about Risky B. I should've not worked her so hard."

"And if you hadn't, her injury might be worse because her muscles wouldn't be as strong."

"I know what I did, Haley."

"True. But you got to give Risky B some of

the credit, too. You had slack on those reins. She was gunning for that cow."

Mateo smiled despite it all. "There was that. I might get the vet to check me out for whiplash."

Haley frowned. "Really?"

She looked genuinely worried, like when Jonah had run a fever after his first round of vaccinations. "I'm fine. Joking."

"Oh. Good." She appeared to bite the inside of her cheek. Probably wondering what to say next. Their times together brushing down Risky B had been good, but he didn't know what to do with all the silence. He'd spent a dozen years deliberately not talking to her, but now, their...difficulties had thrown up barriers.

"You're missing the show," he said.

"That's all right. I was too worried about Risky B to concentrate."

"She'll be okay."

"Are you going to watch the rest of the show?"

"I may just load her and take her back."

"Yeah." Haley drew out the single word as if it really was a question where they shared the decision. "We'd better get on the road now, too, before the storm hits."

Mateo spun to her. "What storm? There was nothing in the forecast. Twenty percent chance of thundershowers. Showers." He checked the barn entrance. Sunlight everywhere, but that meant nothing.

He strode outside and swung to the mountains. Sure enough, a dark blue mess of thick clouds was building. So that was the other reason Risky B was on edge. She could smell the storm coming, feel the electricity. She probably also remembered the hailstorm from her first time in the trailer. He looked to the north and home. Sunny skies right now. If he could clear out now, he might outrun it.

Or he could talk to the organizers and see if he could stable her overnight. But if she was already on edge because of the strange place and she started kicking with her sore back…

Mateo returned to the barn. "I'm loading her now. I'd like her home before this breaks. If I can't get her loaded, then I'll see if I can keep her here overnight."

"All right," Haley said. "I'll go let Dad know what's up and be back."

Mateo stopped on his way to the truck and trailer. "Be back? Why? I can handle this."

"I know you can, but I'm coming with."

She was being stubborn for no good reason. "You'll be in the way. What if I have to pull over?"

"Then we pull over."

Mateo cut to the point. "I don't want Jonah in the vehicle, too."

She gave him a long look. "You and Jonah are neighbors, at the very least. You can't keep avoiding him."

"Not avoiding. Thinking ahead. If I have to pull over, who knows how long it'll be?"

"Have you seen my diaper bag? Commandos aren't as prepared. We're good."

"I haven't time to argue, Haley."

"Finally we agree," she said, turning away. Over her shoulder, she added, "We can argue about this on the drive back."

Not if I'm gone first.

But no such luck. He had barely gotten the trailer lined up with the barn door when she reappeared, loaded down with commando gear.

And then the real work of the day began. The hardest thing on earth was to show patience for an animal that refused to do the right thing. Horses and humans, especially.

Mateo tried to project the same calmness he had when loading the filly at Hawk's, and even this morning, when all was cool and quiet. But now, under the hot sun—made hotter by the mugginess of the incoming storm—he could feel his tension rise. It didn't help to have Haley watching him struggle, either.

"You still have the car seat," she said out of the blue. "Good. I thought I'd have to make a second trip for mine."

He had because he'd no other place for it. He clipped a nod, his focus on Risky B, who was staring off at horses in a faraway corral.

Mateo heard his unlocked truck door open and then Haley reappeared without Jonah and the carrier. "He's sleeping still. Let's see what we can do here."

She stepped into the trailer from the side entrance, placing herself at the front of the trailer. Risky B took note but didn't move.

Haley opened a plastic container. "What have we got here for our hardworking girl? An apple, a banana—" Risky B snickered "—you haven't had a banana, you say? The tra-

ditional carrot, and would you look at this…
strawberries."

"She's a horse, not a toddler."

Risky B ignored Mateo, hesitating only
briefly when her front hooves hit the rubber
mat of the trailer floor.

By the time Mateo came to the side door of
the trailer, Risky B was crunching through a
chunk of apple, and Haley was peeling a banana in preparation.

"Thanks."

She shrugged away his gratitude. "This is
easy. No cooking involved." She gave a sideways smile at him. "Dad misses your lasagna." Then she added softly, "Me too."

Now, how was he supposed to take that?
They had mostly circled each other for the
past month, but any time they had crossed
paths, it was at her doing. Was she having a
change of heart toward him? And if so, why?

Through the open truck window came a
high cry from Jonah. "Uh-oh. That'll be for
me."

She shoved the peeled banana into his hand.
"Over to you." She hopped out the opposite
door. He could hear her making cooing noises

to Jonah. Risky B and Jonah got her loving. He got mushy fruit.

With Risky B tied in, he came up the driver's side of his truck. Haley was already in the passenger seat and—Mateo took a steadying breath—there was Jonah in the back seat in a T-shirt and shorts, bare feet wiggling.

Heart in throat, he slid into the driver's seat and pushed out a quick, "Hey, bud."

Jonah grinned.

Mateo jerked. "He's got a tooth."

"And cutting another one."

A tooth he didn't know about. It hurt, but he better prepare himself for a whole mouthful he would have no clue about. Or any right to know about.

As they pulled away, Haley took shades from her diaper bag and opened the console between them to take out his. The ride back was conducted in silence, Mateo keeping an eye to his left at the clouds. While the air cooled, they appeared to be outrunning it, and the more they angled east, the more the afternoon edged into just another hot late-July day.

"There," Haley said. "I think we're good. Want a sandwich?"

He'd eaten nothing but coffee and dough-nuts. "Your dad didn't make it, did he?"

"No, me. Risk of food poisoning is mini-mal."

He dared a bite. Mustard, beef and... "Rad-ish?"

"For the crunch."

"I don't know how you two can live with yourselves. What are you going to do when Jonah takes solids?"

"Does your kitchen make deliveries?"

She was definitely angling for something. "What are you up to, Haley? Why did you want to come with me? And don't give me that crap about helping me with Risky B. I would've figured something out."

"Company," she said. Her one-word answer threw him, and she repeated. "I came to keep you company. And before you give me crap about that not being necessary, let me say that it is."

"Given our recent history, I don't know why you feel your company is required."

"Because you're here to stay, aren't you? You're building an arena, I hear. You're going to train stock. You're home. Am I right?"

He hadn't put it together like that for himself, but it hadn't crossed his mind at all to walk away when things fell through with Haley and him. "I guess."

"And I'm not moving, either, so at the very least we're neighbors, and we could be neighbors until one of us takes up space in the district cemetery. After the second one of us goes, we could end up neighbors there, too. Forever."

"Okay, so your point is that since we might be neighbors for time immemorial, we might as well get along for the brief time we're on the right side of the grass."

"Pretty much."

Mateo took another bite. He must be hungry to eat this jumble. "Fine. We'll get along."

"And when a neighbor sees the other having trouble with stock, she helps. Okay? Especially when that neighbor has already helped with said stock while as a partner."

"Okay."

"So…until the arena's built, you keeping Risky B where she's at?"

Meaning, had he backed down from his earlier position of leaving after the show? "I think it would be best for Risky B."

"Sure, she's welcome to stay."

"And I'll still help out, as we agreed."

"Sure." From the corner of his eye, he saw her chew on her lip. She was building up to a big ask. She probably didn't know he'd give her whatever she wanted.

"One more thing."

She glanced into the back seat, and her face softened. "Jonah's your neighbor, too."

Except that. "No," he said flatly. "I can do the neighbor thing with you, but not with Jonah. Don't make me, Haley." He had to protect himself somehow. He ached to be in Jonah's life, but not if he couldn't be all in. He didn't know how to do half measures with the boy.

Some of his desperation must have leaked through, because she sat back and said, "Okay. Just you and me, then."

Wheels hummed down the highway another mile or two. Risky B did some footwork and then quieted. Jonah burbled and chattered to himself.

From the outside, they looked like a small family trailering their horse, but Haley had explained away her ongoing interest in his life as pure neighborliness. As help, for crying out loud. She was telling the truth, but he had a feeling there was more going on. Was she too stubborn to admit it? Too distrustful?

Or maybe he just wanted there to be more going on. Maybe this was him hoping for more than was owed to him.

RISKY WOULD MAKE a full recovery. If she got proper rest. If she took her medicine. If she didn't exacerbate the injury. Haley sagged with sheer relief when Mateo passed on the vet's results. She hadn't realized how much she'd become emotionally invested in Mateo's venture.

"Okay, we can handle that," Haley said, watching as Mateo took off the halter in the stall. "I can give the morning or evening dose, if you're in the field."

"I got it covered," Mateo said, swinging shut the stall door. Haley chose to ignore the slight emphasis on the first word.

"It's just fair exchange. If you're already working—"

"I appreciate your concern. If I need help, I will be sure to let you know."

A very neighborly response she had no answer for. Over the next few days, during Jonah's afternoon nap, Haley saddled up Canuck Luck for a quick half hour ride. It was nowhere close to what the mare craved, but it took the edge off and kept her content in the stall.

Seeing the older mare get all the fun made Risky B cranky. She whinnied insistently and circled in her tight stall while Haley saddled Canuck Luck and again when Haley returned into her stall after the ride. By week's end, as Haley brushed the mare down, the filly clearly thought it was her turn.

"Forget it," Haley said. "Just because you feel better doesn't mean you are better."

Risky B snorted her disagreement.

"Canuckie, tell her to be patient." But the mare preferred silent neutrality.

"Right, let her figure that out for herself," Haley said. "Of course, you might be rubbing it in that you're getting all the attention now."

The mare gave a soft snicker, either because Haley had rubbed the sweet spot behind her ears or in agreement. "Aha. The truth comes out."

Risky B stamped her foot.

"Hey, remember your sore back."

She stamped again. Perhaps if there was no reason to feel jealous, she'd calm down.

Haley shortened the mare's brushing and led her into her stall.

It was when Haley dared to exit the barn that Risky B lost her cool. She snorted and struck the board with her back hoof.

"I'm not indulging your bad behavior."

Except that her bad behavior might reinjure her back. Haley retraced her steps to Risky B's stall. The filly stepped into the exact position Mateo liked to have her in when he put on her halter.

"Not happening," Haley said.

Risky B stamped again, as if to prove that she was fine.

This was not good. She'd seen Risky B get more riled with each day she was passed over in favor of Canuck Luck. She hadn't said anything to Mateo because it hadn't seemed like a big deal. It was now.

Haley held up her phone. "You want me to call Mateo, because I will. You'll be in big trouble when he gets home."

Risky B was huffing. Not a good sign. Haley texted Mateo.

Risky B's acting up. Call when you can.

A quarter of an hour passed, in which Risky B became more agitated and Jonah's nap edged toward completion. Nothing from Mateo.

Risky B and her problems belonged to Mateo. Jonah was her sole responsibility and a good deal more important than this two-year-old pulling a tantrum.

Walk away, Haley Jane Jansson.

Except what if walking away caused more problems than taking five minutes of action? She could take Risky B out to the little corral. Maybe having more space would calm her down. Maybe the filly didn't want the movement so much as the freedom to move if she wanted to.

Haley spun on her heel and returned to Risky B's stall. "Don't make me regret this."

Risky B cooperated with getting haltered and taken into the corral. Haley escorted her around the edge of the corral for a couple of laps just to bring her down off the edge.

Her phone rang. "Jonah's awake," her dad said unnecessarily as Jonah raised the roof in the background.

"I'll be right there," Haley said and turned to Risky B. "I'm taking off the reins, and you behave in here. Deal?"

The phone rang again. Mateo. "What's going on?"

"Risky B was acting up, but she's calm now."

"Acting up? How?"

Haley took Mateo through the events, ending off with how the filly was walking nicely in the corral now.

"She's there now? With you?"

"Yes, but I have to get back to the house. Jonah's awake and madder than a stung bear. She's fine for now. I'll deal with Jonah and then come out and put her back in the stall. No worries, I've got it under control."

"Take care of Jonah," Mateo said. "I'll take care of Risky B."

"Do you want me to come back after?"

"No, you've done enough. I've got her." Definite emphasis on the "I" this time. He ended the call.

You've done enough. His way of saying she'd interfered. "He's coming home, and he's not happy," Haley informed the filly. She left out who he was not pleased with.

As she walked away, hooves thundered behind her. Risky B was loping around the perimeter.

"No, no, no," Haley whispered. She had to hope that Mateo could calm the filly down. She had her own little horse to rein in.

While inside with Jonah, she heard the ranch quad rip into the barnyard, and then all was quiet. Several peeks from the kitchen window revealed no movement.

"That horse pen has always been hidden from the house, and no amount of looking will change that," her dad said from his recliner.

"I'm worried," Haley admitted. "For Mateo and the horse."

"You should be worried for yourself. You'll have to answer to him for letting her out."

"I tried to call him. I couldn't reach him, so I did what I thought was right."

"He might not see it that way."

She did owe Mateo an apology, or at least an explanation. She lowered Jonah into his playpen in the living room and waggled a teething toy for him to take. "Jonah's fine. I'm going down there. I'll be back in fifteen, twenty minutes."

"Or," her dad called to her as she left the room, "you could stay here and mind your own business."

"This is my business," she called from where she was now at the back door.

She quickly shut the door on any more of her dad's opinions and hurried down to the pen. Neither horse nor man was there, and Haley turned for the barn. She halted outside when she heard his steadying words to the filly. The clipped prancing of hooves on the floor was a sure sign that stalling her was not going well. Haley hung back for the time being, pretty certain her presence right now would be unwelcome.

"I know," she heard Mateo say. "She's got you thinking one thing, and then she does another. You're not the only one whose head is spinning."

Haley pressed herself against the outside barn wall. This was too good to miss.

"Just the other day, she told me we're nothing more than neighbors. No more than what Howie and me are."

Risky B whinnied, not the high-pitched one of earlier, but still an opinionated one. "I thought the same. I thought we were friends, for sure. We were friends for as long as we were neighbors."

He had a point. Neighbors would call to

let him know that Risky B was acting up. Friends did something to make it better… Though her success in that area was questionable.

"Of course, we were once almost more than that, you know. Yep, she was the first girl I ever kissed."

Haley felt her knees go weak.

"It was pretty good, as I recall. We might've become something more right then and there, but I didn't push it. I didn't want to lose our friendship."

Same here!

"I've always wondered, though. I mean, she was thirteen, so our parents wouldn't have allowed us any real one-on-one dating. We would've lost the freedom to go riding together. But later on, in high school. I could've gone for it then."

Same, same!

"It's too late now. I made my play, and it went south. I screwed up once, and she can't bring herself to trust that I won't do it again."

He spoke with regret, and in a kind of amused, ironic tone, like telling a good story about someone else's bad luck. "You want to give this door another shot now?"

Hooves, slow and reluctant, paced forward, and Mateo continued his soothing prattle. "There, now. That wasn't so hard, was it? Now, I'm going to take this halter off and close the door. Then I'm leaving for the field again. I'm putting up hay so you got something to eat this winter besides snow. Deal?"

Time to step boldly forth and declare her... What? Good-neighbor status? Friend update? Latest reading on the trust meter? No, she had no idea about how to go boldly forward.

She slipped away, taking the long loop back so Mateo wouldn't catch sight of her.

Her phone pinged as she entered through the front door. It was from Mateo.

I've taken care of Risky B. All's good.

Liar. All was not good. And neither of them had any idea how to fix things.

CHAPTER TWELVE

THE THING HALEY liked best about her friendship with Krista was how the blonde chipper got right to the point. They were taking their kids for a walk across the pastures on their properties—Jonah in his front-facing carrier and Krista with her two in an all-terrain stroller.

"So what's going on with you and Mateo?"

Whatever Haley plucked from her whirling thoughts now would get back to Will, and from him back to Mateo. But the other thing she liked about Krista was how good she was at solving problems. And right now, Haley could do with a hint or two.

"We became business partners. Then he wanted more. I kinda agreed, but then kinda backed out. He did not like how I sat on the fence, and he wanted out of the business partnership, which'll happen even though it's a bit tricky with Risky B and the crops. I... I felt bad about us falling out and counterproposed that we be good neighbors."

"Cow mess, cow mess," Ella announced from her forward position.

Krista bounced her stroller off the cattle track and onto the grass. "But you're neighbors anyway. That will take no effort."

"I know. We are sort of friends, but there's been too much water under the bridge for us to go back to the friendship we had when we were kids. And I can't see what this new friendship looks like. There's this huge twelve-year gap in our time together we're not dealing with."

"Why didn't you guys keep in touch?" Krista said, puffing a little as they began their long climb up what they simply called the Big Hill that rose on both sides of the fence.

Haley pulled on the carrier straps digging into her shoulder. Jonah would soon be ready to fit into a back carrier. "He left back when he was eighteen and he... He never kept in touch the whole time, even though we were best friends. He apologized for that, but he says that I haven't forgiven him. Not really."

"Well. Have you?"

"Gopher hole, gopher hole."

Krista veered left.

"Cow mess, cow mess."

Krista veered right, and the front wheel rammed into a gopher hole.

"We're stuck," Ella confirmed.

"And your mom needs a breather," Krista said. "Out you get. Go find me some flowers."

Both Ella and Haley looked about the chewed-down pasture. "There are no flowers," Ella said.

Krista pointed. "Sure, I see yellow ones. Go over there and you'll see them."

As Ella picked her way across the grass, Haley whispered, "Isn't that lying?"

"I'll say I made a mistake. Meanwhile, she gets exercise and I get a break," she said, drinking from her water bottle. With her other hand, she rolled the stroller back and forth to comfort a sleeping Cassie.

"But Ella will figure that out and not trust you anymore. And then where will you be?"

Krista studied Haley from under the shade of a wide-brimmed straw hat. The wind picked at it, even though she had it secured with a wide ribbon. She looked like a modern-day Bo Peep. "So you haven't forgiven him."

"I have."

"You can't talk about trust broken because of a little lie I tell Ella and then say you've forgiven Mateo over a bigger break in trust."

Mateo had said she hadn't forgiven him. Her dad had backed him up, and now Krista was spelling it out. The first two she could dismiss as biased, but Krista barely knew Mateo, and yet she'd joined his team.

"I've got trust issues." Haley drew breath and added, "Mateo thinks it's an excuse to not face what we could have right now."

Her mouth full of water, Krista made a liquidy noise of agreement.

Across this pasture and to the west were the Jansson hay fields. In the moments when the wind died down, Haley could hear the faint rumble of Mateo baling hay. There was a chance that he'd come into sight briefly on his rounds before sinking back down the far side of the slope.

"The thing is, I want to trust him. I just can't seem to…let go. Mateo says I'm stubborn, and I am, but there's more to it."

"You're afraid to get hurt again."

"Yes, I am. His leaving hurt. And if we become involved and it doesn't work out, I'll be totaled. Imagine what I was like after Trevor, but a million times worse."

Krista gave her a sideways hug. "I'd be there for ya again."

"But I don't want you to be there. I don't want that pain ever again."

"But then you give up the chance for happiness, too."

Didn't she know it? She'd experienced happiness in the quiet synchronicity of brushing Risky B, of stepping around each other in the kitchen and sharing quick smiles over Jonah's antics. She really missed those smiles. "How do you and Will make it work?"

"Okay, first off, we're not you and Mateo."

"That's a good thing, you know."

"Maybe." Krista gazed in the direction where Will was baling Claverley hay. "I guess we believe we have each other's best interests at heart, and then we act as if we do."

Sort of what her dad had said. There was something bigger than themselves, even if that something was the other person. "Except I can't believe. At least, I can't believe in Mateo. And maybe not even in myself."

Krista set one hand on her hip, keeping the

stroller still in motion with the other. "Can you at least act as if you do?"

Could she act as if she held his interests in her heart, as if he was worthy of her trust? "You mean fake it until we make it? Or until I make it?"

"You know him probably better than anyone. You know what makes him tick. Likes and dislikes. It should be easy."

"Mommy. I need to pee. I need to pee!" Ella's last word rose on a pitch that had the distant cows turning their way.

"Hold on, hold on. Here, take the stroller." Haley took orders and looked discreetly away while Krista dashed to her daughter. Mateo was coming closer. She heard the particular mechanical huff of the tractor as it shifted for the ascent.

Krista was right. She did know Mateo better than anyone, just as he knew her. His favorite color, his favorite beer, cake, ice cream. Her mind drifted naturally from those foods to birthdays. Yes, she knew the date of his birthday.

It was next week.

As if on cue, the large green nose of the Jansson tractor rose over the ridge. If Mateo was looking directly at the Big Hill, he might see them. As it was, he appeared as a dot in the cab. She waved anyway. A black line grew out from the dot and waved back.

Haley spun to Krista. "Okay, I'm ready to fake this. But I need your help."

Krista held up a yellow brown-eyed daisy like a sword. "We got this, girl."

MATEO HAD GOTTEN used to not celebrating his birthday. The last real party he could remember was when he'd turned eighteen. Jakob and his mother were still together then, and about a hundred to a hundred and fifty people had come out from the district and from his school. Everyone who had ever known him showed. Even his grade-one teacher, though that might have had more to do with her being Howie's sister.

The party had lasted all day, with people coming and going. The day had started off quiet. Jakob had taken him to the garage and opened the door, and there was the truck. Black and shiny, fully loaded, aluminum rims. Mateo had experienced quiet wonder, fear and excitement. He remembered thinking this was it. He was an adult now.

"Keys are in the ignition."

He'd started the engine and reversed out with Jakob watching. Mateo remembered stopping because something was missing. "Dad, can I give you a ride?"

They had driven nowhere in particular that morning: up one country road, down another, out to the highway where he'd opened it up. They had talked about nothing in particular, just let the early morning grow brighter and the land come to life. After they'd turned back into the lane, Mateo had parked outside the house. Jakob reached for the door handle but sat there a moment.

"This was good, son," he'd said. "Happy birthday."

Ten months later Jakob had kicked him out of the house, no longer his son.

Now, on the morning of his thirty-second birthday, there was silence in his house. No dad, no mom. A new truck was parked outside, courtesy once again of the same man who had bought Mateo's first.

And thanks to the same man, he had plans. Plans that he would execute alone because Haley saw him as no more than a friendly neighbor, or a neighborly friend. They were more than that. They'd been friends from birth. No matter what ranch or town or country he'd been in during his years away, whenever her birthday had rolled around, he'd stop and think, "She turns—insert age—today. Happy birthday, Haley." He bet she remembered when his was. You couldn't celebrate each other's birthday for all those growing years without remembering—and if Haley did anything, she remembered.

But all that day, she hadn't mentioned it. Yes, he had hauled hay in the morning and baled in the afternoon, but she could've texted a casual birthday greeting. At about a quarter to five, he called it quits. He swept up his phone and texted her.

Done for the day. Back tomorrow.

Then he added, Closer to noon.

Okay. Any plans?

She'd never asked him that before. Then again, he'd never ended his day so early before. One didn't usually have any more plans for the day at eleven at night except sleep.

He didn't, but his hurt pride prevented from saying so.

Nothing neighbors need to know.

There, let her chew on that.

Back at his place, he showered off the day's dirt as per usual, but instead of heading straight to bed, he got dressed again.

His phone rang. Mom.

"Happy birthday, Mateo." His first birthday wish coming in at quarter to six in the evening. Probably the last, too.

"Thanks."

"What's my birthday boy up to?"

She asked him that every single birthday. Sometimes, he'd really have something to do because the guys he was with happened to be going out on the day coinciding with his birthday. Sometimes, he made something up to get her to move on. But after today's disappointment, he didn't have the energy to come up with a lie.

"No plans, Mom. Nobody here knows it's my birthday. And I'm a little too old to go around announcing it to everyone I meet."

"Surely someone must remember. Haley

should. You two always celebrated your birthdays together."

"If she did, she's got about six more hours left to wish me the best."

"Don't be too harsh. She has a new baby. It's hard enough to remember what day of the week it is, much less someone else's special day."

Mateo didn't care to pursue this. He was caught between wanting to end the call with his mother to avoid any more talk about Haley and to at least talk with someone.

"I guess it's a little hard being back here today," he admitted. "I remembered my eighteenth birthday, when everyone was here, and it lasted all day long."

His mother's voice softened. "I was thinking of that day, too. I wanted it to be special because I knew what was coming."

The breakup.

He could hear his mother draw a deep breath. "And in fairness to Jakob, he just wanted the day to be special because his son was officially an adult."

"Only I wasn't his son."

"He didn't know that. That night, he told me it was the proudest day of his life. To see how fine you'd turned out, to see how so many people cared about you. Eighteen years well spent, he said."

"And then you ruined it for him."

"Not that night, but yes, I did."

Mateo and his mother had not talked much about the fight. It was a topic they'd skirted in order to preserve the few times they visited or their short phone calls. A pile of questions lived inside him like a banked fire. Today, on yet another uncelebrated birthday, he poked at them, felt heat and rage rise and let it flame from him. "Why? Why did you have to tell him? Why couldn't you have just told him you wanted a divorce and leave it at that? Why couldn't you have let Dad and me keep what we had?"

"Oh, Mateo. It was so long ago. Can you not just let it go?"

"No, Mom. I can't. How about you tell me? Consider it your birthday present to me. A little history, a little truth."

"I… Fair enough. I can't honestly remember that conversation, that argument with your fa—with Jakob word for word. I started it, of course. But the thing is, I never meant to tell him. I meant to do exactly what you said, tell him about the divorce and go. It's just that… It all escalated so fast. He wanted us to fix the marriage, fix it for your sake. And I told him that you were an adult now, that there was no reason. But he said you'd feel that your whole life was false. He kept repeating how we were destroying our son. 'Our son,' he kept repeating that. And I… I just wanted out, Mateo. So I said something to the effect that you weren't 'our son.' That you were mine but not his. I remember he went white as a sheet. I'd never seen him go pale before. I thought he'd faint. He told me to explain myself, and I did. He became very, very angry, and then we really fought. That's what you walked into, Mateo. I never intended for you to find out. Certainly not that way. I will be forever sorry for that."

In the end, a flash of anger had spilled the secret and banned Mateo from his father's life. He was making his own way, like Jakob when he'd started his car dealership. But he'd had Crystal.

Mateo was alone. Even if that was of his own doing.

"I understand, Mom," he said. "Thanks."

She gave a soft snort. "That's one lousy birthday present."

"Yeah, I've had better."

"The night is young. You're young," she said. "Go out and do something special. Make a good memory."

How did that work when the one person he wanted to share his birthday with hadn't so much as remembered the day? "Okay, Mom. I'll do that."

The call over, Mateo decided to drive to Spirit Lake, order himself a steak dinner and a drink. Maybe Will could come along, and they could hammer out the details of their partnership in the cutting horse operation, plan for stock and next year's shows. Shake off the past and bring on the future.

Will answered Mateo's call from his truck. "I'd be all over that, but Krista has me going to this birthday party. Why don't you come join us?"

Celebrating a stranger's birthday on his own birthday? "I'll skip, thanks."

Will laughed. "I don't think you have much of a choice."

From outside came a horn blast. The sound echoed through the phone as well. Mateo whirled to look outside his front window. There was Will's truck with balloons tied to the side mirrors. Behind him was a whole cav-alcade of trucks and cars decorated to the hilt.

Mateo came out onto the porch and watched as vehicle after vehicle filed in. It was Dave and Janet, Howie, Dana and Keith, other neighbors, and—was that?—yes, Crystal. They all waved and hooted and lined their vehicles up on the grassy area across from the house. He smiled and waved back, numb from disbelief.

The final truck turned up the lane. The Janssons'. A huge banner arched over the cab: "Happy 32nd, Mateo." In the back of the truck was a huge gift-wrapped box with a blue-green bow the size of a cowboy hat. Knut drove, and Haley was in the passenger seat.

"Happy birthday, Mateo!" she yelled. "Did you think I'd forgotten?"

SHE HAD BOUGHT him a barbecue. The biggest, most recommended unit on the market. It had cost her about the same as the used car she'd bought after high school, but the rush of sur-prise and pleasure on Mateo's face when he unwrapped it was worth every penny.

"Thank you, Haley," he said while the others stood around. His words were quiet and almost intimate, as if they were alone, which they most certainly weren't. Her dad definitely looked on with interest.

"I brought the barbecue," she said. "You do the cooking."

Like any of their district gatherings, duties were divided down gender lines. The women took over Mateo's kitchen, filling the fridge with side dishes and lining up cutlery. The cake, bought by Haley and therefore edible, took up one whole shelf.

Outside, portable tables were flipped open, and a cluster of men stood around the barbecue, Mateo with the assembly instructions.

"I knew I should've put it together for him," Haley said from the kitchen window, where she and Krista were watching the goings-on.

"Don't worry. If they're hungry enough, they'll figure it out."

"I just want Mateo to enjoy his party and not worry about one more thing."

"Haley. Does he look worried?"

He didn't. Beer in hand, he joked and laughed with the others. She hadn't seen him so plain happy. Sure, he'd laughed and they'd shared smiles, but she'd also given him grief. She was delivering a happy memory for once.

"You're right. I need to take a chill pill."

The only task left on her checklist was to keep Jonah away from Mateo. But keeping Jonah away meant keeping herself away, too. It wasn't until everyone had finished their first helping that Haley could park Jonah with Krista and load up her own plate.

Mateo was manning the barbecue. Of course, he would be. She looked at her open burger piled with the trimmings and ready for the sizzling patty. "Please tell me you've eaten."

"Not yet. I'm good."

"It's your birthday. Here, take my plate. And go eat. I'll take over."

Will shot to his feet. "No, no. I'll watch the burgers." He hurried over to the barbecue, where Mateo relinquished the spatula with a serious nod, as if passing on a sacred torch.

"Am I really that bad of a cook?" Haley said.

"Don't answer that," Keith said to the couple dozen people stretched along the tables. "Dana asked me that about her sewing. There's no right answer."

"What you say," Will called, pointing his spatula authoritatively, "is 'Have I told you how much I love you lately?'"

Keith grinned. "Why would I tell Haley that?"

In the general laughter, she looked over at Mateo loading up his burger. Their eyes met. Laughter lingered there, but something more, too. Gratitude…and hope. By making the grand gesture of a birthday party, she had wanted to show him that she was moving on, and he seemed to have read her signals right.

Mateo took up Will's old seat beside Dave.

"You and Will switching places part of the new partnership you to got going?" Howie said from his spot farther down the table.

Mateo had told Haley nothing about this new partnership, beyond some vague talk about stabling Risky B at the Claverleys. Haley darted a look at Mateo. He had his head down, mouth full of burger.

Her dad's head came up. "Not yet. He's still partnered with us."

"You mean with Haley," Howie said over Mateo's head. "And we all know how that partnership works." He waved his hand at the divided crop across the road.

She shouldn't have invited the bachelor busybody. She'd only called him up because she'd called everyone else in the district and it was Mateo's party. She wished she'd left him to eat chips in his rocker in front of one of the two channels on his TV or whatever senior rural bachelors did during their downtime.

But Howie had presented another chance for her to show she was on Mateo's side, even if he had partnered with someone else.

"Whatever the arrangement Will and Mateo have," Haley said, "it'll work out. I highly recommend tonight's celebrity as a partner."

That brought up Mateo's head. His eyes latched onto hers. Before she'd seen hope, now there was resolve and expectation.

From a circle out by the vehicles where a kids' play area had been set up came the distinctive, discontented howl of her son.

Mateo's head swivelled like a dog hearing a coyote.

"I got him," Haley said to Mateo. He nodded but stayed quiet as the howls lifted into the evening air. Jonah was fine. That was his frustrated, overtired cry. It was one that Mateo had once brought to a stop with a bounce and a word. Jonah had been her best contribution to their partnership.

Now if she didn't play it right, all she would ever be able to give him were balloons and a barbecue.

CHAPTER THIRTEEN

ONLY HALEY AND her dad were in his kitchen when Mateo came in after seeing the last of the company off.

"I thought Crystal might be inside," he said. "Her car is still here."

"I saw her head over to the garage about an hour ago," Knut said.

The cars. He'd seen Crystal chatting with others, but he'd caught her sitting alone with an expression of pretended ease, as if eating birthday cake alone was the latest trend. He'd been relieved when Knut had taken up the empty chair beside her.

"I'll go check on her," Mateo said.

Haley was levering birthday squares from the cake platter into plastic containers lined up on the counter. Dodge threaded his way around her legs. "Take your time," she said, implying that they'd still be here whenever he got back.

He did want time alone with Haley, but it looked as if Knut would be part of the deal. He went down the hall to his room to change into a heavier shirt against the evening air.

There, in the middle of his big king-size bed, was Jonah. Thanks to the night light by his bed, Mateo could make out Jonah's tiny body snuggled inside a patchwork quilt. Mateo's pillows were bolstered around him, and his arms were splayed out, his face smooth and peaceful.

Mateo stood rooted to the spot. For six weeks now, he'd kept to his private vow and stayed away from Jonah. He'd especially avoided being alone with him, because he didn't trust himself not to take the baby into his arms and never let him go.

Haley appeared behind him in the doorway. "I'm sorry, Mateo," she whispered. "I didn't know you were coming into your room. I would've warned you he was here."

"It's...all right."

"I couldn't get him to quiet. I brought him in here, and five minutes later, he was asleep."

Mateo tried to move, but his feet stayed planted in the carpet. "He's grown."

"Three pounds this past month. Krista's

greens. And another tooth. He rolled over for the first time yesterday. Back to tummy, even."

"Oh… That's good."

"I'm thinking of starting him on solids soon. Pears, I guess."

Mateo was barely listening. It hurt too much. "I need to change my shirt." He spoke hoarsely, not to keep his voice low for Jonah's sake, but because emotion was choking him.

"Of course, sorry."

She ducked away, and he hurried through the silent business of changing his shirt. He'd almost reached the door when Jonah emitted a little mew.

As if tugged by a string, Mateo turned back and cupped Jonah's head. Like a cat, Jonah snuggled his head inside the curve of Mateo's palm and slept on. Mateo held his hand there one precious moment longer and then pulled away.

He mumbled to Knut and Haley that he'd be right back and then he cleared out, shrugging into his old farm jacket. Good thing the garage was at the far end of the yard to give him time to burn off energy.

What was Haley angling for? Throwing a

huge birthday party sat squarely in the territory of friends. Very good friends. It was the
kind of thing a girlfriend or wife might do.
That sign on her truck might just as well have
announced to the entire community their
change in relationship status. Then she'd de-
clared how she'd recommend him as a partner, but the kind of whispery way she'd said
"partner" and the way her eyes had softened
when she'd looked at him…

And then there was the whole matter of
Jonah on his bed. He didn't think she'd done
it to deliberately force a reaction from him;
he didn't think Haley capable of such devi-
ousness. She had always shot straight from
the hip. But he could believe that she might
be so stubborn she would go to the trouble
of staging a party rather than admit her true
feelings for him.

Or it could all be wishful thinking on his
part. His relationship with Haley was like the
illuminated swath of light from the flashlight
he carried. The way ahead was clear for only
one or two steps, all else lost to the darkness.

The side door to the garage hung open, and
the overhead bulbs diffused a wide daylight
glow over the lineup of three muscle cars.

A black Camaro, a black Mustang and the third—a red Pontiac Trans Am in immaculate shape, though the winged phoenix on the hood was covered in dust. Crystal sat in the passenger seat. He switched off the flashlight and came around to the driver's side. Both windows were rolled down, and he bent over to peek inside. Her face was red and teary, her mascara smudged around her eyes.

Mateo straightened and glanced longingly at the exit. He had no idea how to help a woman he'd met once crying over a man he didn't know how to forgive. Why had Haley even invited her?

"I've put off coming here long enough," Crystal said. "It just didn't feel right to come out."

There was no getting out of this. He opened the heavy driver's door and slid in behind the wheel. The bucket seats in white leather fit around him, and his hand automatically settled on the large steering wheel wrapped in black leather. The dashboard, with its oversize gauges, seemed cartoonish compared to the digital sleekness of his brand-new truck.

"I meant it. The cars are yours."

"I know. I didn't have a place for them at

first, so there didn't seem to be a point. And now, it still doesn't seem quite right. Jakob kept this place to himself." She turned to him. "You know, tonight was the first time ever that I stepped into his house. I used the bathroom, and then I admit I poked my nose into the other rooms."

"What did you think?" Mateo was curious if Crystal saw the place the way he did.

"People were talking and banging around in the kitchen, but in his office, I almost felt him. Nowhere else. I'm sorry, Mateo. I know the place is your home now, but it felt like a shell he crawled into at nights and left in the morning."

That's how Mateo felt in it. Like it was a motel, a place to sleep and shower. Like life was conducted elsewhere, until this evening, when Haley had pressed across the threshold and filled the place with color and noise. He'd left with her owning the kitchen and her dad sitting there as he did in his own house, keeping everyone informed. And when he returned, they'd be there. He'd not return to an empty motel room.

"He should've invited you over," Mateo said. "You would've been good for the place."

"He wanted a different place for the two of us. We bought a house together, you know."

Mateo didn't know. Crystal had been more than a girlfriend, then.

"He insisted that it remain in my name, though. What we had was...odd."

"I guess if it worked for you two, that's all that matters." That was all that mattered for Haley and him as well. If they could untangle the twisted ball of twine their relationship had become.

"Yes, but..." Crystal shifted, the leather squeaking. She brushed her hand along the dashboard and rubbed the dust from her fingers. Her ring with the dark ruby glowed in the light beam.

Crystal caught the direction of his attention. "A gift from your—Jakob. It's my lodestone. I've worked through more than one problem with it. Jakob joked that I treat it like a crystal ball." She flicked a mischievous smile. "Pun intended."

"What I was going to say is that Jakob always kept a part of himself apart from me. And that part was you, Mateo. The house, the property was you, and he didn't want anyone treading on it. I understood, to a degree. But weeks before he… Weeks before, we had a huge fight. In this very car, can you believe it? He'd brought me out to show it off after getting it back from the shop. We started talking about a road trip, where we'd go. South to the States, we decided. We were excited, brainstorming about the stops we'd make, and I took the leap and told him we could stop by your ranch." She laughed shakily. "That crashed the party. He refused. I told him to reach out to you, to make peace. For his sake, for your sake, for our sake. He said there was no reason to change things up. He said he had no right to dig up what was long buried. I said it wasn't buried. Or if it was, then he lived in a tomb. That pulled him up short. We made up, of course. But I've wondered if maybe I pushed him and that caused—"

"No," Mateo said. "Don't go there. You know exactly what Jakob would've said."

Crystal laughed shakily. "Probably what he always said when I doubted any decision I made. 'I didn't fall in love with a stupid woman.'"

Love. Mateo had never heard Jakob use that word. And here Crystal made it sound like it fell from his tongue every day. They gazed together through the windshield. Also dusty. He cleared his throat. "You're always welcome to come out, to keep in touch."

"I'd like that." Crystal's smile faded. "I—I have a gift for you."

"You shouldn't—"

She touched his arm. "No, I must." She opened her purse and removed a card in a pale yellow envelope. "It's not from me."

Mateo took the envelope addressed to him, care of Blackstone Ranch. The return address was marked from Jakob Pavlic.

From the size of the envelope, he'd gone for the biggest one on the rack.

"I found it in his desk drawer at work this morning. I was still undecided about coming, and I went into Jakob's office. I had done nothing about packing it up…and so I thought, as a way of moving on, I should. I opened the top drawer, and there it was."

Mateo's hand shook. He transferred the envelope to his other hand, but it served him no better. He told himself he wouldn't look at it; then his fingers were scrabbling at the flap.

On the front of the card—in broad, sweeping letters—were the words "To my son on his birthday."

Son. Mateo touched the raised letters, read them again. Inside, there was a schlocky, sentimental verse about a man's pride in his son, about the good times, memories, roads now parted…and a father's love that lasts forever, no matter the miles apart.

Above the verse was today's date in his handwriting and the standard greeting, "Dear Mateo." Underneath was the simple closing, "Love, Dad."

Love. Dad.

He had wanted Mateo back. For them to be together again. Hope and gratefulness, the same feelings that flooded him when the vehicles had rolled up his lane, rose again. And then they crashed. Jakob had done it to make the woman he loved happy, to erase bad feelings between them. Mateo had just been the means.

He passed the card over for her to read. It was really meant for her, anyway. She didn't seem to see it that way. She clutched his hand so hard the ruby ring bit into his fingers. "Oh, Mateo."

He wouldn't ruin her moment. "It was good of him."

"You forgive him, then? Even if it came late?"

She searched his face, seeming eager for him to say what he could not feel, to make peace with the man she'd loved. Well, just as Jakob had put aside his pride and stubbornness in order to make Crystal happy, he could do the same.

"Yeah, I forgive him," he lied.

FROM HIS POST at the dining room table, Haley's dad reported sighting Crystal and Mateo returning from the garage. He stood and walked to the door, his bum knee giving a hitch to his step. "So all's well. I'll head out and catch up with you two tomorrow."

"But you're my ride back," Haley said from where she was wiping down the kitchen counter.

"You can't come. Jonah's asleep."

"I'll pop him in the seat and transfer him when we get home." By some miracle, he might actually sleep through the operation.

Her dad donned his cap and jacket. "Mateo can give you a ride back. Might as well put his car seat to use."

"I need to ask him if that's all—"

"I'll ask him on the way out." But he didn't. Haley watched from the front porch as he crossed over to his truck, revved up and left, his high beams catching Mateo as he escorted Crystal to her car. If her dad wanted her to have alone time with Mateo, he possessed the subtlety of a sledge hammer.

She stood on the front porch as Mateo waved Crystal off and then slowly walked across the dark grass to the house, his step slow and careful in the wake of the flashlight beam, his head down, as if wading across a rocky river bottom. Haley's heart sank. It had not gone well with Crystal. She'd invited Crystal because Jakob's girlfriend was part of Mateo's new life, if only on the fringes. She'd hoped this party might draw them closer.

As Mateo climbed the porch stairs, she caught sight of his drawn, pale face. "Uh-oh."

"Yeah," he breathed and went inside. Haley caught the door as it swung shut and followed him in. So much for giving him a good memory.

He was at the fridge, staring inside. She came up beside him. "It's fat with food." He kept staring. "I…uh, moved your drinks to the door." He turned and stared at the selection.

"There's also tea and coffee. Decaf. How about I make you a nice cup of tea?"

He nodded, shut the fridge door and leaned against the sink, facing her. He didn't seem to have the energy to budge, and Haley had to edge around to fill the kettle from the tap.

He said nothing as she put together his tea with a splash of milk, as he liked it. He cupped his hand around the warm mug and pulled a yellow envelope from inside his shirt. "Here."

She read it. "Oh," she whispered. "Oh."

His hands were suddenly shaking. "Crap, not again."

She took the cup from his hands and set it on the counter. He was staring at his shaking hands. She couldn't stand to see him come apart. She wrapped her arms around his waist, and he clamped his tightly around her. Her cheek against his chest, she heard his breath hitch. His own cheek came to rest on her head, and they stayed like that, the only sounds the hum of the fridge and the tick of bugs against the window.

"You know," Mateo said, "this is the first time we've ever hugged."

"We've hugged before," Haley said "We must've."

"No, we've slung arms over each other's shoulders, and maybe when we were really young, we crashed to the ground together, and that looked like a hug, but we've never intentionally hugged."

"Huh."

"Yeah."

Hugs generally had the time span of a fly on food, but this one was floating into something…more. Their first hug was going as well as their first kiss. Back then, they'd not let it change their relationship. This hug might, if she dared to let it. She covered her uncertainty with what could be interpreted as a light and neutral opener. "Birthdays are a good time to get new things."

"They are." He tightened his hold. "Thanks, Haley. For the party, the barbecue…the hug."

"My pleasure." She ought to break away, create space. But right now, after what he'd gone through, it was in his best interest if she showed him a little…support.

"And for inviting Crystal. It meant a lot to her. And me."

Haley released a breath. "This was supposed to be a happy day."

He adjusted his position, another casual opportunity for her to step away. Instead, Haley moved with him. Like they were getting comfortable on a lumpy sofa.

"Crystal thinks Jakob gave me the card as a way of saying he's sorry, but I think he did it to make her happy."

Haley sensed the thread of a question in his words. What did she think? "I don't know," she said honestly. "I can't see Jakob giving into Crystal when he'd held out before. Even if he did it for her sake, he risked your rejection."

"If he even cared what I thought."

"You don't leave your life's possessions to someone you don't care about."

"Who else could he have left it all to?"

Did he seriously not think himself worthy of the Pavlic place? She leaned back to examine his face. His gaze was averted from hers.

"Mateo," she whispered and waited until he looked at her. His face was full of doubt. "Who else but you?"

He opened his mouth, as if ready to object, but abruptly closed it. He straightened but not enough to dislodge their embrace. "I'm sorry. I shouldn't let Jakob interfere on the birthday you arranged for me." He gave her a light squeeze. "Back to us."

Back to us. She liked the sound of that.

"And in answer to your question, yes. I did think you had forgotten. I waited all day for you to mention something, and then I gave up."

Haley had giggled to herself during preparations at how surprised Mateo would be. She'd not thought that he would spend most of his birthday feeling hurt and alone.

"I'm sorry. I didn't think."

"You're forgiven. More than forgiven. But—" He withdrew her arms from around his waist, breaking off their hug but still holding her hands. "Why did you do this, Haley? And don't tell me that it was a neighborly thing to do. This goes far deeper than that."

He had cornered her as if she were a cow he'd cut from the herd. "I... It was Krista's idea."

"Krista?"

"I mean, she suggested I act with your best interests at heart, and a birthday party seemed like a good way to do that."

"But why, Haley? Why did you have my best interests at heart?"

She gave him the squinty eye. "You're not going to let me run back to the herd, are you?"

"Nope."

She scraped her teeth on her lower lip. "Because… Because I overheard you talking to Risky B the other week when she was acting up. I came to help, and you already had her in the barn. I heard you talking about me, us, our first kiss."

Her cheeks burned, and when she peeked at Mateo, he looked embarrassed, too. "That was a private conversation, Haley."

"Yeah, well, you shouldn't have been talking about me. Anyone could've overheard," she said, quite unreasonably.

"So you decided to throw a party because you felt sorry we missed out as teenagers."

"No, yes, no." She blew out a horsey gust. "Because… Because you're right, okay? You're right. We're not neighbors, and we're not friends. We're something else that might become something more. And I don't want to miss out on that, but neither do I want to miss out on who I am…or who I could be."

"No argument here."

"And I know you understand. I get from the bottom of my heart that you do. That's not the issue. It's that…"

He waited, keeping a bead on her, letting her make the first move. A real champion trainer of confused females.

"What if it doesn't work out between us? If we stay neighbors and friends, we can be together forever. But if we turn us into a romance and it goes sideways, we'll be stuck together, being close but apart for the rest of our days."

"No, we won't," Mateo said. "Because I'll leave. For good." There. He said it.

Her hands fell from his. "What?"

"I thought I could make a go of it without us together, but tonight you showed me that you do have feelings for me. We're good together, and I'm good for your son. But I can't go on like this with you forever if you won't give us a shot. We need to at least try to have a relationship, Haley. And if you won't, then it makes sense that if one of us has to go, it should be me."

"You make it sound so easy."

"No. It'll be hard. But I've done it before, so I can do it again."

"You'd…walk away. Go. Anywhere but here."

He flinched. "No, Haley. Nowhere but here…with you."

Haley could barely breathe after hearing his words. All she had to do was reach out and take hold of him, of them. She could have it all.

And when had that ever worked out? "No, what stands to reason is that we don't risk what we have for what we might not get. Never bet what you can't afford to lose. I can't afford to lose what we have now, as mixed up and unpredictable as it is. Don't you see?"

"But the thing is, Haley, you do stand to lose this thing between us, because I can't handle it any longer. My big game plan was not to ask for too much, too soon. To stop trying to make things happen. But that's only led to uncertainty. I don't want to start building something here only to find out that you're not interested. If we commit and it doesn't work out, that will suck, but at least we will both have lived out that possibility and can move on. I need to know… Are you in or not?"

Haley fought the urge to bolt, even as her every muscle tensed harder than rock. It was her fault. This moment was inevitable once she decided to organize the party. She hadn't planned a party, so much as this exact situation. And still she stalled. What was wrong with her? She pressed her fingers to her temples. "Don't, Mateo. Don't make me decide right now. Please."

He tugged her hands away from her head and captured them in his.

"Haley, you must know how I feel about you. I—"

"Don't say it," she moaned. "It'll ruin everything."

They stood so close she could feel his warm exhale on her forehead. "Then what do you want me to say?"

"I don't know what I—" She tripped on the word and took in a deep breath. "I don't know what love is anymore. I thought I did, but Trevor changed all that. Words aren't enough, and actions confuse me. I can't separate what you do for me and what you do for your advantage. Like with the land." She gestured over his shoulder in the direction of the divided field across the road. "At least there, things are neat and tidy. But my heart is a magician that pulls off tricks, convinces me that things are one way when they're actually another." There. She knew what was wrong. "It's not you I don't trust, Mateo. I don't trust my heart. I don't trust to know what love is."

Mateo didn't hesitate. "It's looking right at you."

She ached to believe that, every fiber tensed to take the leap. But this was the same man who had deeply hurt her before, and now there was Jonah.

"Do I know that?" she said. "You've been gone for more than a decade. What did you do? Who did you meet? Who are your friends now? Did you have girlfriends? What was your best day? Your worst? And you don't know what's gone on with me, either. With Trevor, yeah. But there's more to me than him. Maybe I don't know my heart because I don't know you."

Mateo studied her. "Okay, new deal. I want an answer, and you want more information. I'll give you that. Meanwhile, we spend time together. You, me, Jonah."

"Like a...family?"

"Yeah, like that."

"Doing...what?"

"I dunno. It's into August, and I haven't

been to Spirit Lake. The water, not the town. How about we go there?"

"When?"

"Ten. Tomorrow morning."

"Okay, but Jonah might take a while to get back to sleep tonight, and then he'll sleep in tomorrow. It might not be until later."

Mateo cocked his ear to his room. "Get back to sleep? He's sleeping right now."

"But when I transfer him to the car seat, he might wake, and then what?"

Mateo was shaking his head. "No. We're not waking a sleeping baby. You're staying over."

"Oh."

"There's a guest room that's gathering dust. There are extra toothbrushes, towels... I've got an old T-shirt you can wear for pajamas. As for me, I can't tell you how many times I've dozed off on the couch. So we're good. Tomorrow, we'll all wake up and have a day together. Okay?"

In five minutes he'd taken her from panic to joy. He was doing exactly what she'd tried to do—act with the other's best interests at heart. Or pretending to.

Mateo set his hands on her shoulders and

turned her. "Now, call your dad and tell him he's living off his own cooking until tomorrow night, then to bed. We have a big day tomorrow."

As every day with him could be, Haley thought as she later slid between the crisp sheets. But she must decide soon, or she'd lose him again. If he left, she'd have no one to blame except herself this time.

"HONESTLY? ANOTHER PICTURE?"

Mateo grinned at Haley's question. He might be going overboard, but he'd realized that he didn't have a single picture of Haley and Jonah together in all these months. He'd snuck in lots of Jonah in the first couple of months; but then, Jonah had no say in the matter.

Haley was Haley—always on the move, harder to pin down. But today, with her framed by the blue expanse of the lake behind her, he was making up for lost time. Families splashed close by, and farther out were the white triangles of sailboats. Haley was kneeling in the cold lake water, dipping Jonah's toes in and out while he squealed with horror and joy.

Mateo waded in after them, his feet sinking into the soft sand. "One more. This time with a real smile."

"Give me a reason to."

He stepped back into a natural sand hole, lost his footing and fell butt-first into the foot of water. His phone, held high, escaped the splashes. Haley laughed and laughed, and Mateo captured a ton of pictures.

"That's the last you're getting," Haley said and stood. "Middle of August, and the water's still cold enough to freeze a polar bear."

Back at their staked-off territory of blankets, coolers and a beach shade borrowed from Krista, Haley wrapped Jonah in a bath towel with a hoodie. Stretching out on either side of them along the mile-long lake front, families and couples and friends hung out in their own spots, just like when he and Haley had come as teenagers. Back then they'd shared ice cream instead of a baby. "What's with the pictures all of a sudden?"

He draped a towel around his shoulders and handed another to Haley. He'd been taking pictures since Jonah woke at five in the morning raring to go. Mateo had been, too, despite the late hour his head had hit the couch cushion. He'd brought Jonah to a very mussed-hair Haley. Dodge had blinked sleepily from the foot of the bed. That was when he'd taken his first picture. "A throwback from my days working at a photography studio."

"A photography studio?" Mateo slid Haley a sideways glance now. She wore a cloth base-ball cap and a red-and-white-striped swim-suit that she warned him not to make any comments about, given her post-pregnancy pounds. It was a trap. Say nothing, and she'd see it as him agreeing with her. Say some-thing, and it had better be carefully worded. He'd told her that he couldn't see the extra poundage, but he'd take her word for it.

"Yeah. In Toronto." He did a mental calcu-lation. "Eight years ago."

"You went to Toronto? You, in the city?" She gave another laugh, this one tinged with disbelief.

How much truth should he divulge? An-other dilemma like the swimsuit. "I went with my girlfriend at the time. She got a job there, and I was between jobs."

"Oh." Haley's laugh lines faded away. "She was a photographer."

"Yeah. She joined a big studio where there

was a team. I came on board to help with the setup. I shuttled models around, staged settings, looked for locales. I was head gofer."

"Okay." Warm now, Jonah stretched, and Haley opened the towel and laid Jonah on the picnic blanket so he could kick and punch the air. Mateo stuck out his finger, and Jonah latched on, trying to draw it into his mouth.

"I picked up techniques for taking a good picture. But mostly, I came away with how much people would pay for a good picture of themselves and their family. This one family had millions to their name, and they dropped ten grand on family photos out at their summer retreat. I remember the dad saying when he wrote the check that governments have war chests, but they had a memory chest."

"That makes sense."

"Yeah." Mateo didn't know if he should continue down this same memory hole, but he'd promised full disclosure about their years apart. "My girlfriend didn't see it that way. She was more into the modeling gigs, the big-money assignments. We parted ways after a year or so."

Jonah let go of his finger and heaved himself onto his side to face Haley. It took a full minute and involved legwork and back muscles, giving Mateo time to word his next confession carefully. "I still keep in touch with her parents and two brothers."

"They live in Toronto?"

"Yeah. One brother lives with his wife and kids north of Toronto, but they're all within a three-hour drive of each other. I think that's why I went east. Because of her family. I didn't realize that until we broke up, and I found myself missing her family more than her."

"Huh." Haley looked out over the shimmering lake abuzz with splashes, squeals and the slaps of powered-up motorboats. Mateo poked Jonah in the shoulder, and he wobbled his head over to him and grinned. Mateo grinned back and reached for his phone.

"That's what I wonder with you," Haley said quietly.

Mateo snapped a picture and looked up.

Haley was biting her lip. "I sometimes wonder if you want a relationship with me because of Jonah."

"No, never." Jonah flopped to his belly, and maybe because of uneven ground underneath, he rolled the other way to Mateo. "Look at you, buddy. Regular gymnast."

Haley gestured at them. "What did I say last night about words and actions?"

"But the two of you are a package deal, like it or not. If it helps, it's not Jonah who comes to mind when I think of kissing someone on a horse ride."

Haley blushed, which was his intention, but he also wanted to distract her.

"But you want a family, right?"

She was relentless. "I admit, I always wanted a family. Years after I left Ontario, after I'd drifted from one job to another, I finally ended up at Hawk's ranch. I got there when the twin boys were still babies. Their mother was pretty much out of the picture by then. I changed diapers, gave them bottles, bathed them. Not all the time, but enough to know that I was good at it."

He opened his phone to his photo stream and turned it to show her the picture of two toddler boys in matching outfits hugging each other so tightly they looked as if they had choke holds on each other. "Amos and Saul."

"Don't blame you for going soft on them," Haley said. "Cute enough to eat."

"I resisted the impulse."

"Send me the pic," Haley said. "I'll forward it to Gracie. She and Hawk were buddies, remember?"

"When they weren't trying to outdo each other."

"Yeah, can't see them having an experimental kiss."

Mateo couldn't help but drop his gaze to Haley's full lips. "We should try another round of experiments. See if the results are the same half a lifetime later."

She wagged her finger at him. "You know as well as I do that the outcome is not in question. And you are good at this baby thing. Better than me, at times. It's just that…if there wasn't Jonah, would there still be us?"

"Yes. Us first, and then a whole whack of Jonahs after."

"Because you're such a family man?"

She was prying, getting under his floorboards to the treasure chest of memories underneath. "I don't want to be lonely anymore, Haley. I haven't had a Christmas with family since I was eighteen. I've always been on the outskirts, the pity invite. You said you didn't know your heart, but I know mine. It's a big plain, empty and howling. Whenever I was at my loneliest, I was always this close to calling you. But there was so much distance between us, and I didn't know how to make it good again. You said you think it's wrong to want to have it all, but it's all there is, Haley."

She couldn't ask for more. He'd given her all he had. She leaned across and kissed him. On the cheek. "Okay," she said. "I hear you."

"Is it enough?" he pressed.

She gazed out over the glare of the lake and drew a deep, deep breath. Her back straightened, her shoulders lifted and she turned to him.

He held his breath.

"Yes," she said. "It's enough."

And then she kissed him.

CHAPTER FOURTEEN

THE DRIVE BACK to the farm was quiet, perhaps out of consideration for Jonah napping
in the back. But Haley thought it had more to
do with their kiss. It had been off. Off like old
stew. They had carried on afterward as they
had before, talking and eating, but it had felt
forced. When Jonah had started fussing, and
Mateo had suggested they head back, Haley
had packed like a tornado was bearing down.

For the life of her, she couldn't figure out
what had gone wrong. There was no reason
not to trust Mateo. She had felt his tale of
loneliness as if it were her own. She wanted
him. She wanted him to become a true part of
her family. She was all kinds of attracted to
him. He loved Jonah. He loved her. Okay, she
hadn't allowed him to say the actual words.
And she hadn't said them to him, either. But
it was understood, otherwise she wouldn't
have kissed him.

They just needed time to ignite their romance. After all, it had only just started. In the meantime, move on to something their relationship could handle—business.

"I'm thinking we should sell the yearlings," Haley said. She'd deliberately chosen the "we" pronoun. She had only ever used it with her dad. Trevor only used "I think" and "you should." But if she wanted to partner with Mateo, if she wanted to act with all their best interests at heart, it was time to at least talk the talk.

If Mateo noticed her use of the inclusive pronoun, he didn't let on. "All of them?" There were nearly a hundred head, fifty he'd bought.

"It's the end of August," Haley said. "In another month, we'll have to start feeding them. We won't be the only ones. This way, we keep ahead of the rush, maybe get a cent or two more a pound."

Mateo hooked his wrist over the top of the wheel, like on a pommel. "That's not really answering my question."

"We can keep some, but—" she really hated saying this "—you were right about the feed. We... *I* should have gone with planting the whole quarter to greenfeed. The wheat's not

going to yield. Even the straw won't be there."
She hitched around in the leather seat. She'd
worn jeans, and they stuck to her even though
it was eight in the evening.

Mateo ticked his head one way, then the
other. "There'll be straw."

"But the hay's only half of what we got last
year, and we were down to our last thirty bales
this year before turning the cattle out to pasture. And that was before you bought your
bunch."

"So…what do you suggest?"

His don't-offer-up-too-much routine really
wasn't helping.

"Let's sell the equivalent of yours."

"Half?"

"Give or take. But we won't worry about
whose is whose. Treat it like one herd and
sell the best."

"All right."

"What? Just like that? I've made bad decisions before. Don't let me make another one
if you have something to say."

"Happens that I agree with you on this one.
We'll decide together which ones will go."

We. That one word sounded so good. "Auction day is Tuesday," Haley said. "We should decide sooner rather than later."

"You want to make the arrangements or me?"

"I can. I was thinking of watching them sell before I go to my doctor's appointment."

Mateo frowned. "Jonah due for another round of vaccinations?"

"No, it's for me."

His frown deepened. "Anything the matter?"

"No. I'm a fine, strapping farm girl. They're taking blood samples to figure out how to breed a bloodline of Haley stock."

"Not surprised."

"I've got Krista covering for me with Jonah."

"I can take him."

"It's all right. I'm swapping with Krista next week when she works at her spa."

"I can take him part of the time, then. Pick him up from Krista's. What about food for him?"

"I'll leave you a bottle."

"He takes a bottle?"

"I've got him on to it. I figured there will be times going forward I won't be around."

"Makes sense."

Yes, everything made sense. Why, then, did everything feel wrong?

Mateo turned up the long lane leading to the Jansson house, and Haley immediately noticed a familiar truck parked in front.

"Brock. What's he doing back? The rodeo season doesn't end for at least another month."

Mateo swung in beside Brock's truck. "I guess he has his reasons." Maybe it was her already-buzzing imagination, but he sounded a tetch put out.

As they got out of the truck, her dad stepped out onto the front deck and announced, "Brock's come back."

The return of the prodigal son. She suspected that her dad viewed the hired help as the son he never had. Brock never seemed to mind the paternal affection, even though he had parents of his own living in the States somewhere.

As if to prove his existence, the man of the hour joined her dad on the deck. "How was the lake?"

"Good," Haley said. "Hot. Wet. Sandy." *Weird. Disappointing.* She hauled the beach paraphernalia out while Mateo unlatched Jonah. There was no use debating who did what. If Mateo had empty arms, he'd be taking Jonah.

Mateo and Brock exchanged nods and subdued hellos. A stiffness had entered Mateo's posture, and he became absorbed in swiping sand from the car seat. He didn't meet her eyes. What was with him?

Haley switched her focus to her father. "What's for supper?" she joked.

"Whatever you bought."

He knew her too well. It was an unspoken law that if either of them dared to be in town all day, they'd better come home with supper.

Once Jonah's tummy was full, they tucked themselves around the table for the adult meal of fried chicken and coleslaw, Mateo one-handing it with Jonah tucked in his other arm.

"Why are you back so early, Brock?" Haley asked.

He wiped his mouth and his fingers and then used the napkin to mop up crumbs around his plate. "A buddy came off a bull wrong. He won't walk again."

Heads lowered around the table. Accidents were an inherent risk in rodeos, and the longer you played the game, the more likely you ended up in the hospital.

"I've seen too much of that happen to friends."

"Will still feels it in his shoulder from time to time," her dad said.

"I was lucky, too," Brock said. "My arm came right, but luck is one thing I've pushed for too long. I'm already waking up like an old man."

"Wait until you are one," her dad said. "It hurts more because there's nothing you can do about it."

"Yes, there is," Haley said. "You got your knee replaced, and now you're following the instructions of professionals."

Her dad raised a warning finger to Brock and Mateo. "Don't expect sympathy from your children. They get annoyed you won't live forever."

"They get annoyed," Haley corrected him, "when you *act* as if you will live forever."

Her dad didn't respond, probably because he knew she was right. He turned back to his prodigal son. "Glad you're back."

"Yeah," Brock said. "Me too. I can start tomorrow, if you like. Where are you at with the hay?" He addressed the question to her dad.

He rubbed his nose. "I've been out of commission for most of the summer. Mateo's taken over pretty much."

When Mateo finally spoke, his voice was quiet, dull. "I have, but now that Brock here has arrived on the scene, everything can go back to the way it was."

He looked at Haley then, and his question was clear in his steady gaze. They'd said Mateo would stay until she found a replacement, but now that they were together, what would happen? Clearly, somebody needed to say something.

"I'm not sure how this will work, Brock," Haley said. "Mateo and I partnered up, and part of the deal is that he helps in the fields."

"Oh," Brock said. He had clearly expected his job to be waiting for him, was probably why he hadn't called ahead. Usually, life on the Jansson ranch was pretty much like a painting—nothing changed. "I understand. I guess I thought I'd pick up where I left off, like I usually do, but I did leave you-all in the lurch this time. You moved on, and I can, too."

Haley felt bad, and her dad looked as if he'd run over the family dog. "No, no," he said.

"Between the two places, there's lots of work. We'll get you set up."

As if the situation wasn't confusing enough. "What two places?"

"This one and Mateo's."

Was her dad suggesting the ranches join together formally via a hired hand? "Mateo plans to build a training arena over at his place for cutting stock," her dad expanded "We could use someone like you."

"We?" Haley squeaked. "Don't Mateo and I have a say?"

Brock gave her a deep, considering look. He gave Mateo, holding Jonah, the same long look and then pushed back his plate. "I'm going to step outside for a moment."

Haley wished he would go. More to the point, she wished he'd never come back in the first place. Not when her emotions were in the spin cycle. But whether or not he was physically present, the matter still needed sorting.

"Stay," she said. "You're not the lowest person in the pecking order here. We all have a say in the matter."

She looked to Mateo. "What do you think?"

He finally met her eyes. "I think you know what I want."

She bit her lip, hoping the flush heating her cheeks wasn't obvious to the other two men. He wanted her. Family. Not to be lonely. Brock wanted the same thing in the end. That's why he'd come here. It was the one place he trusted would take him in.

It's all there is.

She lifted her eyes to Mateo's and kept them locked on his as she told the others, "Mateo and I are working out a much more long-term partnership that might involve household changes. If we get the terms down right, there will certainly be an opportunity for you to work or even buy in, Brock."

Mateo's lips flattened in disapproval. But hadn't she said exactly what he wanted to hear?

Brock cleared his throat. "Sounds good to me. I…uh, still think that I should step outside."

"I'll come with you," her dad said. "I'll show you the new filly."

"Don't let her out," Mateo and Haley said together.

"Sixty-seven going on seven, the way I'm treated around here," her dad muttered to Brock as they headed for the back door.

Haley waited for the door to close and their voices to trail away before she spoke, but Mateo beat her to the mark.

"This won't work, Haley."

Jonah arched his back and raised his arms to Haley. She automatically shifted him onto her lap, welcoming the distraction. "What do you mean?"

"You were cornered, Haley. You did the right thing by everyone, but it isn't what you want."

"If it isn't what I want, I wouldn't have committed to you today."

"Yeah, you committed. And then we kissed."

She touched her lips. "You felt the same way, then?"

He sighed. "Yeah, Haley. I did. I'm not saying there should've been fireworks, but there should've been some kind of spark. Maybe there's too many years of hard feelings between us. I don't know. All I know is I laid myself bare for you today. I gave you all I had, and I wasn't enough. Was I?"

"I… It's not you. It's us. There's something wrong with us. Or me and my tricky heart." Would there ever come a day when she wasn't in a constant state of confusion?

"I think both of us need to stop trying to make it happen."

How many times had he come back to that mantra. "We can't break up after not even a day together, over a bad kiss. That doesn't make sense."

"And there's the 'something wrong'. We always choose to do what makes sense. We expanded our business deals into our personal lives because it made sense. That's when we hit bumps. You and I want the best for each other, but your heart isn't in it, Haley. When you kissed me, you were holding back, Haley. It felt as if you were trying to cheer up a lonely guy, and all it did was make me feel even more alone."

He had read her right. She was still a scared rabbit when it came to her heart. She had failed him. Mateo stood slowly, as if sore all over. *Say something, Haley. Don't let him leave.*

"We still have a plan, right? Even if things don't work out between us, there's still you and Jonah. I don't want us to come between what you have with Jonah."

The stiffness left Mateo, and he rested his hand on Jonah's head. "I only said I'd leave if we didn't give it a try. And we did. I'd like to be a part of his life, if you don't mind. We're… good together."

In other words, he didn't feel lonely around her son.

Mateo slipped his hand away. "I'd still like to take him next Tuesday."

"Of course." They sounded like a couple arranging custody.

At the door, he paused with his hand on the knob. "About the cattle. Sell all mine."

At least she knew which deal they were operating on. The one where she wasn't part of his life.

MATEO PICKED JONAH up from Krista's and brought him back to his place. That morning, Haley had offered to make other arrangements, but he'd refused. He didn't know how often he'd get to see Jonah going forward, and he wasn't about to pass up any opportunity.

In the entryway, Mateo lifted Jonah out of the car seat, and the little guy immediately rubbed his face against Mateo's shirt, a sure sign of tiredness.

"Dozy? Want the big bed again?" But as soon as Mateo had spread out the bedding,

Jonah seemed to revive. He lifted his arms to be picked up, and Mateo couldn't resist.

"All right. Let's hang out for a while." He carried him to the kitchen, the place that saw the most action in the house, and opened the fridge. "What should I have for lunch?"

He hadn't eaten all day, having spent the morning helping to load the cattle at the break of dawn and then meeting with Will to go over plans for the training arena. Will had mentioned that it was good Brock could help out, and Mateo hadn't said anything to the contrary. Yeah, it was good Brock was back, but it only cemented the separation between him and Haley.

What a short-lived disaster that had been. They hadn't lasted a day before they both concluded that she just wasn't that in to him.

There was ground beef. He could fix up a couple of patties and throw them on the barbecue. Haley's gift. He suddenly didn't have the energy. He shut the fridge and opened the cupboard to his old comfort food.

"Peanut butter–jelly time," Mateo said. "Hold the jelly, double the peanut butter."

He lay Jonah on the counter inside the circle of his arm while he prepared his sandwich, troweling on the creamy spread. Jonah reached out, and Mateo pulled the sticky bread away in time. "Not until you've more teeth, buddy."

Mateo slapped on the top half of the sandwich and bit down. "It's all right," he informed Jonah, "but I prefer burgers."

Jonah shoved his fist in his mouth. "Fingers are okay, too. I prefer chicken fingers myself." Jonah sucked on and Mateo chewed on.

He was halfway through his sandwich when he spotted red patches on Jonah's cheeks. "Getting tired?"

Jonah coughed.

"And catching cold?" Jonah never had a day of sickness before, and it was kind of unusual he'd have one now.

Mateo froze and then flung his sandwich in the sink. He examined the hand Jonah had in his mouth. Nothing, but he could have sucked the peanut butter off. Mateo was sure he'd pulled the sandwich away in time, but what else could it be other than a reaction to the peanut butter?

Mateo called Haley, but she didn't pick up. "Call me back as soon as you can." He didn't go into details, because he hardly knew himself what was going on.

"And I'm not waiting around to find out. You're going straight to the hospital."

Haley called as he was barreling down the highway forty clicks above the speed limit. She sucked in her breath as he filled her in.

"Yes, it's a peanut butter allergy. Trevor practically went into anaphylactic shock if he had peanut butter. No peanuts or peanut butter anywhere, anytime. How's he doing?"

Mateo risked turning in his seat. "He's red and blotchy, coughing."

"Okay, I'll meet you at the hospital. He's going to be okay." Yet, he could hear the strain in her voice.

"See you there," Mateo said and pressed on the gas. Never a better time to test Jakob's belief in the quality of this truck.

Haley met them at the emergency room doors. One look at Jonah, and she led the way to the front desk. "Excuse me," she said in her cattle-calling voice. "We have a five-month-old experiencing a severe reaction to peanuts." Her voice cracked. "Help, please."

They were promptly swarmed by caregivers, and Jonah was lifted from his arms.

Mateo related his side of the story while Haley inserted notes about family history. Jonah was taken down the hall. Haley followed them and looked over her shoulder at him. "You can come, too."

Mateo stood frozen. He felt strangely light-headed. *This is not happening. This is not happening* "Go on," he said to Haley. "I'll wait here."

He took a chair in the waiting room. There was a teenage boy with his mother, his foot busted. An elderly woman breathed heavily through her respirator. A young woman in her twenties played a game on her phone, her sneakered foot shaking in agitation. Mateo put his elbows on his knees and stared at the floor's abstract, splotchy pattern. He saw a horse head, a car, a boot, a butterfly...a little hand.

He'll be okay. He'll be okay.

Into his vision appeared a pair of white shoes. "Hello. You're Jonah's father?"

In his heart, he'd angled for that connection since the day of Jonah's birth. "No. I was just with him when it happened. Is he okay?"

"He's been treated now. We have him in a

room under observation. His mom invited you to join them, if you'd like."

He would've rather not shown his face, but he trailed after the nurse to a half-lit room. Haley sat on the hospital bed, cuddling Jonah, who'd been stripped down to his diaper. Jonah looked the same but more relaxed. He wasn't in pain.

"See?" Haley said softly. "He's fine."

Mateo reached out to cup Jonah's head but withdrew. "I'm sorry, Jonah."

"It's not your fault, Mateo."

"No one else pulled peanut butter out of the cupboard," Mateo said.

"And no one thought to warn you about the possibility. I knew the risk. Why didn't I warn you today or yesterday or a couple of months ago? It's as much my fault as yours. More, in fact."

There she was, trying to make him feel better, when he didn't deserve her sympathy. "I was out of Jonah's life for a month, and I made it clear that I didn't want to talk about him. I didn't give you the chance—"

"I didn't tell you he was allergic. And I knew there was a chance he could be. Usually babies are way more resilient to allergens, so

I didn't make it a priority to inform you. And there was no way you could've known unless I told you."

"His dad would've known."

"His dad? Trevor, you mean?" Haley made a scoffing noise. "Yeah, he would've known. But he isn't here, and he never has been. I don't even know where he's at. I called him the day after Jonah was born to let him know. I left a message. He never replied. I haven't heard from him since. You're better than him. Jonah's teddy bear is more useful than him."

"He gave Jonah life. I nearly took it away."

"No," Haley said. "Don't go there. It was an accident. Accidents happen all the time, to everyone. You can't get through life without some things going wrong."

Jonah was drifting off in Haley's arms. "Is he falling unconscious?"

"Yes," Haley said dryly. "It's called sleep."

"But maybe he's passing out."

"Mateo, listen to yourself. Has Jonah napped today?"

"Not with me, no."

"Does he normally nap in the afternoon?"

Here she was having to calm him down,

when she was the one who ought to be upset, angry. It was her son. "Yes."

"Well, then, he's doing what he normally does, despite being in a strange environment, and despite listening to his mother talking you off a cliff."

"I'll check with a nurse."

Haley sighed. "Sure, you do that."

The nurse came to the room, confirmed Haley's prognosis of sleep induced by tiredness and left. Haley eased herself back on the upraised bed. "Not so long ago, I was on one of these a couple of floors up."

Mateo sat in the one chair. "I was scared that day, too."

"You were? Why?"

"A million things could've gone wrong."

"Yet nothing did. Like today."

"No, there is a difference. The first time, I felt this urge to be there for Jonah. That I could replace his real dad. No, not replace. Be better than. It's like I told you before, Haley. I'm good at this stuff. With Hawk's twins, I stepped in when the mom was away. I'm a natural father, I thought. Until today."

"Do I need to remind you again of how this

is not your fault? That it could've happened to anybody?"

"That's my point. I thought I wasn't just anybody. I thought it my special gift."

"So your ego took a bruising. Welcome to my life with Jonah. It hasn't always been easy to see how much he prefers you to me. Get over it."

Haley's cheerful callousness should've righted his plunging emotions. It wasn't working. "Since the day Jonah was born, I've been trying to win your trust back, Haley."

"And when it comes to Jonah, I do trust you. Whatever hang-ups you and I have, I've always trusted you with Jonah. God's honest truth."

"Okay, then look at another truth. I hurt you when I left all those years ago. I knew I'd hurt you, and I could've come back and owned up, but I didn't. I let you hurt because I didn't want to face up to the crummy jerk I was. Is there truth in that?"

"Yeah, but you made good. We all make mistakes. Welcome to the human race."

"And Risky B. I wanted to impress the judges at the show, impress the horse association, rustle up clients for myself. I did it for others to see that I was worth their time, their money. And the result was an injury that could've been disastrous. Truth?"

"Some," Haley conceded. "But don't continue with that line of reasoning with Jonah. You've given Jonah everything you could."

"And why did I do that? Because Jonah loved me back. He made me feel good about myself."

"Because you don't want to be alone," Haley said. "That's normal, don't you see? We all do things, good things, to make sure we stay part of our family. We do it without even thinking that's the reason. You're not alone in your actions, Mateo."

"But it didn't work. I pushed and pushed, and you couldn't commit because the truth is, you know me best, Haley. You know that I push into places where I don't belong."

"You're the one with the 'don't ask too much, too soon' mantra. Doesn't sound pushy to me."

She defended him like a good friend would. That was Haley to the core. Even when he'd hurt her, she'd left him a plate of food. Even when he'd endangered her son, she defended him. She always treated him as if he was worth her energy. Her loyalty was deep but misplaced.

"I know that about myself," he said. "I'm always fighting my basic nature, which is that I'm a solitary beast. Things didn't work out with us, and I should've let you and Jonah be—but no, I didn't want to give up Jonah's love for me. You're right, it's not about peanut butter. You planned to have Jonah stay with Krista, but I had to interfere. I used Jonah because I felt bad about myself. I'm unbelievably selfish, Haley."

She frowned. "It's not like that."

"Then tell me what it is like."

"It's... You're wrong." She stopped there because she must know that he was right.

"I am alone," Mateo said, "because I'm no good with others. And in your heart of hearts, you know that about me. That's why you couldn't commit. You are right not to trust me." He stood, suddenly clear for the first time about his path ahead.

But to have the courage to do what he must, he had to leave fast, for the sake of the two people he loved the most. And yes, for his sake.

"I'm going now. There are a few things I need to take care of."

OVER THE NEXT WEEK, Haley discovered exactly what those few things were. Back from combining the wheat, Brock reported that a "For Sale" sign had gone up at the Pavlic place. Krista told Haley via text that Mateo had pulled out of his partnership with Will. She asked Haley what was going on and attached a series of sad broken-heart emojis.

Haley went over to his place after Jonah went to bed with a check from the proceeds of the sale of his yearlings. His truck was parked outside, so she figured he was home. She knocked, waited, knocked again and waited. She went around to the back where the barbecue was in case he was out there. The barbecue sat there, gleaming and cold.

Impulsively, she hollered his name. Silence. From the corner of her eye, she saw a blind flicker open and shut. So that was the game.

"I've got a check for you," she addressed the silent house. "Your share from the sale of the cattle. I'll leave it for you under the mat."

She placed the check where she said she would. She tried to think of something to say to get him out of the house. "You know where to find me." It was the best she could come up with.

The next morning, Haley was chopping

vegetables for stew when Mateo rolled in with a brand-spanking-new horse trailer. He didn't come to the house but took the lane to the barn. Knife paused in the air, she followed his progress as he pulled up to the stables. "Well," she said over her shoulder to Jonah in his playpen, "looks as if he's taking Risky B who knows where."

She turned back to her vegetables. "He's well within his rights, of course."

Jonah burbled a response.

"That's right, we're doing just fine. I wonder where he's taking her." Back to his place, but where would he keep her?

"I'm rather proud of this stew, you know. I'm following a recipe this time. I braised the meat in flour, got a thick gravy from that. Sautéed the onions. Chopped up celery and carrots. Now for the potatoes and maybe a turnip."

Jonah squealed.

"Yeah, screw the turnip." She whacked a few potatoes into cubes, and it felt good. All the while, her ears were trained to detect any action from the barn, and she spared a glance or two or three out the window. No doubt

Risky B was giving Mateo trouble about getting into the trailer.

"Probably using that slow and steady approach," Haley said, giving the stew a good stirring. "Coming along nicely."

She bent over the playpen and tickled Jonah's soft roly-poly belly. "Who's my big boy?"

Jonah giggled. He had the best giggles. She'd texted a recording to Mateo once. Had he kept it? From across the yard, she heard the distinctive clatter of the back of the trailer closing. She peeked from the kitchen window in time to see Mateo slide behind the wheel and slowly pull away. "Hey, Jonah, want to sit on the front deck?"

Mateo might pull around to the front of the house and park. He might come and apologize for his silent treatment last night and at least leave her his forwarding address. He might wish her well, invite her to keep in touch, promise not to change his number. He might smooth his hand over Jonah's hair and tell him to be a good boy. Something like that.

She settled Jonah and herself on a deck chair. From there, she could see across to the barn lane when he came around.

He drove slowly over the cattle grate. She

could see him looking straight ahead. He would see her if he so much as shifted his eyes.

She stood and moved to the stairs, took a step down. Her movement would surely catch his eye. He could obviously see that she was standing there. But he didn't turn her way; he kept right on driving without giving even a single wave.

Haley rested her forehead on Jonah's head. "Fine, then. We don't need him anyway, do we?"

She dropped to the stairs and stared down the empty lane to where the cloud of dust was settling back down. She stayed there until she could no longer detect any trace of his presence. She reentered the house through the front door in time to hear the back door opening. Her dad came to the kitchen entrance and gave her such a look of sympathy and sorrow that stupid tears rose.

She swiped at her eyes and hitched Jonah in her arms. "Well, that's that."

Knut rubbed his chin. "He said he's taking the filly back to Hawk's."

Haley set Jonah back in the playpen. "Oh, yeah?" She aimed for nonchalance and yet clung to the nugget of information. She went back to the stew she'd left while out on the deck.

"At least this time you know where he's taken himself off to."

"Sure do." She gave a mighty stir that unearthed a blackening gunky load of vegetables to the top. "Want some burnt stew?"

The sigh from her dad was strong enough to lift curtains. "I guess there's nothing for it."

"Nothing for it."

"Then dish it up."

"HERE WE ARE," Haley announced to Jonah as they pulled into Howie's yard. "The chicken place. Hopefully, your mom can get through this without getting into a fight with the world's most annoying man."

She bought eggs from Howie, as did practically everyone in the district. With his small flock of a hundred or so hens, he kept everyone supplied. He even offered deliveries, but Haley preferred to come to him. Then she could choose when to leave.

As she carried Jonah out into the barnyard where Howie likely was, a border collie came over, friendly but watchful.

"Hey, Tula. Have you met Jonah before?" Haley crouched for the two to meet. Tula nosed at Jonah until his squeaks and baby flails alarmed her, and she skirted to the side to receive Haley's much more predictable petting.

Howie emerged from the barn a ways off. "You're not Krista."

Normally, Krista picked up Haley's cartons of eggs as well as her own and dropped them off. It was a good excuse for a visit, but Haley had insisted that she would go today and deliver to Krista for the exact same reason she had come to Howie's. She could choose when the visit would end. She was determined not to dissolve into a crying mess over Mateo the way she had with Trevor. One week in, and so far, so good. But it would only work if she didn't stay in anybody's company too long.

"No sweet dimples and polka dots today, Howie. I'm doing the egg run for the both of us." She held up her bag of empty egg cartons.

"She working? I didn't see her car go by."

Howie's place was situated at the intersection of three other properties, right in district central. There wasn't a truck or piece of farm equipment that didn't pass under his watchful eye. And if he couldn't figure out what his neighbor was up to, he'd come over and ask. He'd missed his calling as an investigative journalist. Still, she had to give it to him. He'd farmed his section of land every year for the past half century all on his own.

"No. Time I took a turn."

"Okay," he said. She waited for him to get her the eggs or tell her where to get them or something. Instead, he approached and she suddenly noticed that a kitten rested in the crook of his arm. Pale gray and tiny, its pink mouth stretched wide in a mew. "The other three have opened their eyes, but his are all gummed up. I thought I'd wipe them and see if that helps."

Howie stroked the soft fur, his finger as big as the kitten. "Hard start to life."

"Howie, you got a heart as soft as that kitten."

"For those who deserve it, I do." Howie tipped his head toward a garage. "I got my stuff there. The eggs, too."

She knew the place from pre-Jonah days. The wide garage was split down the middle, with his truck on one side and a mini-suite on the other side. There were kitchen cupboards and a counter, a rocker with the green vinyl torn across the seat, and a mini-fridge.

"Cozy as ever," Haley commented from the entrance. Tula nudged her from behind, and Haley stepped aside to allow her to enter. She headed for a water bowl by the fridge and lapped away.

Howie opened a cupboard where there was a neat stack of toweling. He took out a washcloth, old and threadbare, that may have once been blue and was now gray.

"My home away from home," Howie said without irony. "I crash on the rocking chair during calving sometimes."

He walked over to a water cooler. The nozzle was directly above Tula's water bowl. His arm still curved, he dampened the cloth and settled himself on the edge of the rocker. "There now, let's see if we can fix you up."

No hurrying Howie this morning. She supposed the eggs were mere steps away in the fridge. She couldn't exactly load up, pay and exit like a self-serve checkout. And where did she have to be, anyway? Brock had done the morning chores already and was now hauling in his first load of bales. And Jonah seemed enraptured with his new surroundings, especially Tula.

"The cat shouldn't have kittens this late in the year," Howie said. "Winter'll come, and they won't be big enough to handle the cold."

"I'm not sure she had much say in the matter," Haley said. Farm cats weren't fixed, since they ran through their nine lives in short order, picked off by hawks, coyotes, tractor tires, hooves, anything bigger than them that moved. A constant resupply of mousers was required.

Howie gave her a faintly accusatory look. "Two of the kittens are calico. Orange and gray. That tom on the Pavlic place came over."

She'd forgotten all about Dodge. Surely Mateo hadn't left him to starve.

Howie answered her unspoken question. "Mateo dropped him off before he left. Along with a bag of cat food and twenty-two cans of tuna. Wasn't much point to it all. The tom turned around and went right back. I have to go over and feed him every second day. As if I don't have enough to do." He sounded as if her whole breakup with Mateo had landed more work squarely on his shoulders.

"For the record, I didn't tell him to leave.

He could've stayed for the rest of his life, for all I care."

"We talking about Mateo or the cat?" With the care of an eye surgeon, Howie dabbed at the edges of the kitten's eyes.

"Both."

"You can't blame him for having a mind of his own. You got one, too."

"Him or the cat?"

"Both."

"Can we pick one? I'm trying to reduce confusion in my life."

Howie shrugged. "Him, then, since there's no telling a cat what to do."

Haley didn't trust Howie enough to tell him a thing about her love life, but it was her one chance to direct the story that got out there. The whole world was about controlling the narrative, but in this district, it was about controlling what Howie heard.

"It wasn't my idea that he leave. It wasn't my idea that he left a dozen years ago. You probably blamed me then, too."

"No, he and his dad had a falling out."

"Yeah, they did. And don't ask me what it was over."

"I don't care to know." Her face must've

registered disbelief, because he continued, "I cared that he left, and I cared that he came back again."

"And you care that he left again?"

"Of course. I got to take care of his cat and put up with you telling me about how none of this is your fault."

"It isn't my fault. I wanted him to stay, but he got it in his head that since he accidentally exposed Jonah to peanuts, he doesn't deserve to live here." There were a few more connecting dots to Mateo's reasoning, but that was really what it came down to.

"Peanuts, you say? I've got peanut butter in the fridge with the eggs. Dog likes it as a treat. Is that okay?"

"Yes, it's okay. It was always okay, but he couldn't get that through his head."

"So you don't believe him?"

"No. And I really hate saying this, but it only proves that I was right not to believe him in the first place. He said this time it was different, that he had no plans to leave, and then he got scared and did."

Jonah flung himself forward, his signal that he wanted down to explore, but she didn't want him to whack his noggin on the cement floor. Howie looked at the thickly cushioned dog mat. "You can set him there. It's mostly clean."

Mostly clean worked. She crouched beside Jonah, her arms like bolster cushions. "You read all kinds of babies well."

"You sound surprised."

"I am. You're a lifetime bachelor."

He grunted. "Could've gone either way. Your dad ever tell you about my near miss?"

Keen to get off the subject of Mateo, she shook her head. "Sounds juicy."

"She was a friend of your mother's. She lived in town but came out to visit your mom quite a bit. I dropped by one time when she was there, and we started going out. We were pretty regular together, and then she was offered a position in Southern Alberta. Head nurse at a hospital. She asked if I would come with her. I said I preferred my life here. So we parted."

"And you never saw her again?"

"No, but I heard lots." He met Haley's eyes. "She married a rancher there by the name of Blackstone."

Haley inhaled. Hawk's mother, Angela.

"Yep. That friend. She'd come up in the

summers, and all you kids would play together. I wouldn't go over, but every summer, I'd drive by and see her vehicle and see you kids riding and running and biking together, and I'd think that maybe if I'd budged a little, it might've been my kid playing with you and Grace."

She understood what Howie was driving at, but there was one important difference. "Mateo didn't ask me to join him. He left me."

"And if he had asked, would you have gone?"

She hesitated. "This is different. Mateo has a life here, a job. He gave all that up to do I don't know what." Whatever it was likely involved Risky B. "And I have Jonah to think of. Why should I be the one to give up everything?"

"For what you might get in return," Howie said.

"And what might that be? A guy who has given up on me, on Jonah? I don't trust him, Howie. And I don't trust myself to know what's best. I told him as much. I told him my heart plays tricks like a magician, and you don't trust a magician."

Howie set his cloth on the cupboard and

tapped the kitten's head. "Ready to open your eyes?" The kitten mewed and crept shakily up Howie's flannelled arm.

He seemed so absorbed in the kitten that Haley wondered if the topic had changed. She picked up Jonah. "Anyway, I suppose I should get over to Krista's with the eggs. She's planning a sponge cake for—" Haley searched her mind for the right name. "I dunno. For somebody's birthday."

"Dave's," Howie said and rose to go to the fridge. "He invited me over."

"Hey, I didn't get an invite," Haley said in mock offense.

"That's because you're not single."

"Yes, I am."

"Then let me put it another way. You have a chance not to be. No one pities you." He opened the fridge to trays of eggs. "Help yourself. I'll hold Jonah." He widened his free arm. The kitten was snuggled into his other one.

"Are you sure?"

"I got him."

He did, too. Jonah laid his head against Howie's chest in the same trusting way he had with Mateo. A teary lump clogged her throat. She quickly transferred eggs from the trays into the cartons.

"The thing is, magicians aren't all bad," Howie said.

"What?"

"You said your heart was a magician, but the thing about magicians is that you still come out to see them, even if you know it's all tricks."

"I guess," she said and kept on slotting in eggs.

Howie eased himself into the rocker with his double load. "Because everyone knows that the trick isn't the important part. The important part is that the rabbit comes out of the hat."

"You telling me that I shouldn't care that I'm getting tricked?"

"I'm saying that the heart makes the impossible happen." Howie pulled down a corner of his mouth. "If you're prepared to be amazed."

His gaze drifted out the garage window across the road to the Claverley pasture. Across that pasture lay the Claverley home quarter. Haley imagined that Howie and Angela might have ridden in those same pastures. It was all in the past for Howie, but he seemed to think it wasn't for her.

Hard to believe, but if she took Howie's word for it, not impossible.

CHAPTER FIFTEEN

RISKY B TROTTED around the edges of her corral, occasionally stopping to lift her head to whatever sound or smell she could catch on the steady Foothills breeze. On her own, she crossed over to where Mateo waited at the gate entrance.

"She's back on familiar territory," Hawk said, coming up beside him on the outside of the fence.

Mateo clipped the lead reins onto Risky B's halter. "And she's ready to work." It had been nearly two weeks since he brought the filly down, and the most he'd done was hour-long rides at the occasional trot. Just enough to keep her from outright rebelling. Time to step up the game.

"More than ready, I'd say."

Mateo heard the quiet criticism in Hawk's voice. Hawk was now his landlord and no longer his boss or his occasional childhood playmate while visiting the Jansson ranch, but that didn't change a lifetime of Hawk speaking his mind.

"I already had a setback. Don't want to double it." He smoothed his hand along Risky B's flanks to where her reddish coat was lit up in the midmorning sun.

Hawk looked out to the hills and mountains beyond. "You mean with the horse?" It was the closest Hawk had come to introducing the subject of Haley. Mateo had simply told him that it hadn't worked out. He'd hoped that his rigid tone had conveyed his disinterest in pursuing the whys and wherefores.

"Yep. The horse."

Hawk kept his attention on the scenery. "You give any more thought to my offer?"

Cash-strapped, Hawk had decided to sell his most westerly quarter. The land there began to lift into the mountains and had two creeks running through it. Pretty country, but not good for growing anything but grass and wildflowers. The original homestead had been kept up until a few years ago. He could live in it and have his training arena there. He could make a go of it.

From the corner of his eye, Mateo caught

the metallic wink of a vehicle barreling down the main road. Not too many vehicles came this way. The Blackstone ranch was more or less on a dead-end road. There was still a chance it might turn right or left at the next intersection and avoid the ranch.

"When do you need to know?"

Hawk brought his gaze back to Mateo. "I'm thinking yesterday."

The creditors had to be leaning on Hawk hard for him to say that. Mateo knew it tore at Hawk to sell land that had been in his family for the past four generations. "Better to lose a foot," Hawk had said, "than the whole body. And I'd rather my neighbor not be a stranger."

The vehicle shot through the intersection toward the ranch. "Looks as if you got company."

Hawk turned and tipped back his hat. "What now?" His ex-wife's sister had taken the twins and was scheduled to bring them back at suppertime. Mateo had avoided time with the toddlers as much as possible, though they'd welcomed back their *Ma-tat-o* with open arms. He didn't trust himself to have them under his care—and more to the point, they reminded him too much of Jonah. As the vehicle resolved into a defined shape, Mateo groaned.

"The company's for me, not you," he said. "Grace."

Hawk straightened. "This about Haley?"

"No doubt."

Hawk pushed off the railing as though ready to flee the upcoming storm. But then he grinned and leaned back. "This," he said, "I have to see."

They watched the sports car crunch gravel and stop in front of Hawk's ranch bungalow. Grace popped out and scanned the yard. She locked on to them. Mateo tensed, and he swore Hawk braced himself against the steel fencing. She'd poke and poke, and he'd just have to hold on until she went away.

She bore down on them. She wore a professional skirt and jacket and shoes with heels. She stripped off the shoes after a short ways and kept coming barefoot.

"That's gotta hurt," Hawk remarked from the side of his mouth.

Not as much as what would fly from her mouth. She let loose as soon as she was within calling distance.

"Three thirty in the afternoon. That's when

I'm due back in Calgary for a video court date that has been seven months in the making. I should be going over my final arguments right now, but instead, I'm here dealing with you." Her final clipped words brought her up to the fence.

"I didn't invite you here," Mateo said.

Grace spoke through the railing. "I warned you before that if you screwed Haley over, I'd come for you. We had an understanding. You've given me no choice."

"Really?" Mateo unhooked his lead from Risky B to let her move freely around the corral. The filly didn't need to listen to Grace's scorching. "Because I don't remember signing any document to that effect."

Grace narrowed her eyes. "Are you going to deny that I told you on your property on June fifth that if you did wrong by Haley, I'd make certain that you pay?"

Mateo stood toe-to-toe with her, an arm's length and a fence separating them. "I remember that, but that all hangs on whether I did wrong by Haley, and you need to demonstrate that first."

"According to the signed agreement, you were to give sixty days written notice of withdrawing from the partnership. I think you gave sixty seconds."

Mateo acutely remembered every single word that had passed between Haley and him that evening, not a word of which he would share with Grace, but he pulled out his phone and opened up his photos. He presented his screen inches in front of her nose. "Recognize Haley's signature on that check? That's payment from her for my share of cattle sold on the date in the memo line. I consider that piece of paper its own kind of agreement between the two of us. I also think that Haley is fair-minded enough not to take this to court, so I think we're finished here." He turned and called for Risky B to come over.

Grace stepped onto the bottom railing, putting her right beside Hawk, her toes curled around the steel pipe. It had to be heating up some under the sun, but she hung on like a bull rider. "How can you be fair-minded when you admit to selfishness?"

Mateo flinched. Haley had shared. Then again, a person had to be made of the fencing Grace stood on not to give way to her questioning. "I call it fair, if we both get what we want."

"And what exactly do you want?"

Mateo swept his hand around the corral. "You're looking at it."

"This? Really? You gave up a newly renovated house, six quarters of land, a promising partnership in cutting horses and a community for what? A bunkhouse, a horse and the right to ride on someone else's land? Are you kidding me?"

Just like that, she'd gotten underneath his skin. "As a matter of fact, it may interest you to know that I'm picking up Hawk's quarter to the west."

Grace swiveled to Hawk. "The one with the old homestead?"

His eyes to the ground, he nodded.

"You can't sell that land. It's the Blackstone homestead. It stays in the family."

Hawk raised his eyes to her, his expression bleak. "I've got no choice."

Grace's toes curled harder on the railing. "There has to be a way. There has to be. But first—" she flashed her eyes at Mateo "—you're not taking Hawk's land when you own six perfectly good quarters situated in a way-better part of the country for training up stock."

"That's what selfish people do," Mateo shot back.

"That's what stupid people do."

"Last I checked, stupidity isn't a crime."

"It should be when it leads to land grabbing. Pack up your horse and go back and work it out with Haley."

The weak part in him jumped to do her bidding, but he knocked it back. "I don't take orders from someone who has seen her family only once in the past five months, and that's only because Haley put in an emergency call to you. And now you cut into me for disturbing your workday. You could've driven the same distance north instead of west and spent your precious time with them. But where's the fun in that, right?"

Grace flushed. But if he'd struck home, she didn't give another sign. Instead, she continued, her voice lowered, "I've made choices that keep me from family. I admit that. You don't need to make those. Do better than me."

Her voice had taken on a soft, pleading edge that dug deeper than all her harshness. He looked away. "I wish I could."

Her expression remained soft, but her last

words to him remained unrelenting. "Wish harder."

She hopped off the railing and turned to Hawk. "Don't sell the land until you've heard from me."

"Grace—"

But she'd already spun away and was making her way back across the prickly grass and sharp stones. Hawk and Mateo tracked her progress.

"I'm pretty sure I see burn marks where she stepped."

Hawk's relaxed humor was the first Mateo had heard in a long time from his old boss. Grace had provoked opposite reactions from them, but then again, Hawk hadn't been the target of her attack.

An unfair attack. She was all wrong. Haley had not called him since they'd broken up. He had promised himself that he would pick up if she called and would not change his number. But her silence meant she agreed with what he'd said. Or she'd given up and moved on. It amounted to the same in the end. They were done.

"I'll tell you what," Hawk said, "Grace

doesn't call in a week with a plan, I'll hand the land over to you. Deal?"

Mateo nodded, his eyes to the same dusty patch of ground Hawk had been staring at.

"Meanwhile," Hawk said, "there's Risky B to work."

Yeah, there was always the horse. And, as Grace pointed out, not much more. He'd smashed his chance to build his own legacy with the woman he loved.

Grace had told him to go back and fix it. But he had no idea how. He couldn't change who he was at heart.

HALEY FLOPPED ONTO the couch, exhausted to her very marrow. Early September had to be the busiest time of the year with all the chores, the bales to haul, the potatoes to dig. She wasn't doing all of it, but her fingers were in every pie.

And, of course, there was Jonah. He seemed to think himself too grown-up for a morning nap now, and he rode her arm like a little lord everywhere. Mateo had spoiled Jonah. She'd only just now gotten him to bed at quarter past eight. Brock was combining, and Knut was hauling grain. All she wanted to do was fall asleep right there on the couch.

Her phone rang in the kitchen. *Please let it not be Knut or Brock with a machine breakdown.* Another week, and they'd have the crops off.

She dragged herself upright and headed to her phone. It was Grace.

"Twice in one week," Haley said. "This is special."

"Did you know Hawk is selling his homestead quarter?"

Haley sifted her sluggish mind through old conversations. "I remember Mateo talking about that. I can't remember if he said it was the old-home quarter. Why?"

"I was out there today, and Hawk plans to sell it. To Mateo."

Mateo was putting down roots. Somewhere else. "No law against that."

"I told Hawk to wait a week, but I don't know if he just won't go ahead and sell it anyway."

Two of Haley's weary brain cells rubbed together. "Wait. You were out there? Why?"

"To see Mateo. And this business of the land came up."

Oh, no. "Grace, why did you go see Mateo?"

"Why do you think? I told him to fix his mess."

Mateo had let drop that on her last visit, Grace had come to see him en route to Calgary. He didn't go into the details, but he'd summarized it as an interrogation. Haley had rolled her eyes at Grace's interference, but since Mateo had seemed happy to let it go, so had she. She should've put Grace in her place back then.

"Grace, this is none of your business. You had no right to get involved. I don't even know if I want us to reconcile."

"How could you not want it? He's great with Jonah, shares the same interests in ranching and he obviously cares for you."

"If he cares so much, why did he leave?"

"How do I know? He went on about how you both agreed that it's for the good of all, yadda, yadda."

"He… He actually said that?"

Grace blew out her breath. "Which is it, Haley? You tell me to butt out, and then you ask me to give a play-by-play of what happened today. If it's not my business, are you going to make it yours?"

The heart makes the impossible happen.

"I… I'll think about it."

"Too much thinking is going on. But hey, I did what I could. Anyway, what are we going to do about Hawk's home quarter?"

"Uh… How is this any of our business?"

"Because if you don't try to stop Mateo, you're basically giving up on him. That's why it's your business. And it's my business because—" Grace stopped.

"Because…?"

"That's my business."

Ranching had never interested Grace, not like the way it ran in Haley's blood. Why now? But if she expected Grace to respect her privacy, she had to reciprocate. "Fair enough. I'll talk to Dad when he comes in."

"What's Dad got to do with any of this?"

But an idea was already percolating in Haley's mind. Or her heart. "Let me talk to him first."

Grace let off a cry of frustration. "Thinking and talking. We've got a week at best, Haley."

Didn't she know it? She heard the loaded grain truck growl its way up the lane. Dad. "I've got it from here."

HALEY HAD ABOUT a half hour to talk to her dad before he had to return to the field to pick up the next load of wheat. He came into the house and sat heavily at the dining table. The workload was taking its toll. Brock was enough for the daily responsibilities, but she had to line up additional help fast.

She set a cup of instant decaf in front of him. He took a tentative sip. His eyebrows shot up. "This is good."

"Dad, it's instant coffee."

"Still." He added, "Thanks."

"That's fine. How about I bring in the next load? Jonah is out like a light. It's all good."

She thought he'd put up an argument. Instead, he rubbed his knee and said, "I'd appreciate that."

Haley bit her lip. A change was underway. A whole shift in which her dad stepped aside and the next generation—hers—rose up. Well, she had always wanted to be in charge of her destiny. That didn't mean simply coping with whatever came her way. Every now and again, it meant creating the way.

"Dad, you know how you said that you'd only sell Jakob's quarters if I okayed it?"

"Yep."

"So I give you permission to sell."

Her dad blinked and took a long, noisy gulp of coffee. "All right. To who?"

"To Mateo, of course."

Her dad scratched his forehead. "I don't know, Haley. I think that ship has sailed."

"It's sailed, but it hasn't quite docked in another port yet." Haley went on to fill her dad in on Grace's visit to Blackstone and Mateo's intention of buying the home quarter.

"But that land has been in the Blackstone family for generations. Shame to have that change because of a bit of bad luck."

"Yes, it would be. That's why I propose we buy it. Or more specifically, you buy it. Assuming you have the money."

Her dad sat back in his chair. "I have the money, but I'm not sure why I would."

"Because Mom was a Blackstone."

"Not exactly. Her mother's sister-in-law married into the Blackstone family. We're not blood relatives."

"There was no blood between Jakob and Mateo, and yet they were father and son. Dad, we have a duty here. To Mom. It wouldn't have sat right with her, just like it doesn't with you."

"If we buy the land, it'll sit there, a five-hour drive away. No way could we ranch it. What's the point?"

"That's fine. For now. Hawk can have first rights to buy the quarter back. That'll give him time to straighten out his finances."

"Seems a shame to let a perfectly good quarter sit there."

"You could let Hawk run his cattle on it or—" Haley bit her lip and plunged on "—give it to Grace."

Her dad looked as if Haley had proposed putting a turkey in charge. "Grace? She has no interest in ranching or the farm life. She couldn't wait to leave here. She's got her own life in the city. And a busy one at that."

"I hear you, believe me. But Grace called me about that quarter. She never cared two hoots about the land here, but that place… You'd think Hawk intended to saw off her leg. Maybe she got attached to it during the summer visits there as a kid with Mom." Haley had never gone with them, preferring to be on the Jansson ranch. And yes, near Mateo. "Anyway, it's only fair. Grace might not want any part of this ranch, but she deserves something. You buy her a quarter of land she does want and give her the right to operate it as she sees fit. If she wants to sell it right back to Hawk, she can. If she wants to go all survivalist and subsist on gophers and roots, she can do that, too."

Her dad snorted. They both knew that their urbanized Grace would never do that.

"The point is," Haley finished, "is that you can trust that whatever she decides, it will all be for the best."

Knut spun his spoon, and the metal clicked rhythmically on the wood surface of the table. "What about you? Why would you sell the land to Mateo now when you wouldn't before? You would lose the land. There's no recourse for you. And nothing I can do once the papers are signed."

"But it's my choice, right?"

"Not a choice I'd recommend, Haley."

"But you'd do it?"

"Haley—"

"You're the one who told me to let go of my grudge. You're the one who wanted Mateo here right from the start. What's changed?"

"Nothing, except what's changed between you two."

It wasn't what had changed between them; it was what hadn't. They still loved each other, but they still didn't trust themselves. That was what needed to change. Starting with her. "Let me take care of that." Haley stood. "I've got grain to haul first."

Outside, Haley dragged in the night air—nippy now, with the first frosts of the season. Her earlier exhaustion had vanished; she felt wide awake.

THREE DAYS LATER, Haley rolled up the lane to the Blackstone Ranch.

She eyed the plastic folder on the passenger seat, a printout of all the information that Grace had also put onto a flash drive tucked inside the folder. She'd offered to present the terms to Hawk, but Haley had insisted that since it was her idea, she would talk to him. Besides, she had said it was the only way she could fix things with Mateo. That had settled Grace down.

"Pretty wild-looking country," Haley said to Jonah in the back seat. He slouched in his seat, contemplating some piece of the blue sky. The huge foothills rose brown and rugged over the homesteads. There were no trees around the Blackstone buildings, but farther west, autumn yellows mixed with the greens of the pines in a thick layer across the base of the mountains. And then there were the blue and gray mountains, like permanent storm clouds.

Haley felt far more kinship to her family land, but she could see why Grace was drawn to the Foothills. She always craved a challenge.

Haley parked in front of the house, right beside Mateo's truck. He was here. Anticipation fluttered through her. She'd not called ahead to Hawk, fearing that if Mateo got wind of her coming, he'd take off. But scanning the yard, she saw only Hawk coming across from the horse pens. He was holding the hands of two little boys. His twins, she assumed.

"If Mateo's hiding in the house," she informed Jonah, "I'm going after him this time." Jonah squirmed and gave a questioning burble. "Yeah, we're getting out."

"Haley," Hawk said as he came up, his toddlers now riding in his arms. They observed her from their perches. "I didn't recognize you at first."

"It's been a few years. Seven, eight?"

"At least." He hadn't changed. He was still tall and not given to elaborate speech, but there were faint lines around his eyes and something more…a tinge of defeat. She hoped her proposal would sweep that away.

"Trip down good?"

Technically, it was a trip up into the Foothills. "Came through a rainstorm south of Calgary, but otherwise dry roads all the way."

Hawk shook his head. "We got an inch the other night, but too little, too late."

"We didn't get that," Haley said. "But at least we got the crop off." What there was of it.

Having gone through that necessary ritual of commiseration about weather, they moved into introductions of their kids, even going so far as having Amos and Saul shake Jonah's hand as Haley outstretched it for them. She stole glances around, hoping to spot Mateo. Nothing. "You two are as handsome as your pictures."

"You've seen pictures?" Hawk said.

"Mateo showed me." And now that his name was out there… "He around?"

"Sort of." Hawk looked over to the hills where the trees rode up the mountains. "He's taken himself up there for a few days."

Haley's heart sank. She'd planned a surprise visit so he wouldn't take off, but he already had. "Alone?"

"Yep. But he's got a gun, so he should be okay."

"A gun?"

"Bears. Cougars. Sometimes a moose, especially at this time of year."

"Did he say when he's coming back?"

"He said he wasn't sure, but I imagine in the next day or so. Or maybe the day after that."

If he wasn't clawed or rammed to death. "What's he doing in the bush?"

Hawk shrugged. "Said he needed to be alone for a bit."

No, he didn't. "And I suppose there's no cell reception up there?"

Hawk shook his head. She'd have to wait for Mateo to reappear. In the meantime… "I didn't come just to see him. There's business we need to discuss."

If Hawk was the least bit interested, he didn't let on. Arms full, he nodded to the house. "Come on in. Time to fill the kids' troughs."

While Hawk organized an early supper for his boys, Haley nursed Jonah in the living room. It had been built for Hawk's mother according to Western style. There was a high ceiling, and a stone fireplace ran counterpoint to a modern kitchen. But there had been no recent upgrades, and the furniture wasn't fancy. It had a bare-bones feel to it, and Haley wondered if Hawk had sold off items. Or if his ex had taken them.

That was none of her business. Her interests lay in that folder beside her on the couch. But Hawk didn't seem anxious to bring up the purpose of the visit, and with them managing three kids who were two years old and under, there wasn't much room for adult talk. Haley got a glimpse of where she was heading with Jonah. He watched the antics of the twin boys with deep absorption, even going so far as to pick up a plastic spoon and attempt to feed himself his pears.

In turn, the twin boys abandoned their own meat and potatoes to take turns feeding him. Haley oversaw the operation, her hand guiding theirs.

The tension in Hawk's face eased as he watched. "Anything to do with taking care of animals, they're all over it."

"That's good," Haley said. "They'll be a big help around here down the road."

Hawk visibly sagged. "Yeah, if there's still a road."

Forget the right time. This whole trip was about not waiting around for the ducks to line up. She steadied Saul's hand and said, "Look, here it is in a nutshell."

She filled Hawk in about the proposed purchase, and sure enough, a new energy seemed to swell up in him. "Grace agreed to this?"

"Stayed up all night to prepare the papers. I picked them up this morning on the way out. She's serious."

Jonah batted away Amos's offering, and mushed pears fell to the floor. Amos scowled at Jonah, tossed down the spoon and returned to his meat and potatoes. Saul tracked his brother and did the same. Haley bent over to pick up the pear, and when she straightened, she saw Hawk's face had settled back into tired, resigned lines.

"I offered it to Mateo, and he accepted. It's not right to go back on our understanding. He's been good to me. To the kids."

Not as good as he was for her and Jonah. She didn't even think about what she said next. Her nest egg couldn't go to a better cause. "How about for an additional twenty grand?"

Hawk regarded his twin boys. She thought she'd swayed him, but he sighed. "Can't."

"Mateo will have to back out of the deal before you'll take ours."

"He tells me he's out, and I'll sign."

Simple enough, but hard. She'd have to wait for Mateo to return to change his mind. Who knew how long that would take?

Hawk followed her gaze to the hills where Mateo was. "You can stay here. Plenty of room."

"Thanks. I guess I have to, seeing as there's no other option."

"You might be able to drive out to him," Hawk said. "There's a fair hike afterwards, though—two hours at least, and it won't be easy with Jonah."

But she'd brought the back carrier. "How long is the drive?"

"A good half hour. Part of it's along an access road. Lots of twists and turns. Then you hike for a couple of hours. A pretty spot with a little lake."

"Why didn't Mateo take his truck?"

"He didn't want to run the risk of damaging it. He's become as attached to it as he was to his first one."

It was probably his way of honoring his dad, of not ruining things. That was why he'd left, because he thought he'd ruined the chance to be part of her life—and Jonah's. She couldn't wait here for him to come back.

"Show me a map. I'm going after him tomorrow."

Hawk glanced at Jonah.

"And he's coming with me. And yes, I know the risks. If I have to turn back for Jonah's sake, I will."

Early afternoon the next day found Haley shouldering the back carrier at the trailhead, her chest backpack stuffed with baby supplies. Hawk had loaned her a tent, just in case, and she'd strapped it to the bottom of the carrier. The roll bumped against the backs of her thighs as she headed off into the bush.

"Here I come, Mateo. Ready or not."

CHAPTER SIXTEEN

MATEO EMERGED FROM his afternoon swim in the lake nearly frozen to death. For the last three days, he'd gone for one. He'd swum all the way across and all the way back. Thirty minutes of such torture that he couldn't think of anything else except getting into warm clothes and sunning himself. Thirty minutes away from thinking about how he'd screwed things up with Haley.

Grace had ordered him to wish harder. He'd spent the last two days doing exactly that, but he could see no way back to Haley. He'd left. Again. Not even told her of his decision to sell. Not even tried for a goodbye, painful as it would be. He'd hightailed it out of there. She had forgiven him once for leaving. He couldn't expect her to forgive him twice for such rashness.

He'd dragged on his jeans and was tugging on a shirt when he heard rustling along the path that led to the access road. Bear. A cougar or a coyote was quieter. Even deer were. He gauged where his rifle was stashed by his tent.

He could make it, even in bare feet. He had the rifle pointed when the bear broke from the bush into the small meadow.

"Haley!" With Jonah.

She looked as shocked as he was. "Crap, Mateo. Can you point that thing somewhere else?"

He threw on the safety and set it down, his hands trembling. He'd put Jonah in danger. Again.

"Help me with this, will you?"

He turned to find Haley had dropped a backpack humped out like a turtle shell from her front and had moved on to the carrier straps. Jonah had spotted him and was squealing with excitement. He had no idea how bad things could've gotten.

Mateo helped to lower the carrier, toeing the tent aside. She couldn't possibly think of camping out here with Jonah. It was too dangerous.

"Man, that water looks good," Haley said.

"My feet are screaming for a treat. Watch him, will you?"

He didn't have time to object. He couldn't just leave Jonah in the unstable carrier.

Mateo set him on his arm and grimaced. Full diaper.

He could wait until Haley came back and let her do the diaper change, but she had already stripped off her socks and boots and was wading in. He reached for Haley's backpack.

Once Jonah was good to go again, Mateo carried him down to the edge of the small lake, where Haley stood knee-high in the water. She looked much as she did on their excursion to Spirit Lake short weeks ago.

"It's so cold I think my legs will break off at the knee," she said cheerfully. She indicated his hair. "Looks as if you've already had a dip."

"Just finished swimming the length and back."

She looked across to where pines crowded down to the edge. "You're braver than me."

"Stupider, maybe."

She stood with her hands on her hips and her head tipped to the side, studying him as if he and Jonah were a painting she might purchase.

"Haley, what are you doing here? Especially with Jonah. It isn't safe."

She kicked the water, and droplets rose high and splattered him and Jonah, who squealed and giggled. "You're telling me what's safe and what isn't? You're the one who aimed a gun at me."

"That was an accident. Can we leave it at that?"

This time, her kicks came hard and fast, and the splash soaked them. Mateo backpedaled with Jonah, and Haley surged forward, kicking with both legs until she ran out of the water and stood on the edge.

"No, we're not going to leave it at that, Mateo Jonah Pavlic. Jonah. Your name, his name. I told you I called him that because I like the name, but you know why I like the name? Because back when we first kissed, I started dreaming about you being the father of my babies, and I swore that the first one would be called Jonah. And you know what? My dream came true. I had a son, and I named him Jonah."

"Except I'm not the father."

"You mean like how your father wasn't yours? You know that it doesn't work that way. Jonah's yours as much as he's mine. Maybe even more, because you two chose each other the second he took hold of your finger the day he was born, and you let him. You can't break that promise."

Mateo shooed off a wood fly hovering around Jonah. "I already did."

"So what?" Haley said. "It didn't hurt that you left, Mateo. It only hurt that you didn't come back. I'm asking you now...come back."

He longed to. In less than an hour, they could return this lake back to its pristine stillness, pack up and leave together.

"You might as well," Haley said. "Hawk is considering another offer on the quarter. Dad wants to buy it."

Mateo had to replay her words in his mind to make sense of them. "Why?"

"Grace wants it, so he's going to give it to her. He'll get reimbursed from the money he gets from the sale of my land."

It felt as if Haley was still kicking cold water on him. "You're selling? But why? The land was everything to you."

"It is, so I hope you appreciate the offer I'm making you."

She was selling him the land, her most treasured possession next to Jonah.

"That's right. I'm giving it all to you, Mateo. At full cost, just as Dad paid market price to your dad." She closed the distance between them. "All you have to do is come and get it."

"Haley—"

"It's not so hard, you know. I thought I was stuck, too. I thought I had to wait for you to come to your senses. But I decided I wasn't going to wait another dozen years while you and Jonah both miss out on an incredible relationship. So I came to you. And now I'm asking the same, Mateo. Come back with us. To us."

Her words swayed him, filled his emptiness, his loneliness. They were what he wanted to hear. He loved her, loved Jonah.

Until he'd pushed things too far, assumed too much and something happened. Like a gun going off. There was no coming back from that.

"I can't, Haley. I just…can't."

Her lips flattened, and she stared out at the lake and then back up at the campsite. Without a word, she sat and pulled on her boots. She dropped a kiss on Jonah's head. She returned to the backpack, retrieved a water bottle and filled it from a creek entering the lake. Finally, she turned to him.

"When you're ready, you and Jonah come back. I'll be waiting at Hawk's, and we'll all go back home together." She smiled. "And we'll kiss. And this one…" She frowned, as if searching for the right word. Her face cleared and split into a wide grin. "This one will be magical." She turned and headed for the path.

Cold fear gripped him. "No, Haley. You can't," he called out to her. "You can't abandon him."

She didn't break stride. "I'm not. I'm leaving him with his father."

"I'm not his father."

"We've already covered that ground." She was angling toward the path not twenty yards away. She was really going to do this. He ran after her, but he couldn't move as fast in bare feet.

"Haley, stop. It isn't safe. There are bears. Cougars."

"Keep the gun close, then."

She was at the edge of the bush when he

made one last desperate plea. "Haley, I can't do this. Please."

She paused and turned. "Mateo. I trust you with all my heart, and with all I love."

Then she vanished into the trees.

"OKAY, BUDDY, looks as if she packed you enough bottles, food and diapers for the next couple of days," Mateo informed Jonah. They sat on the grass before the lake, Jonah within the secure curve of Mateo's legs as he rummaged through the backpack Haley had left behind. There was a onesie and his favorite flannel blankie—as if she'd anticipated an overnight outing.

Had she also planned to leave them behind? "Your mom's one wild woman," Mateo opined to Jonah. "But one way or another, I've got to get you back to her."

He had three choices. Pack up and follow in Haley's direction until he got onto the access road. She had enough of a headstart to have already left by then. Then he could walk it until he got to the main road, where he might catch a ride for the forty miles back to the ranch. If he could flag someone down, otherwise he'd have to camp overnight. He could pack up and head back the way he'd come, following human and animal trails cross-country, shaving off a good ten miles. That would still mean roughing it for a night. A night with animals that preyed on humans.

Or he could wait it out in a game of chicken and count on Haley returning when he didn't show up with Jonah after a couple of days. There'd still be the nights, but at least there was a water supply close. Besides, she was still breastfeeding. She'd have to circle back eventually.

She was testing him, and it was up to him to pass or fail. Failure in her eyes was doing nothing. He could live with that. Failure in his eyes was not protecting Jonah. He couldn't live with that.

The prudent thing to do was wait it out. Who knew, she could be on her way back right now after coming to her senses.

"All right," Mateo said, "We'll hang out here for today. If your mom doesn't show by tomorrow morning, I'll—" What would he do? "Let's hope she shakes out of a bush before then."

Jonah let his soother drop from his mouth and inserted a couple of knuckles. "Hungry?"

That was one problem Mateo knew the answer to.

The rest of the day, Mateo's thoughts were occupied with taking care of Jonah. He fed him milk and applesauce, flicked stones and grass out of his grabby paws, swished his hands and feet through the water, strapped him into the baby carrier and checked the area for any tracks of wild animals. Thankfully, there were none.

He made a fire in the pit and warmed up the chili he'd brought along. Jonah's mouth opened suggestively every time Mateo brought a spoonful to his own mouth. "Nope. You're only—" Mateo calculated. Jonah was six months today.

Technically, according to the baby books he'd read and from what he could recall with Amos and Saul, Jonah was ready for meat. He didn't know if Haley had introduced it yet, but from the looks of her supply, it wasn't high on the list.

She trusted him to take care of Jonah. But what if Jonah was allergic to something in the chili? Surely Haley would've told him of other food allergies after the peanut butter episode. And Haley had said that babies were resilient to allergens.

"No one has died from my cooking," Mateo said. He mashed a thumbnail-sized chunk of beef between his fingers and offered it to Jonah, who gulped it down.

Jonah's eyes widened, and he smacked his lips. "I take it you approve." Too bad Haley wasn't here to see Jonah's reaction. Too bad she wasn't here, period.

Now, with losing the power of the sun, he hoped she wasn't stumbling along the path somewhere out there, but had driven back safely to Hawk's. He and Jonah would get through the night on their own. Mateo checked again and again for red blotches on Jonah and for difficulty breathing. Nothing.

MATEO EXPECTED HIS sleep to be as troubled and fitful as the other two nights he'd been out here, especially with the small, live package tucked next to him. Instead, they both slept like logs. Mateo woke to morning light filtering into the green nylon tent. Beside him, Jonah slept on, cocooned in Mateo's hoodie and jacket shirt. They'd survived the night.

So far, so good.

He unzipped the tent and poked his head out. Clear skies and no wind. A beautiful fall morning. Jonah stirred and his eyes flew open. He gazed up at the unusual green light.

"Morning, buddy."

Jonah pivoted his gaze to Mateo, and a smile broke across his face. "Da."

Da. Dad. No. It wasn't a word. It was a sound. An accident of the tongue. But Jonah looked at him with the same trust as if Mateo really was his father. There'd been a time when he thought he could be. Now Haley had placed him in a position where he was forced to be one. Maybe she was right.

No, once again his arrogance was taking over. He had lucked out with Jonah last night. He wasn't going to push it. He'd get back to Haley for Jonah's safety—not so they could all be together.

He broke camp right after breakfast. "I'm a mule," he shared with Jonah as he strapped on the back carrier. He'd come in light with a single pot, a two-person tent, a lighter and a gun. But the smaller the human, the more the stuff. He'd weighted down the carrier and his front with all the gear, including the tent Haley had brought in.

"If we get out of here alive, I'm going to have a talk with your mom," Mateo said and then amended, "*When* we get out of here."

He hit off across country, opting for the faster route. After a short walk, he spotted cougar feces along the trail. He gripped his gun. "A long talk," he muttered.

Jonah and the extra weight slowed him, and the growing heat didn't help. Even the stretches of trees provided shade but no break from the heat. Every half hour or so, he shed everything to hydrate Jonah, who had burbled and chattered the whole morning. At least his noise would keep animals at bay.

At noon, Mateo unburdened himself again by a creek. "Big break this time. Lunch, diaper change, play for you, sit for me." Except he couldn't sit. With Jonah, the hike back was taking twice as long as hiking in, spiking Mateo's anxiety to keep moving. To return Jonah to Haley and to deal with the matter of Hawk's quarter. He still intended to buy it. He would not return north with Haley and Jonah. Her trust in him was misplaced.

No sooner were bellies and bottles filled than Mateo piled on the gear and struck out. An hour in, Jonah slumped to the side and fell asleep. Mateo had lost his animal detractor. His senses sharpened. Predators slept by day usually, but that meant nothing in the end.

Nor did it help that there was a fresh pile of cougar scat with scraps of rabbit fur and bones mixed in. Mateo scanned the trees. "A very, very long talk."

Despite the weight, he picked up speed. He couldn't wait to reach camp. There, he could set up, get a fire going, stake his own territory. Another night out, and by tomorrow noon be back at the ranch.

His legs wobbled from exhaustion and relief when he reached the camp. "Never have I been so happy to see a piece of ground," he said over his shoulder to Jonah, who'd awakened earlier.

He dropped the gear, and with Jonah in one arm and water bottles in the other, he headed for the creek past the campsite. The creek was at a trickle compared to the spring runoff, and he had to balance himself and Jonah far out to catch a stream of water.

Mateo was tightening the lid on one of Jonah's baby bottles when his hackles rose. He pivoted slowly, and further up the creek bed sat a cougar, tail twitching. A full-grown animal not even a stone's throw away. Which was the only weapon he had. He'd left the gun back at the campsite. Left it when he'd known there was a cougar roaming about. He'd made a mistake that had once again placed Jonah in mortal danger.

Jonah had also spotted the cat and let loose with an excited squeal. Yellow eyes narrowed in annoyance or speculation.

Sudden anger surged through Mateo. "Don't even think about jumping him," he yelled at the cougar. "It'll be over my dead body because that's what it'll take. He's mine. Do you hear me? Mine!"

He hucked a rock and another and another. All fell short, but it was enough to make the cougar spring up the bank and away into the trees. Except how far had it gone?

Mateo hurried back to the campsite, throwing glances over his shoulder. He set up camp, practically one-handed since he was afraid to set Jonah down. Only when the tent was up did he set Jonah inside and close the zipper before pounding in the stakes.

The whole evening passed in high-alert mode. The gun close, Jonah closer. Jonah didn't seem to pick up on Mateo's anxiety.

He didn't fuss as much as he had when Mateo and Haley had their falling out. Or maybe he was imitating Mateo and staying quiet.

Not fond of fire or humans in general, the cougar had likely passed on or didn't care to engage. But Mateo wasn't taking any chances. When Jonah fell asleep in Mateo's arms, once again wrapped in the blanket and shirt, Mateo transferred him into the tent and then came out to sit between the tent and the fire, ready to protect Jonah from the whole wide world.

"No one's coming between you and me," he muttered. He stopped. He'd said it. He'd claimed Jonah for his own. Thrown stones, yelled, said he'd sacrifice himself for Jonah's sake. Even now, in the calm of the night, he would do anything to keep Jonah safe. Not to get him back to Haley. Not because that was the right thing to do.

Because Jonah belonged to him. To him and Haley alone.

Hadn't Jakob said the same with the card? *Love, Dad.* The single-word claim. Mateo would never know why Jakob had signed the card the way he did, but he did know for a fact that a man could feel powerful love for a baby who didn't share his genes. The run-in with the cougar had proved that. And wouldn't that love continue as the baby grew into an adult? *Eighteen years well spent.*

Jakob had kicked Mateo out, but he'd not rid himself of the memories. He had remembered Mateo's birthday, had discovered where he lived, had preserved his old home for him. That's what it was to love your child. Even when they were not around, they were still yours. Even when you made out to the world that they weren't yours, they were.

"You figured that out before I did," Mateo said to the fire. "I'm sorry you didn't get the chance to mail that card. I would've opened it, and I would've come back. A wise woman said it wasn't the leaving that hurt but the not coming back. Staying away hurts, too. And I've grown tired of hurting."

He poked the fire, and a spray of sparks shot up into the dark. "I'm coming back. All the way back to my home. Thanks for keeping it, Dad."

The name fell as easily from his lips as Jonah's chirpy syllable. Haley was right to say that he was Jonah's father, but it was something even more. It was a bond founded on the purest of chance. He'd arrived in the hour of Haley's need and helped bring Jonah into the world. By all rights, it shouldn't have happened. It was a bond forged in an instant that neither peanuts nor a cougar nor his own inner torments could break.

Fear for Jonah had surged through him at the creek, but he'd stood his ground, claimed Jonah for his own, heard himself say it.

"You're mine," he repeated now softly, testing himself. It still felt right.

"You're mine." This time he was thinking of Haley. He listened and nodded.

Tomorrow, he'd deliver the results of the test she'd given him.

HAWK HAD SAID that the earliest to expect Mateo was noon, supposing he'd camped out and not walked out via the access road. Haley figured Mateo would come back the way he'd gone, by way of walking trails.

There was no way to prove her hunch. She just knew him. The same certainty that had bloomed inside her when she walked away from him and Jonah had carried her through the hike and drive back to Hawk's place.

It had washed over Hawk's visible worry and sailed her through helping to watch over his twins yesterday and this morning. She'd cut free to drive to town for groceries and takeout. No way would she inflict her cooking on Mateo for his first meal back.

She returned shortly before noon. The house was quiet. Hawk had likely taken the twins with him into the yard. She settled out the groceries and turned her gaze to one particular hill, the one Hawk had said Mateo would come across before descending into the yard. He would appear as a single dark mark, but he would come.

He would.

A half hour passed, during which she glanced up at the hill about once a minute.

She slipped on her jacket and boots, and walked out to the pens, where Hawk watched over the twins playing in loose straw.

"I'm going out to meet Mateo and Jonah."

"You've seen them?"

"No, but they'll be coming along soon."

"I don't think—"

Haley continued on in the direction of the hill. "We'll be back soon. Wings, noodles, rice and club sandwiches. Something for everyone."

She was skirting a bluff at the base of the hill when she heard voices from the other side.

"I'm telling you, bud, there's nothing better than cranberry juice. Once you're weaned, I'll introduce you to a tall glass."

Jonah let off a long series of babbles. Not two days away, and she missed that noise.

"Yes, served up with meat, no matter the kind. By the way, how about I be the one to tell your mom about you and the chili?"

Jonah burbled something like agreement.

They rounded the bush, and there they were. Mateo, a little more unshaven, his ball cap pulled low. And Jonah, riding high in his carrier and wadded in Mateo's plaid shirt. His smile grew larger at the sight of his mom, and he let off a high-pitched greeting.

Mateo lifted his blue-green eyes upward and then settled them back on Haley. "I kinda agree with Jonah."

The warmth in his eyes tingled through her. "You came back."

He reached for her hands, and she slipped them into his hold. "I did. To you," he said. "To the three of us. To what's mine. To what's ours."

Joy as bright as the light on the hills broke within her. "Welcome back," she breathed. "I—I—" Emotion choked her.

He smiled. "Are you ready for me to say it first?"

She nodded.

He twined a loose tendril of her hair around his finger. "I love you, Haley Jane Jansson."

It took a couple of tries, but she finally found her voice, although it was high and croaky. "And I love you, Mateo Jonah Pavlic."

She rose to her tiptoes, and they kissed. When they drew apart after a long while, Mateo whispered, "You're right. Pure magic."

They had leaned in for a repeat performance when Jonah grabbed hold of Mateo's hair. Mateo winced and said over his shoulder. "Jonah. Drop hands."

Jonah did, and Mateo grinned. "That's him yanking on my reins. I know what Risky B feels like now."

Haley grinned in return. Not because it was really funny, but because her happiness had to find a way out, or she'd float off.

Mateo sobered, though his eyes stayed warm. "Haley, I will buy your land, but there's a condition I want to see in writing."

She waited, trusting.

"I want it put in both our names. And I want you to sign the papers right after signing the wedding registry."

Yes, she was sure her feet lifted off the

ground. She gripped his hands. "You mean…
our wedding?"

"Yes, Haley. Do we have a deal?"

"Yes, Mateo. Yes. Sign me up."

They got in a quick kiss before Jonah pulled
on the reins again. "Later," Mateo whispered.

Later. Tonight, tomorrow and every day
from this moment on.

"Later," she agreed, and the three of them
headed home.

* * * * *

COUNTRY LEGACY COLLECTION

19 FREE BOOKS IN ALL!

EMMETT
Diana Palmer

COURTED BY THE COWBOY
Sasha Summers

THE RANCHER AND THE BABY
Marie Ferrarella

Cowboys, adventure and romance await you in this new collection! Enjoy superb reading all year long with books by bestselling authors like Diana Palmer, Sasha Summers and Marie Ferrarella!

YES! Please send me the **Country Legacy Collection!** This collection begins with 3 FREE books and 2 FREE gifts in the first shipment. Along with my 3 free books, I'll also get 3 more books from the **Country Legacy Collection**, which I may either return and owe nothing or keep for the low price of $24.60 U.S./$28.12 CDN each plus $2.99 U.S./$7.49 CDN for shipping and handling per shipment*. If I decide to continue, about once a month for 8 months, I will get 6 or 7 more books but will only pay for 4. That means 2 or 3 books in every shipment will be FREE! If I decide to keep the entire collection, I'll have paid for only 32 books because 19 are FREE! I understand that accepting the 3 free books and gifts places me under no obligation to buy anything. I can always return a shipment and cancel at any time. My free books and gifts are mine to keep no matter what I decide.

☐ 275 HCK 1939　　　　☐ 475 HCK 1939

Name (please print)

Address　　　　　　　　　　　　　　　　　　　　　　　　　Apt. #

City　　　　　　　　　　　State/Province　　　　　　　　　Zip/Postal Code

Mail to the **Harlequin Reader Service:**
IN U.S.A.: P.O. Box 1341, Buffalo, NY 14240-8571
IN CANADA: P.O. Box 603, Fort Erie, Ontario L2A 5X3

HARLEQUIN
PLUS

Try the best multimedia subscription service for romance readers like you!

Read, Watch and Play.

Experience the easiest way to get the romance content you crave.

Start your **FREE TRIAL** at
<u>www.harlequinplus.com/freetrial</u>.